Misleading

A NOVEL BY

WINK Katme

PUBLISHING

Ailam Publishing LLC
P.O. Box 43413
Chicago, IL 60643
www.ailampublishing.com

© 2011 by Winkk

ISBN 978-0-9837759-0-4

Library of Congress Control Number: 2011911282

First Ailam Publishing LLC trade paperback edition September 2011

Book Cover Concept by: Winkk and Graphix by Dzine
Book Cover Design by: Graphix by Dzine
Book Cover Photography by: Reginald Payton
Book Cover Model: Jonathan Thompkins

10 9 8 7 6 5 4 3 2 1

Manufactured in the United States of America

To order additional copies of this book contact:

Ailam Publishing LLC
P.O. Box 43413
Chicago, IL 60643

ailampublishing@aol.com

www.ailampublishing.com

Acknowledgements

Giving thanks to God is something I do daily and I will continue to give him the praises for every step I make in life. I'm very grateful. This is my third novel and I'm jumping up and down right now. I had a great time writing this book and creating the video book trailer. I get to use my creativity which is something I must do daily. Ride with me as you read another one of my novels, and know that I always try to give you the best I can give.

I love writing and entertaining readers with words. It's my passion to write and I'm driven to keep creating great novels. So many people have been so supportive that I can't thank them enough. My family has been incredible, and they have never doubted me. They believe in me and want me to succeed. I'm happy I have such a strong foundation and I surround myself with positive people. This keeps me grounded and normal.

The readers have been so encouraging and I thrive off of their responses and questions. I'm here because of the readers and their loyalty to my work. I thank you so much and always look forward to meeting people and discussing my books. To the authors that has been kind enough to talk to me, or share some advice, I appreciate you. I will continue to be helpful to authors that are trying to see their books on bookshelves. If you know me, then you know I will try to assist you and give any information to help you succeed with your dreams. I believe in inspiring, motivating and supporting others. Be confident in your talent and the gift of giving. Okay, I've preached enough. ☺

Thanks to my husband for always supporting me no matter what and listening to my creative craziness every day. I love you and thankful that you are a part of my life. To my daughter who I love so much, you're mommies little angel. I'm glad you are learning how to work hard and stay focus on your dreams, by watching me daily. Thank you to my family, friends and everyone who supported this project. You are always there for me and I'll always acknowledge you. Marcia, Montoya, Alven, Mom, Dad, Anita, Rob Hewz, Joy Hughes, Tamala, Jessica, Jeffrey, Phil, Ebony, Teseiee, Troy, Vida, Regina, Sharon, JM Benjamin, Quincy, Reginald Payton Studios, Marvin, Kyra, Jonathan, Martel, Chiara, Lala, Karisia, Let's Face It, Angie, Marty, Kristine, Johariel Hair Salon, Urban Reviews, APOOO, AAMBC, Worldwide readers, Parle Magazine and Rolling Out Magazine. I thank all the book clubs and publications that continue to give authors a platform to display their work.

Now you know I'm probably forgetting someone, but please forgive me. You know how my memory is after I finish a book. Please don't feel forgotten if your name was not listed, I love you and I don't have to list your name for you to know that. Blame my memory, not me personally. Motivate, inspire and support.

Love ya,

Misleading

Sexy, wealthy and handsome is what best describes Jarvis Denttin, the owner of the exclusive popular Denttin nightclubs. His posh lifestyle has women flocking to him regularly, and they feed his strong appetite for sex. Having his choice of any woman, has created a selfish, deceiving, controlling man. Women are attracted to his alluring demeanor, until they are invited into his life and introduce to his devious side.

Expanding his company, Jarvis Denttin is excited to open a new nightclub in Chicago. He is devastated when his close friend is killed and his businesses become in jeopardy, that he is now reconsidering his move to the Windy City. Just as attractive and charming as Jarvis, his friend and employee Antonio Flink is being well trained to become a duplicate of him, but Antonio proves that he is more conniving then Jarvis could imagine.

Candace Mourton, the personal assistant to Jarvis Denttin is a smart opportunist and knows that he is capable of providing the lifestyle she deserves, and she is willing to do whatever it takes to keep the money flowing. She enjoys her professional and sexual relationship with him, until she breaks her own rule and falls in love. Jarvis takes care of her financially, and she caters to him daily, but realizes that isn't enough to keep him interested in her.

With money dominating Jarvis' successful life, he is unaware of the scheme being orchestrated to bring him down and he gets caught up in a web of deception. Knowing all the wrong he has done to people, he's ready for a fresh start, but karma gets to him first. Oblivious of his acquaintance motives, puts him in a deadly situation. Will his life crumble before he finds out that the people around him have been misleading him the entire time?

Misleading

by

W I N K K atme

Prologue

"Ashes to ashes, dust to dust," the minister said while standing over the custom-made white casket.

"Why, why, why!" Mrs. Moeky screamed as she fell on top of the casket, not ready to see her daughter disappear six feet underground.

Family members pulled her off the casket and helped her back to her seat, while friends and the remaining family cried as the casket was lowered into the ground with Jennifer Moeky's body inside. No one understood why such a beautiful prosperous woman would end her life by committing suicide. Jennifer's death just didn't make any sense.

Her family wanted to believe it was a homicide; however, the suicide letter left next to her body was a clear indication that she had given up on life by taking an entire bottle of sleeping pills. Everyone's hearts were broken, and they were missing her dearly.

Once Jennifer's body was lowered into the ground, the attendants started dumping dirt into the deep hole. As if the earth was sucking up the shiny casket, it instantly began to vanish. The gray skies added to the depressing day, and the light mist of rain fell on the cheeks of weeping family and friends.

A handsome young man sang his heart out as the dirt continued to cover the casket, making it apparent she was never going to be seen again. Loved ones bellowed out in sadness while watching and holding each other for support. Jennifer's parents were hysterical and couldn't move from their chairs. The crowd continued to watch in sorrow as the hole was filled with dirt.

Jennifer was only twenty-five years old and too young for her life to have ended so soon. She was Jarvis Denttin's executive assistant and worked hard to keep her job, professionally and sexually.

She had an intimate relationship with Jarvis and fell in love with him, but he didn't feel the same about her. She did anything he asked her to do, even scouting out women so they could have threesomes.

She was not gay or even bisexual, but after dating him, she started sleeping with women on a regular basis, most of the time while Jarvis watched. She only wanted him to love her like she loved him, but he had no intention on loving her the way she needed him to. He didn't respect her or care about her feelings. He wasn't attached to her mentally, because for him, it was only physical.

Jennifer lived each day trying to make him look at her as more than just a piece of ass. He was nice to her in public, but behind closed doors he treated her awful. She hated seeing him with other women, but it was what she signed up for. Therefore, she had no ground to stand on. When Jarvis decided to end their sexual relationship, she flipped out and couldn't imagine not being with him.

He realized she was becoming too attached, and he was not interested in a committed relationship with her. He just wanted to have fun, and the fun ended when her heart got involved. When he pushed her away, she became depressed and her performance at work suffered.

Jarvis ended up firing her. Even though she begged to keep her job and their intimate relationship, he declined both pleas. He was done with Jennifer and on to the next woman. He stopped giving her any attention and shut her off from any connection they ever had.

This drove her crazy, and one week later, Jennifer committed suicide, leaving a letter behind that explained she couldn't live without him. She never mentioned his name in the letter, but her friend Karen knew exactly who had caused her pain.

She had given all she could give and didn't understand why he no longer wanted her. The pain and rejection was too much for her to handle. She warned Jarvis that she would kill herself if he didn't take her back, but he didn't believe her.

He even told her that he didn't care what she did, just as long as she stayed away from him. His mean comment was followed by him slamming the telephone down. That was the last thing he told her before her death.

The next day, Jennifer's parents found her dead in her apartment from an overdose of sleeping pills. From the empty bottle on the nightstand, it appeared she washed down the pills with a bottle of Vodka.

Jarvis tried to pretend like he didn't care, but actually, he was shaken up by her killing herself because of something he said. He kept trying to brush off her death, but it kept haunting him.

Always wanting to be in control, he pretended like he wasn't the cause of it, but he knew he was the person to blame. He disrespected and abused her, and when he was tired, he dismissed her, causing her death.

Choked up, Jarvis couldn't fight back the tears trying to escape from the corners of his eyes. He fidgeted in his chair as he quickly wiped away the tears. He wasn't a crier and didn't plan on showing his vulnerable side now.

"Are you alright, man?" Jarvis' friend, Kevin, asked him.

"I'm good," Jarvis responded in a macho tone, while clearing his throat and continuing to shift around in his chair.

"I'm ready to get out of here. I hate funerals," Kevin said, discreetly nudging Jarvis on the arm.

"Chill out. I don't want to be the first person to leave," Jarvis whispered as he slowly put on his dark sunglasses.

Once the man finished singing the slow, depressing song that brought everyone to tears, people gradually started getting up and walking away. With heads down and tears flowing, Jarvis and his friends slowly approached Jennifer's grieving parents.

"You have my deepest condolences," Jarvis said, while giving Mrs. Moeky a tight hug as he whispered in her ear.

He then turned to her husband and gave him a strong handshake, nodding his head to acknowledge his sorrow. Jennifer's parents thanked him for coming then strolled away in sorrow.

A gloomy look came across Jarvis' face, but quickly disappeared as he watched Jennifer's parents. Jarvis observed Mrs. Moeky as she walked arm in arm with her husband. He couldn't resist staring at her because she didn't look like a woman in her late fifties. She had the body and face of a thirty-year-old. It was obvious she took good care of herself.

He was burning up inside watching her clench to her husband for support. Not only had Jarvis been sleeping with Jennifer, he was also sleeping with her mother, which was something Jennifer never knew about.

Jarvis was no longer interested in her after seeing her display feelings towards her husband. The pleasure of sleeping with a mother and daughter turned him on every time he thought about it. Now that Jennifer was dead, he no longer had an interest in her mother. He watched Mrs. Moeky, knowing he would no longer sleep with the mother, daughter duo again. The thrill was officially gone.

It only took Jarvis one time meeting Jennifer's mother before they started having sex. He had that effect on young women and cougars, as well. Her mother definitely was not the type of woman who would cheat on her husband, but in a weak moment, he took advantage of her. Jennifer's mother was going through a separation with her husband, and Jarvis quickly stepped in to console her heart and body.

Jarvis talked to Jennifer's mother about how her husband was cheating on her, and how she needed to be treated better. He told her what she needed to hear to get her in bed. It only took two weeks of talking to her daily before he had her bent over his desk banging her from behind. It was almost too easy for him since she was trying to get back at her deceitful husband.

Jarvis' dream was to sleep with Jennifer and her mother together, but he knew that wouldn't happen. Eventually, Jennifer's mother reconciled with her husband. After twenty years of marriage, she wasn't ready to get a divorce. Since Mrs. Moeky was only using Jarvis for sex, they were even.

Jarvis Denttin was handsome, selfish and controlling. A self-made millionaire, he was the owner of the popular Denttin's nightclubs in Atlanta, Chicago and Detroit. Looking like the identical twin to the model Tyson

Beckford, he had the looks and muscular body.

Jarvis complexion was smooth as dark chocolate, as if he received facials daily, and his white perfectly-straight teeth were a complement to his luscious lips. His well-groomed, low-cut beard shaped his face to perfection. His tall, lean body helped his clothes fit just right, with dark brown eyes that had a dark rim around each pupil, made them stand out even more. His dark, thick eyebrows complemented his eyes, which made him look like he was wearing eyeliner. There was no denying that Jarvis was gorgeous and exotic looking.

Jarvis was ruthless and only concerned about making money and becoming more successful. He had made a name for himself and his businesses. People knew if they were able to get in his clubs, they would be bumping elbows with the most elite.

He opened up his first nightclub seven years ago in Atlanta and had branched off, opening up more popular clubs in different cities. Now that he was living the life he knew he was meant to have, he was determined to enjoy every bit of it.

He was scandalous and didn't care what people thought about him. He believed in having things his way, and he didn't believe in monogamy. The only way he would settle down was if a woman would submit to him one hundred percent. Basically, women needed to do whatever he told them to in order to make him happy.

It wasn't hard for him to find women, because they were lined up waiting for their turn to date the infamous Jarvis Denttin. He was a devious man disguised in an impeccable wardrobe, charming personality, chiseled body and handsome face. To top it off, he was rich.

Jarvis grew up watching his father work hard to keep his three restaurants and two nightclubs the number one places to attend. His father was a hard worker driven by money and power, which Jarvis duplicated. His parents were never married, so he was always back and forth between his mother and father's houses.

At the age of thirteen, he begged his mother to let him live with his father permanently. He loved his mother and had nothing against her, but she wasn't able to provide the lavish lifestyle he received when he was visiting his father. His father gave him anything he wanted, and like any other child; he wanted to be where he was getting pampered the most.

His father was wealthy, while his mother was living paycheck to paycheck. He wanted to live with his father where there was a maid, chef, and nanny. His mother agreed to let him move in because she felt he needed to be around a male figure.

His father taught him everything he needed to learn about being successful and staying on top. Along with the great entrepreneurial advice, his father also taught him how to be a controlling womanizer. He was the exact image of his father and did everything for his approval. Jarvis was always destined for success, and his father was going to make sure he succeeded and lived the life he expected him to.

Stopping him from going completely into a daze, Jarvis' friend shoved him. They started walking across the cemetery, ready to leave and forget about the day. One of Jennifer's friends looked at Jarvis as he headed for his vehicle. She mumbled to her friends as Jarvis pretended not to notice them. By the unpleasant looks on their faces, it was obvious they didn't care much for him, and he could sense their disapproval.

"I see the cackling crew is about to get started," Kevin commented after noticing the women looking at Jarvis.

They had made it through the funeral with no problems, and Jarvis wanted to keep it that way. However, before Jarvis and his friends could make it to their cars, Jennifer's friend stopped them.

"Is your name Jarvis Denttin?" the tall, slender woman asked curiously.

"Yes, I'm Jarvis Denttin, and your name is?" he replied, flashing a sexy smile while flirting with the woman.

"My name is Karen Law, but that's not important," she said with an attitude.

He checked her out while focusing on the low-cut black dress she was wearing that revealed her cleavage. He was used to women boldly approaching him and trying to seduce him, so this wasn't out of the ordinary. He knew he was a good catch; he also knew women wanted what he had to offer. They were enticed by his wealthy businessman status.

When Jarvis and his friends arrived at the funeral earlier that day, Karen Law watched them and tried to figure out which one was Jarvis. He was dressed sharp in a tailored black suit, which screamed expensive.

He walked with confidence and power. He was strong, and she could sense it from the moment she saw him. She picked Jarvis out of all the men because he showed he was running things by his body language. She watched him closely at the funeral and at the burial site. By this time, she knew she had the right guy.

"You dated Jennifer, right?" Karen asked.

"We never dated, but she was a friend and one of my employees," Jarvis replied.

He tried to walk away, but the questions continued.

"You're the reason why Jennifer killed herself. You are a cruel man," Karen said, scowling.

"I think you have your information wrong. I know you're mourning your friend and don't know what you're saying, so I'm going to excuse myself," Jarvis told her, while taking off his sunglasses and looking directly at her. All the sexual thoughts he had for her suddenly rushed out of his mind.

She couldn't help but be mesmerized by his beautiful brown, almond-shaped eyes with long lashes women would kill for.

Taking a deep breath, she said, "You're the man who broke my friend's heart. I've never seen you, but I know who you are because your expensive clothes make you stand out from everyone here. Jennifer described you well."

"It was nice to meet you," Jarvis simply responded as he tried to walk away, but she quickly grabbed his arm.

"You should be ashamed of yourself. Jennifer loved you and would have done anything for you. You took advantage of her. It's because of you that she isn't here today. You should be in that coffin!" Karen shouted, drawing attention to them.

"Don't ever touch me!" Jarvis calmly said, gritting his teeth as he forced a smile on his face. He then took a deep breath and adjusted his black suit jacket. "You don't know me, so I suggest you watch what you say."

"I know exactly who you are. You're the devil in disguised. How dare you come here after what you put her through! No one knows you because you wouldn't allow Jennifer to talk to her family or friends. Well, she told me everything you did to her," Karen revealed while her friends looked on.

"Goodbye, Karen," Jarvis said as he put on his sunglasses.

"You think you can do what you want to people just because you're charming and rich. That's not how it works."

Jarvis walked up to her, close enough for her to smell the spearmint gum he was chewing. Not trying to cause a scene, he put a smile on his face and said, "You better watch who you're talking to. I suggest you walk away before you're six feet under like your friend."

His tone was frightening to her. She hated him and wanted him dead. She knew all the horrible things he put Jennifer through, but she always promised her friend that she wouldn't tell anyone.

Even though she had never seen him, she had painted a picture of him in her mind from Jennifer's description. She knew exactly who Jarvis was, especially when the two brand new black Cadillac Escalade trucks with tinted windows pulled up. Six men dressed in black suits emerged from both trucks, and all eyes were on them as people wondered who they were. One can always pick rich men out of a crowd of poor people.

As everyone started to stare at them, Jarvis and his friends got into the trucks.

"What's up with her?" His friend, John, asked from the backseat.

"I guess she's just upset that her friend passed away. You know how people act when they're grieving," Kevin replied.

"She got me confused with someone else," Jarvis said, laidback.

"She really thought you were the cause of Jennifer's death. That's fool-ish because you never dated her," John added.

"It seems like they're looking for someone to blame her death on. They just need closure," Kevin said, glancing over at Jarvis.

"Did you hit that?" John asked, looking at Jarvis suspiciously.

"Every man in town hit that," Kevin responded before Jarvis could answer, and they all started laughing, even though Jennifer was not the type of woman who slept around.

"You got women killing themselves over you? Damn, Jarvis!" John said jokingly while shaking his head.

"I didn't have anything to do with her killing herself. I don't give a damn about these crazy-ass women. I'm just trying to keep money in my pockets and my clubs up and running."

"I'll kill someone over my money, but I'm not killing myself over a woman. The person she killed herself over must have really messed up her mind," John commented.

"I paid my respects. Now it's back to business. I need to stop by my club to check on things. Let's get out of here because this is making me depressed," Jarvis said as he drove off.

"You're supposed to put it down in the bedroom and bang her back out. Not drive the woman to kill herself," John said, cracking up laughing, but Jarvis didn't find it amusing.

"I can't help it if I got a deadly package," Jarvis replied, then started laughing along with him.

He knew Jennifer's friend was right, and the only one in the car that also knew she was right was Kevin, who wasn't saying a word.

"Man, if you're the reason she killed herself, you're a dirty dog. I know how you get down, and I'm sure you had her losing her mind. These women better be careful dealing with your ass. They're lined up to date you, but don't have a clue what they're getting into," John said, smiling.

"The things women are interested in are powerful men with money. They don't care about us, so why the hell should we care about them?" Kevin stated.

"The only thing a woman can do for me is have sex, cook, clean and do what I tell her to do. If I'm going to allow her to have a good life off of my money, she's definitely going to submit to me," Jarvis said seriously.

"Keep them in line," John added mockingly.

"Keep them on lockdown, and they will always stay in line," Jarvis told them, trying to school his boys just like his father had taught him how to manipulate a woman and get them to do what he needed them to.

They drove off laughing, talking, and unconcerned about Jennifer's death, family, or friends. They headed back to the club to do what they did best. Make money.

CHAPTER 1

Two weeks after the funeral, Jarvis filled Jennifer's position by hiring a new executive assistant named Candace Mourton, and his personal assistant, Michelle, gave her an intense training. He felt Candace would be able to handle the job, but wanted to put her to the test to find out.

She had the look he liked, and based on the information provided on her resume, she had all the skills to get the job done. Jarvis had a private office away from his clubs because he wanted to keep things separate, and since his business was growing so fast, he needed more space.

To others, Candace Mourton appeared to be strong and confident, but she was actually weak and insecure. She always had her game face on and could charm mostly anyone. Candace was stunning and had a confidence that made people flock to her. Just like society awarded Halle Berry the most beautiful woman in the world, Candace must have been a mirror image of her, because she definitely deserved that award, also.

Her petite body was complemented by a small waist, nice-size breasts and a round butt. She took pride in her body and made sure she worked out every day to keep it tight. She had long flowing hair, with light brown eyes, small lips and high cheekbones. She was striking to the eyes, even without make-up.

Candace watched her mother work a nine-to-five job five days a week and listened to her complain daily about how much she hated her job and manager. Hearing her mother complain all the time, she knew she had to make money doing something she enjoyed.

Since her mother raised her alone, she wanted a man in her life to take care of her, like she had seen her friend's father do. Since Candace's father left when she was a child, she didn't know him. She was an only child and had a decent childhood, not wanting for anything. Still, she longed for the love of her father.

She learned that her beauty and nice body made men want to take care of her financially and pamper her. With her well-paid job, she would do whatever it took to keep a luxurious lifestyle.

Jarvis also hired Antonio Flink as his new assistant manager to help run his new club. He saw something in Antonio that told him he was the right person to hire. Antonio appeared to be a hard worker and eager to learn, which were two things Jarvis loved and respected. Jarvis wasn't ready to give him the title of manager, he wanted him to prove himself in his position, and Antonio didn't waste any time showing his worth.

Antonio met Jarvis when he walked into his nightclub in Atlanta and told Jarvis that he was his new manager. Jarvis was amused by his cockiness and decided to give him a chance to prove himself. Jarvis liked the way he carried himself and hired him on the spot.

Jarvis planned to teach Antonio everything he knew about business and women. Antonio had many jobs, which most people would have complained about, but since he was well paid, he wanted to keep the money flowing.

Antonio Flink spoke English, French and Spanish fluently, which Jarvis knew would be helpful in sealing many deals. Antonio was smart, loyal, handsome and a perpetual cheater. His mother was African American his father was Puerto Rican, and with that mixture, he was definitely handsome.

He had black curly hair, a light caramel complexion, clean-shaven face, and reminded people of the rapper Nelly. His body was very muscular, and he didn't disappoint the eyes. His deep dimples were the first thing people noticed when he smiled, which lit up any room. He was charismatic and sexy without trying to be.

There would definitely be a competition between Antonio and Jarvis with the women. They were both attractive and the women were already going crazy over them. They were double trouble.

Candace knew she had big shoes to fill because Jarvis always talked about how great Jennifer was. Determined to erase Jennifer's memories, she wasn't going to let the most wanted job in town slip through her hands. She was going to do whatever it took to keep her position.

Jarvis' personal assistant, Michelle, had been working with him for over two years and was just as tough as he was. She was his right-hand woman, and he trusted her with his businesses.

Jarvis was building his dream team, and since his businesses were expanding, he had to keep filling the team positions. All of his clubs were upscale, and he was known for giving elaborate parties. He only wanted the best people working for him and never settled for less.

If you couldn't hold your weight, you would be fired immediately. No exceptions, no excuses. He knew the secret to succeeding was having the right people working for him.

Every woman who met Jarvis wanted him, and his reputation made women lust after him even more. Word around town was Jarvis was very good to his women and employees, but demanded a lot from them.

As long as you did what he wanted, you wouldn't have a problem keeping your job. He was successful and wanted to stay that way, so if you were going to work for him, you had to damn near be perfect. Candace was up for the challenge, and she also had a motive. She wanted a rich, successful man in her life, and that man was Jarvis.

During their first couple weeks of work, Michelle was hard on Candace and Antonio. She had them rethinking their career choice. Michelle helped Antonio get adjusted to his new surroundings and taught him all the rules to survive working for Jarvis. Antonio was tough, and she knew he would do fine. Once she was finished teaching him all the rules and regulations, he began working with the manager of one of the clubs.

After weeks of strenuous training, Candace got the swing of things and started feeling comfortable with her job duties. Michelle finally eased up on her because she knew Candace was able to handle her job, and was very much aware of the things expected of her. Only the strong survived, and Michelle would make sure Candace was a worthy candidate.

Candace admired the close relationship Michelle and Jarvis had, and she dreamed of being just as close to him. Michelle was always out of the office working on deals for Jarvis, and it appeared she was just as powerful. Candace worked in the office most of the time and assisted Michelle whenever needed.

Jarvis didn't believe in chaos in the workplace and was adamant about everyone working well together as co-workers and friends. Therefore, Candace was forced to be friends with Michelle if she wanted to keep her job and make a good impression on Jarvis.

Now that her training was over, she actually enjoyed Michelle's company and thought she was fun to be around. With a Bachelor's degree in Marketing, Michelle was on top of her game, and Candace had nothing but respect for her.

Months later, Michelle decided to move to Los Angeles to go back to school for her Master's degree. It was hard for her to resign because she loved her job, but she knew she was making the right decision for her career. Jarvis didn't want to see her leave because she had been working for him for such a long time, and he trusted her.

Once she was gone, Jarvis moped around and appeared to be slightly depressed. He always said it was hard to find trustworthy employees, and when you found people you could trust, you should hold on to them. He tried to persuade Michelle to stay by offering her more money, but her mind was set on getting her degree and eventually starting her own marketing company.

Candace was torn because she was happy to see her leave since it meant she had a shot at her position, but she was also sad because she had grown to like her. Candace learned a lot from her and appreciated her generosity of knowledge.

She didn't waste any time trying to prove to Jarvis that she was the right candidate for Michelle's position. With Michelle gone, Candace had to take on her job responsibilities until the position was filled.

She needed him to trust her, so she did everything she could to show him that she was capable of doing the job. She had a lot of responsibilities and had her hands in everything pertaining to the business, including bank accounts, insurance papers, and other important elements of the company.

Ready for a change of scenery, Jarvis contemplated moving to Chicago to look after his new club he had opened a few months earlier and to also explore other business opportunities. After five months of working his employee's non-stop, he invited Candace and Antonio to move to Chicago with him to help with the new club.

They didn't hesitate to follow him from Atlanta to The Windy City. He paid them very well, which made it easy for them to agree to continue their careers with him. He also brought along his close friends and a few other staff members to train the new employees and help maintain the club.

He couldn't take all his star employees because he needed them to take care of his other clubs, but he took Kevin and John, who had been with him since he opened his first club. They would manage the clubs while Antonio assisted them. Kevin was a traveling manager who visited the other clubs to make sure things were running properly.

Jarvis brought along everyone that he trusted the most and who he could rely on to help run all of his businesses. He had the ultimate dream team and was ready to have another successful club.

Two months later, they made the quick move to Chicago and settled into their new homes. Jarvis rented luxury apartments for his staff in the downtown area of Chicago and purchased a posh condominium for himself until he was able to find a house. He leased them cars, which were nothing but the finest. Treat them right and they will be loyal was his motto. He knew money ruled the world, and he was controlling his staff with it.

The nightclub in Chicago was already known as the hottest place on the scene. The Denttin nightclubs already had a name for themselves, so it wasn't hard to make an impression in the Chicago nightclub circuit.

His staff had shown him true loyalty, and he was grateful for them. They were dedicated to keeping him on top. With the strenuous work schedule he demanded of his staff, he always showed his appreciation by giving them substantial commission checks that kept them around longer. Although he worked them hard, they were happy to be part of his empire. He just asked that they always be honest, loyal, and never steal from him.

CHAPTER 2

Six days a week, ten to twelve hour days, and now Candace understood the meaning of working hard for the money. She was working hard enough to earn every bit of her salary. She had a difficult job and a demanding boss. It was hard for her to keep up at first, but she learned fast and her endurance increased.

She was exhausted and didn't have a life of her own. However, her bank account was growing, and she was becoming more popular. As she learned her way around Chicago, she fell in love with the city and had already made new friends. Chicago was much more congested than Atlanta, but she was adapting. Shopping on the Magnificent Mile on Michigan Avenue helped keep her mind off of the hustle and bustle of the downtown area.

Chicago was definitely a place she could call home permanently. The way Jarvis set her up was exactly how she wanted to live. Living in a tall, luxurious high-rise building with a doorman, she brushed shoulders in the elevators daily with doctors, lawyers, and entrepreneurs who made her feel like she was important. She was feeling great about her career, living arrangements, and the new city.

After working a long, stressful day, it was already after six o'clock in the evening when Jarvis called Candace to his office. She jumped up from her desk with her notepad in hand, ready to work. She quickly slid on her four-inch stiletto heels because he required the women employees to dress sexy, yet professional and with heels on. The men had to wear suits at all times while at the clubs.

With her feet in agony, she hated to put her heels back on, but knew she couldn't walk into his office without them. So, she suffered through the pain and adjusted her skirt. She took a quick glance in her small compact mirror to make sure she was flawless. Her white blouse was stylist, and her breasts were peeking out just enough to show the goods, but also remain professional.

Jarvis hadn't said too many words to her since she started working for him, and he kept a professional attitude towards her. However, since Michelle was gone, he had no choice but to communicate with her more on a daily basis.

Since he was always on the telephone or away from the office, Candace hardly saw him and was thrilled when he was in the building. Whenever she was around him, she noticed him checking her out on the sly. She knew he liked what he saw and was turned on by her appearance.

Candace walked into his office and closed the door behind her. She was a little nervous, but ready to handle any task he threw her way. She had butterflies in her stomach just looking at him. The very sight of him intimidated her but made her even more intrigued.

She looked at Jarvis sitting behind the desk, and her heart skipped a beat. He was gorgeous and always smelled wonderful. This day he was dressed casual, with a pair of nice-fitting dark colored jeans, a white t-shirt, an exclusive designer belt and watch, and one diamond stud earring.

"We have a big party next week and I want to make sure everything is set. I have a lot of people coming in town, so make sure all of my guest's hotel suites are booked," Jarvis said without looking up.

"I've reserved all of the rooms," Candace told him proudly.

"Make sure the bar is stocked with enough top-shelf liquor and the VIP room is set up ahead of time. Also, make sure there are enough gifts bags for all the guests," Jarvis said, still not looking at her, but making sure everything was covered.

"I'll take care of it," Candace replied as she started writing down his instructions on her notepad.

"Every athlete, actor, entertainer, you name it, will be at this party.

Things need to be perfect because my reputation is riding on this," Jarvis said, sounding anxious.

"I will make sure this event is the talk of the town. Don't worry. I have it all under control."

"Make sure you print out the final guest list for me. Remember, this event is invitation only," Jarvis reminded her.

"A lady by the name of Karen Law keeps calling regarding attending the party. She said you would remember her because she was a friend of Jennifer Moeky. Should I put her name on the guest list?"

"Don't put her name on the list because I don't know who she is," Jarvis said, even though he knew it was Jennifer's angry friend who approached him at the funeral.

"Should I put Jennifer Moeky's name on the list?" Candace asked.

"No. Jennifer passed away."

"I'm sorry to hear that. What happened to her?"

"It's not important, but the next time Karen Law calls, tell her to fuck off," Jarvis said, annoyed.

"Do you really want me to tell her that?"

"You have my permission to say whatever you want to make sure she doesn't bother me again," Jarvis said with no emotions.

Candace wondered who the woman was and figured it was some old girlfriend trying to get back in his life. So, she was more than happy to tell her to go to hell and get out of her way.

"I need to ask you something, and I need you to be honest," Jarvis said as he folded his hands and leaned on the desk while looking at her strangely.

Candace wasn't sure what he wanted to talk about, but by the look on his face, she could tell it was something serious.

"What's going on?"

"Do you know a man name Mark who was involved in some illegal activities?"

Candace hesitated before answering because she knew where the conversation was going.

She responded with caution, "Yes, I know Mark."

"How do you know him?" Jarvis asked as he sat up straight in his chair, anxiously anticipating her answer.

"We were in a relationship."

"Finish the story."

"Huh?" Candace responded, knowing he wanted her to tell the entire story, which was something she wanted to put behind. But, it seemed like the past was revisiting her.

"Never let them see you sweat. I taught you how to do that, but right now, I need to see you sweat a little and tell me what happened. I already know the story, but it seems you forgot to mention this incident to me when I hired you," Jarvis said, demanding answers.

Candace wanted to sit down, but this wasn't the time to get relaxed while he was waiting on a response. Besides, he didn't invite her to sit down, so she remained standing. Her palms began to sweat, and she hoped her past wouldn't jeopardize her job.

"You're not going to fire me, are you?" Candace nervously asked.

"Tell me what happened," Jarvis said, tired of her hesitation.

Without further delay, Candace started telling him the story about how her life changed five years ago. She was in a relationship with Mark for almost a year and thought he was an employed, hardworking person.

Mark wined and dined her, and she was happy with their relationship until the day he asked her to pick him up from work. He called her before she arrived at his job and told her where to meet him, which was on the side of a bank.

Mark instructed her to meet him at exactly three-thirty in the afternoon. Since she was always late and wanted to make sure she was on time, she arrived fifteen minutes early. Once she got there, she waited until three-thirty exactly and called to tell him that she was outside waiting.

He told her to wait and he would be right out, so she sat in the car and waited for him. After turning the radio on, she fixed her hair in the rearview mirror and listened to music.

Ten minutes later, she got a call from him telling her to start the car and unlock the doors because he was in a rush and wanted to make the dinner reservation he had made for them. She found that strange, but did as she was told. She was excited because he always pampered her and took her to the most expensive restaurants. So, she was ready to eat and see her man.

When she looked in the rearview mirror, she saw her boyfriend Mark and two other men running extremely fast toward the car with two large black bags on their shoulders. She knew if you saw people running, you also ran without asking questions. She thought maybe someone was chasing them. Panicking, she almost drove away, but she waited until they got in the car.

After they jumped in the car, Mark shouted, "Drive! Drive!"

Candace kept asking, "What's going on?"

They never responded, instead, they laughed and gave each other high-fives as their adrenaline rushed through their veins. Once they arrived in front of a house Mark instructed her to drive to, which was a place she had never been, she now knew they had just robbed the bank.

Mark had set her up as the driver of the getaway car without her knowledge. She was young, dumb, and never saw it coming. Mark never worked at a bank, but he robbed them on a regular.

Several people saw Candace while she was waiting for them and they also saw her pulling off with Mark and his friends. A full detailed description of Candace, her car, and license plate were given to the police. They arrested Candace the next day when she returned home.

The police were waiting at her front door, and in exchange for her freedom, she told the police where Mark and his friends were hiding. She didn't have anything to do with the robberies that had taken place and was misled by Mark. She testified in court against Mark and his friends, and she got off free of all charges.

She was terrified at the thought of going to jail. She didn't want to snitch on her boyfriend, but her freedom meant more to her, especially since he had set her up. She walked away from that incident, moved to Atlanta, and started a new life.

She was scared Mark would find her and kill her for taking his freedom away. He is serving twenty-five years in jail and was never convicted for the two other banks he robbed while they were together.

"That's the whole story. I was young and naïve, but that was a long time ago," Candace explained, feeling like she was on the witness stand again.

"It wasn't that long ago. Why didn't you tell me this information when you got hired?"

"I didn't get charged with anything. I don't have a record, so there was nothing to tell."

"I think that piece of information is something you should have disclosed to me."

"I'm sorry, Jarvis. I didn't think I needed to tell you that. I'm not a thief or snitch," Candace said, wondering if that's what he was concerned about.

"You are a snitch, but it's understandable."

"I just want to put that behind me. He threatened me and I was scared. I've always thought he would kill me if he ever got the chance. That's why I moved to another city to feel safe," Candace said as tears streamed down her face.

"You don't have to worry about him harming you. I knew the story. I just wanted to see if you would tell me the truth, and you did. I don't respect snitches, but I guess there are some incidents when it is acceptable. Right?"

"You're right. Are you going to fire me?"

"No, I'm not going to fire you. I guess I just have to be careful of you snitching," Jarvis said, flashing a smile.

Candace didn't find his comment funny.

"I'm not a snitch, but I will put myself first. I'm not going to go to prison for something I didn't do," she told him.

"Did you know Mark is getting out of jail next week?"

"He's supposed to be in jail for twenty-five years. How can he be getting out?" Candace asked, starting to panic.

"I'm not sure how he's getting out so early, but he will be out soon."

"How do you know that?"

"I'm like God. I know everything because my ears are always in the streets."

Candace didn't respond. Instead, she just looked down at the floor.

"You don't have to worry about anything. As long as you're working with me, he won't bother you. You're safe, so don't worry."

"Are you sure?" Candace asked, sounding relieved.

"I won't let anything happen to you as long as you're my employee," Jarvis said, looking sexy and yummy to her.

It was something about a man that protected her and who looked good doing it that turned her on.

"So, basically, I need to keep my job in order to save my life," Candace said quietly.

Although she was feeling scared, her intuition told her that she would be safe with him.

"If that's how you want to look at it," he replied.

Silence filled the room as Candace stood still and thought about their conversation. Jarvis started writing something down on a notepad and then began typing on the computer. He ignored her like she wasn't in his office, but she didn't say anything. She just waited patiently.

She was trained to wait until he dismissed her. Otherwise, she needed to wait for further instructions, which is what she was doing.

She prayed he would say something soon because her feet were aching and starting to swell from being in heels all day. She wasn't sure if discussing her past was the only reason he called her in his office, but she was going to wait to find out.

Finally, Jarvis looked up as if he had just noticed her, and took in every inch of her body starting with her four-inch stilettos. He slowly glanced over her physique and didn't stop until he reached her breasts.

He stopped and stared at her ample breasts that were trying to break free from her blouse. Then he stopped his sexual thoughts for a moment and looked at her face.

"You should take your hair down. It looks better hanging instead of being pinned up. You look old with your hair like that," Jarvis said before putting his head back down and continuing to write.

A few seconds later, he glanced back up at Candace, who was still standing there looking at him confused. Again, he looked down and kept writing. By the look on his face, she knew he meant for her to let down her hair at that very moment.

She removed the pin holding her beautiful, black, silky hair together in a bun and let it fall down past her shoulders. She used her fingers to quickly comb through her hair and prayed it was styled correctly.

"Come here," Jarvis said calmly as he put his pen down, leaned back in the chair, and waited for her. His eyes showed he approved of her instant makeover. Candace did exactly what she was told and walked over to him.

"Sit down," he said, instructing her to sit on the edge of his desk.

Candace sat down, arched her back and crossed her legs. The telephone rang, but before Jarvis answered it, he told her to uncross her legs. His voice was calm and smooth.

With her heart about to jump out of her chest she did exactly what she was told. His sexy presence was intimidating, and she was now very tense. He was a man of few words, but when he did speak, everyone listened, and she was anticipating his next words.

He hung up the telephone, and without saying a word, he slid his chair between her legs, gently spreading them open as he placed his hand on her chest and softly pushed her down on the desk. Without permission, he buried his head under her skirt and began to taste her through her panties. He pulled her lace thongs to the side and licked between her legs slowly, then at a fast pace.

Candace started breathing heavily and was not about to stop him because she wanted him just as much as he appeared to want her. She just didn't know it was going to go down like this, in his office on his desk. Hell, she didn't even know they were at that point in their relationship.

He had a mysterious way about him, which made him more fascinating. He was a man who knew what he wanted, and when he found it, he took it. Candace wanted him and was determined to make him hers forever.

Once Jarvis slowed down from tongue wrestling with her clit, her body began to shake from pleasure. After grabbing a condom from his desk drawer and sliding it on, he slowly entered her. Candace laughed inside thinking about how men would perform oral sex on women without a condom but were quick to get a condom to have intercourse. That never made any sense to her, and she knew he was no different than any other man.

She held on to his neck and allowed him to get more acquainted with her insides. Jarvis pumped harder, then faster, then harder, then in a slow motion until Candace's legs started shaking. She wanted to explode again, but didn't want the pleasure to end. Her hips gyrated fast, and he moaned as he grabbed her waist to slow down her movement before he had an orgasm too soon. Candace knew she had him and decided to show him all her tricks.

She moved her hips to the same rhythm of his thrust. The banging became intense as she leaned further back on the desk, wrapped her legs around him, and continued to ride him until he came hard. His body shook as sweat dripped off of him. She smiled inside as they both continued to breathe heavily.

Jarvis got up and fixed his clothes. She did the same. No words were exchanged, and Candace was unsure of what to do next. He sat back down in his chair, threw the condom in the trashcan, and leaned all the way back, feeling relaxed as he gazed at her.

Candace sat back down on the desk feeling confident that she had just put it on him. She wasn't sure if she was the best he ever had because of the number of women he had been with, but she knew he wouldn't forget the pleasure he had just experienced between her legs.

"Can I help you with anything else?" Candace asked softly as she seductively licked the corner of her mouth.

"You've done enough," Jarvis said with a smile.

The sound of the telephone interrupted them, and he picked it up on the first ring, not wanting to miss anything pertaining to his business. Candace sat patiently waiting for him to get off the telephone, but a few minutes later, he was still talking.

"I'm sorry, can we talk later?" Jarvis asked her as he covered the mouth-piece of the telephone.

"Sure," Candace replied then swiftly got off the desk.

Before she walked away, Jarvis stood up, leaned over, and kissed her on the neck. She walked out of his office feeling confident that she had her man on lockdown. She knew when a man didn't kiss a woman in the mouth after making love; it was only sex and nothing more. Still, she was happy with the situation for the moment because she knew it would all change soon.

CHAPTER 3

Months passed, and Candace was continuing to have sex with Jarvis whenever he was in the office, which was usually a few times a week. He wanted their sexual encounters kept confidential and their relationship professional while in the public's eye.

Jarvis was a charmer and always sent her flowers, gave her expensive gifts, and allowed her to go shopping on him. Even though she couldn't tell anyone who her secret admirer was, she had a plan and hoped one day she wouldn't have to hide their relationship any longer.

Candace enjoyed sleeping with the boss and the perks that came with the job, but their secret relationship was starting to bother her. She was upset that they had never been on a date and had never been seen in public as a couple. It was obvious she was just a booty call to him.

At the moment, she didn't mind filling that position because she had plans on changing her status. She just didn't know it would take so long. Locking down Jarvis in a committed relationship was harder than she thought.

Candace worked overtime every night and offered to help him with projects whenever she could. However, as hard as she worked at providing him sexual pleasure while running the office and his affairs, Jarvis still hadn't promoted her to his personal assistant, nor did she get promoted to being his girlfriend.

She was doing her job, but not given the title or salary. When she asked him about it, he told her that she had to earn the position, and he wasn't sure if she was ready. She knew that only meant he needed to trust her fully before he advanced her.

After a few months of sleeping with Jarvis and working herself to death, she decided not to continue going after the position. Instead, she would just do the job she was hired to do, because it was obvious Jarvis wasn't going to give her the position and wasn't looking to fill it anytime soon.

She had sexed him down several times a week, and he still wasn't comfortable enough to trust her. So, she would focus on making him her man and being able to tell the world she was dating Mr. Jarvis Denttin. She was going to be as patient as she needed to be.

Candace had been working non-stop with no break and her body was slowly shutting down. She had been working hard and was tired and irritable. Jarvis left the office for a meeting and left her there to continue working. The phones were ringing continuously and Candace was cranky. She kept thinking about meeting up with Jarvis later on that night for some much needed sex. When Candace looked up from her computer, a tall beautiful woman was standing in front of her.

"Hello, may I help you?" Candace asked.

"Is Jarvis here?" the woman asked.

"He went to a meeting. Can I assist you with something?" Candace pleasantly asked.

"I'll just wait in his office," the woman said.

"I'm sorry I can't allow you to do that," Candace said shocked by her boldness.

"I'm sure he won't mind his fiancée' waiting for him," the woman said, as she walked into Jarvis office and sat down.

Candace followed behind her completely caught off guard by her comment.

"I didn't know he was engaged," Candace said, eager to hear her response.

"I guess Jarvis hasn't told everyone yet."

"I guess not," Candace said as she noticed the huge sparkling diamond ring on her finger. "I'll call him to let him know you're here."

"Don't bother. I'll just meet him at home."

"It was nice meeting you. I'm sorry I didn't get your name," Candace said.

"It's Kora, soon to be Mrs. Kora Denttin."

"Well, congratulations on your engagement. I'll tell Jarvis you stopped by," Candace said, trying to pick her heart up off the floor.

"Nice meeting you too," Kora said as she walked out of the office.

Candace couldn't wait to call Jarvis to find out if there was any truth to the mystery woman's visit. Just when she thought things couldn't get any worse, Jarvis re-introduced her to his fiancée, Kora the next day.

Five months later, Jarvis made Kora his wife when they eloped on an island in Barbados. Candace's heart was broken, her feelings were hurt, and her pride was destroyed, especially since she had to help plan the wedding ceremony and honeymoon.

She didn't know what went wrong. She did everything he ever asked of her, and she was puzzled. Things were going great between the two of them, so she didn't know how he slipped away from her. Jarvis didn't even seem to care that he was breaking her heart. It was always about him making money; no one else ever mattered.

Candace didn't know that Jarvis was exclusively dating someone, and was totally shocked that someone had beaten her to the finish line and took the most available bachelor off the market.

Kora Denttin, the wife of Jarvis, was stunning and a retired model, not by choice but by the orders of Jarvis. He felt there should only be one star in the family, and that was him. So, she put her career on a permanent hold.

Kora was definitely making the wrong decision of retiring so early from modeling. She had the look, body and skills to be a supermodel. She was 5'9" with no shoes on, a size two, and beautiful. She looked like a mixture of supermodels Gisele Bundchen, Heidi Klum, and Cindy Crawford.

She had an exotic look, and Candace knew she had a lot of different ethnicities tied up in her. Candace couldn't hate on her. She was gorgeous and made Candace stare at her a few times impressed by her beauty.

Kora was hardly seen in public unless Jarvis wanted to show her off, and even then people didn't know she was married to him when they were out. She was a well-kept woman and accustomed to the finer things in life.

Kora was from a dysfunctional family with an alcoholic mother and drug-addicted father. She struggled throughout her childhood and moved in with her grandmother who raised her.

She never wanted to be broke, and after meeting Jarvis, he offered her a deal she couldn't resist. She could be his wife, do what she was told, and live the glamorous life, which sounded like a good deal at the time. She was once a secure woman, but being married to Jarvis broke her down and had her feeling like a trapped bird.

Kora didn't know her life would be this way, but she dealt with it because she loved her environment. She was addicted to the charmed life she had, being married to Jarvis.

After getting to know Candace, Kora confided in her with her deepest secrets. She was unaware of the sexual relationship Jarvis had with Candace and the way they both manipulated her. She was clueless and sheltered from the world. Even though Jarvis cheated on her with many women, he pampered Kora constantly.

Jarvis didn't allow her to have friends that he didn't approve of, and being married to him, she had to disown her family. She hadn't spoken to them since she married him. He kept her away from anyone who he thought would speak some sense into her. He controlled her every move, and she couldn't leave the house without asking him. Since she wanted to marry a rich man and live comfortably, she paid for it with her life and freedom.

Candace spent many days trying to figure out what made him marry her so quickly. Kora was beautiful, but so was she. She just figured Kora had game and knew how to lock down a man quickly. She needed to study her, find out who she really was and why she had married her man.

Kora was very nice and seemed to be kind. Candace was unaware that Jarvis had been dating her for a few years before he decided to put a ring on it.

Candace was so devastated by his marriage she almost quit her job because she couldn't handle the thought of never fully being with him. Things became worse for her when Jarvis didn't want to end their sexual relationship. He continued on as if he wasn't married. She never stopped him because she still had feelings for him and just couldn't walk away.

She had to wake up and remember her purpose for being with him was to live a nice lifestyle. Working and sexing him on a regular, guaranteed that she would continue to be financially stable. Therefore, she sacrificed her pride and feelings to live comfortably.

"Can I talk to you?" Candace asked as she walked into Jarvis' office.

"Sure. What's up?" he asked cheerfully.

"I'm not sure what to say, but I thought I meant something to you."

"What are you talking about?" Jarvis asked, confused.

"We've been sleeping together for a long time, and you married someone else. What did I do wrong?" Candace asked, lowering her voice.

"You didn't do anything wrong?"

"Well, why didn't you marry me?" She probed, shocking herself by the question.

"Candace, I thought you understood that we are grown adults just having sex."

She felt like a ton of bricks had fallen on her. She had never felt so used and cheap.

"I thought I was more than just a sex partner to you. I thought we had something."

"We do have something. We both have orgasms a few times a week," Jarvis said with a smirk.

"Jarvis, I'm serious. We are still having sex and you're married."

"Candace, if you can't handle these arrangements, then we can stop. I don't want to have this conversation anymore. I need to get back to work and make this money."

"It's like that?" Candace asked, feeling hurt and angry inside.

"Just because I fuck you once in a while, don't get your mind confused and think you can come in my office stepping to me like that. You need to get yourself together or walk away from me and this job," Jarvis said with a frustrated frown on his face.

Candace stared, but knew to walk away quickly. She left out of his office feeling stupid.

CHAPTER 4

Things became harder for Candace when Jarvis insisted that she become his wife's personal assistant until he could hire one for her. Candace had to make spa appointments, dinner reservations and anything Kora requested. Jarvis treated her like a precious gem, and made sure Candace was available whenever Kora needed her.

Candace didn't understand why he trusted her to be around Kora, knowing they were still having sex. Jarvis knew Candace's type and wasn't worried about her telling his wife their secret, because Candace was ready and willing to take Kora's place. Jarvis didn't care if Kora found out and wanted to leave, because she would be replaced just like he did all the other women.

Candace witnessed how special Jarvis treated Kora, and she felt envious of their relationship. She had never experienced that behavior from him and yearned for the attention he gave Kora. She could tell Jarvis was in love with Kora and would do anything to keep her happy.

Although Jarvis tried to act like he didn't care about Candace, she knew the true story and didn't know why he pretended like he wasn't that interested.

Candace also observed several surprises he gave Kora, especially whenever he was away from home for long periods of time. She always helped Kora put away her expensive designer clothing courtesy of the regular shopping sprees Jarvis set up for her while he was out of town on business.

One day while Candace was assisting Kora at her house Jarvis called Candace's cell phone and told her that he had a surprise for Kora and to have her open the front door. So when the doorbell rang, they both rushed to see what was going on. When they opened the door, there was a man dressed in a black tuxedo, with white gloves and a top hat. He was holding a silver serving tray with two large cups on it.

"Good morning Mrs. Denttin. Have you had your coffee today?" the gentleman asked.

"Who sent you?" Kora asked in amazement, while Candace remained quiet.

Candace had no idea what the surprise could be, and after watching Kora shop all day, she didn't think she could handle watching her receive another gift from Jarvis. She couldn't help but feel jealous.

"I was sent by Mr. Jarvis Denttin. He said you love coffee, so I'm delivering a fresh cup for you," the gentleman informed her.

"That is so sweet," Kora said, smiling as she covered her mouth with both of her hands. "Jarvis knows what I like. I love that man."

"This is for you," The gentleman handed her the cup of coffee.

Kora couldn't stop smiling as she took a sip of coffee, closed her eyes and savored the taste.

"It's perfect. Thank you," Kora said, feeling special.

Candace noticed there were two cups of coffee on the tray and thought to herself how nice of Jarvis to think of her, too.

"Who is the other cup of coffee for?" Candace asked.

Before the gentleman could respond, Jarvis stepped from the side of the house and asked Kora, "Can I drink a cup of coffee with you?"

Kora was surprised by his unique gesture. She didn't know when he was returning home from his business trip. Needless to say, she was ecstatic to see him.

"What are you doing home?" Kora asked.

"I've missed you," Jarvis said.

Kora placed the coffee cup back on the tray and jumped in his arm, hugging and kissing all over him. Candace watched them tongue each other down as Jarvis rubbed all over her body, like Candace and the gentleman were not standing there.

Jarvis pulled a blue gift box out of his pocket and handed it to her. She opened the box, and upon seeing the beautiful expensive diamond bracelet, she hugged him again.

As if he hadn't already outdone himself, they walked hand-in-hand back into the house as Kora rested her head on his shoulder. To Kora's surprise, the entire living room area was full of colorful exotic flowers. Even Candace's mouth fell to the floor when she saw the gorgeous arrangements that continued up the staircase.

While Jarvis kept the ladies distracted at the front door, he had flowers placed all over the house . He made sure the back door was unlocked so the floral delivery service could enter his home and strategically set up the flower arrangements.

Candace's jaws tightened as he continued to act like she wasn't there. As tears of joy were running down Kora's face, they kissed and hugged like a happily married couple. Candace just stood at the door watching them.

While Kora's back was to Candace, Jarvis continued kissing Kora's neck and eyeing Candace as she awkwardly watched her boy toy fondle someone else right in front of her. They walked passed Candace and went upstairs to the bedroom, going at it like two horny teenagers. From the headboard banging on the walls, Candace heard every thrust Jarvis was giving Kora. She listened to Kora's moaning as her heart continued to break into tiny pieces.

After months of feeling like the third wheel, Candace finally accepted she would never be with Jarvis exclusively. She had tried several times to break away from their sexual relationship, but he had a hold on her, and whenever she tried to distance herself from him, he kept pulling her back.

He wasn't the person she thought he was and there was more to him than she was aware of. Jarvis knew Candace was seeking monetary gains, and he planned to hold that over her head to get what he wanted from her. She wanted to bow out gracefully and move on to the next sucker. However, he was too good of a catch for her to just walk away from their arrangement.

For now, she would continue to assist his wife, whom she had become friends with, and be the best executive assistant and sex partner she could be. She now had her sights set on Jarvis' assistant manager, Antonio.

Antonio was fine, but didn't have the money or status that Jarvis possessed. He would simply be someone to spend her time with. Candace was becoming a mini version of Jarvis, which was scandalous, selfish and dirty. Her heart had turned hard and cold, just how Jarvis wanted her to be.

The next day, Antonio walked into the office looking handsome as usual. This caused Candace to become even more attracted to him. Now that she couldn't have Jarvis the way she wanted, she needed to focus her attention and feelings on someone else. Even though Antonio didn't show any interest in her, she was going to work her magic on him anyway. She knew it would take some time, but she felt it might be worth it.

"Hey Antonio," Candace said with a flirty smile.

"What's up, Candace? Is Jarvis here?" he asked.

"He stepped out for a moment, but he will be back shortly."

"I'll just call him on his cell phone. Thanks," Antonio said, walking away quickly.

"I hardly get to see you. How's the job going?" Candace asked, trying to make small talk before he left.

"It's going good," Antonio replied.

"Have a seat. You're always in such a rush. Relax."

"It's been very busy and I don't have time to relax. You know how Jarvis hates his employees sitting around doing nothing. You trying to get me fired?" Antonio responded with a chuckle, but with truth to his statement.

"You're right. I better get back to work, too," Candace said, ending the conversation.

She knew it would take some time to get him to be interested in her. Right now, he was too focused on his job to let her sidetrack him.

"I'll talk to you later. Stay out of trouble," Antonio told her before quickly walking out of the office.

Antonio knew Jarvis had a strict policy about employees dating each other, and he wondered why Candace was trying to cross the line. It was obvious that she was flirting with him, and although he thought she was attractive, he wasn't interested in being with one of Jarvis' women.

CHAPTER 5

"Make sure you're there at a reasonable time tonight," Jarvis said, trying to rush off the telephone because he had a million calls to make before the charity event.

"I'll be on time," Candace replied.

"They're auctioning a lot of wealthy people tonight, and I need to make sure I generate the most money," Jarvis told her.

"That's nice you're doing a charity event. I hope these broke women can afford to bid on you," Candace joked.

"There are plenty of women who can afford to win a date with me. Plus, the money will go to support cancer charities, so tell your friends to bring their credit cards," Jarvis said.

"I hope the women attending have some money because the starting bid is five hundred dollars," Candace said.

"That's actually not enough. I'm worth more than that," Jarvis teased. He was in a good mood and ready for the charity event.

"I'll see you tonight. I'll be ready to start the bid with a dollar," Candace said, cracking herself up.

"Funny! Just make sure you're dressed in a nice business suit or something professional. Please don't wear any party clothes," Jarvis said seriously.

"Party clothes! I know how to dress for an event like this," Candace responded, annoyed at his comment.

"I just want to make sure you look presentable," Jarvis said, sounding preoccupied.

He knew Candace was not ashamed of showing her body at social events, and sometimes that could be perceived as slutty. He had class and style, so he didn't want her to embarrass him, which is something he hated.

"Oh, so you think I dress like a hooker? I dress professional every day at work. I know what to wear," Candace said, hiding her huge attitude.

"I don't have time for this. Just make sure you're dressed professionally," he told her rudely.

"Okay, Jarvis."

"What are you doing after the charity event?" he asked.

"Going home."

"Change of plans. Meet me at my house naked after the event," Jarvis said, changing the tone of his voice.

"I thought we both decided our sexual relationship was over," Candace said.

"I never agreed to that."

"What about Kora, your wife?" Candace asked.

"She will be at the house and will not disturb us. You know how it is. She will do whatever I tell her to do, and tonight, she will stay her ass in the bedroom," Jarvis said arrogantly.

"I thought we were going to be strictly professional from now on?" Candace said, trying her best to resist him.

Her conscience was bothering her because she was sleeping with a married man and also friends with his wife. She knew she was going straight to hell. Candace was his eyes and ears, telling him everything Kora did, and she made sure to do whatever Jarvis instructed her to. Having his mistress and wife as friends made Jarvis' life easy, especially since Candace was willing to cooperate.

"That's something you want. It's not what I want," he told her.

"We really need to stop this. You need to focus on Kora," Candace said, trying to fight the urge to sleep with him.

"Are you trying to tell me what I need to do with my wife?" Jarvis asked harshly.

Feeling uneasy, Candace said, "What we're doing is wrong."

She knew he didn't allow her to question the way he ran his life, but she tried to slip her comment in without any consequences.

"Just do what you're told," Jarvis said.

"Okay," Candace responded.

She frowned and rolled her eyes. Since he couldn't see her through the telephone, she continued to release more frustration.

"Did you make the spa appointment for Kora?" Jarvis asked in a businesslike tone.

"Yes. I've even arranged for her favorite flowers to be waiting in the limousine with a nice card from you," Candace said.

"You know how to keep my wife happy."

"She should be very pleased," Candace added as her jaws tightened.

"So do you want some dick or not?" Jarvis asked.

"I want some dick," Candace replied, smiling and reminiscing how great their love making was.

She had been his personal sex toy for so long that she was use to their agreement. Besides, her body was craving him. Even though she was sleeping with another man she was seeing off and on, she only wanted to be with Jarvis.

"That's my girl. Make sure it's wet for me," Jarvis said as he licked his lips and hung up the telephone.

Their relationship was bizarre, but something she had become accustomed to. She knew it was wrong what she was doing, but couldn't control her feelings; she was in too deep. Jarvis was manipulative and she couldn't stop from having sex with him and allowing him to control her body and mind.

"Hey, Lisa, I will be at your house at seven o'clock tonight. So, make sure you're ready because Jarvis is stressing out. We can't be fashionably late," Candace said.

"Everyone is talking about this charity event. They are auctioning off a lot of single, rich men tonight, and I'll have lots of money available," Lisa said, excited.

"Jarvis definitely wants us to bid on him, so be ready," Candace warned her.

"I'm bidding high to win that date with Jarvis. You just make sure you have your butt here on time. See you tonight," Lisa said, hanging up the telephone.

Lisa Cotus was a confident, strong, outspoken, businesswoman who was ready to take on the world. Her exact measurements were 34-25-38. Shaped like an hourglass, it was difficult sometimes for male clients to stay focused.

She never walked out of the house without her hair done, her make-up properly applied and dressed professionally. Her shapely body was complemented by long hair, a golden bronze complexion, large piercing brown eyes and high cheekbones.

As a successful interior designer, she created beautiful designs for just about every wealthy person in Chicago. Although it was costly to have her decorate your home or business, her services were worth every penny.

Her designs had been seen in the most popular magazines, and she was always on television talking about or displaying her unique designs. Her career was the most important aspect of her life, and her personal life had suffered because of her passion for designing.

After talking to Candace, Lisa immediately dialed Stacy's number. "Make sure you're at my house no later than six-thirty. We must be on time tonight."

"I'll be at your house at six because I want a drink before we leave," Stacy said.

"Can't you drink at the event?" Lisa asked jokingly.

"I like to be relaxed before I go out, and you know a glass of wine always hits the spot. Someone is calling me on the other line, so I'll see you tonight," Stacy replied before clicking over. "Hey, baby. Will I see you tonight?" Stacy asked while blushing. She wanted to make sure her night was going to be enjoyable.

"Most definitely. I can't wait to see you," Antonio said.

"I hope you're leaving your girlfriend at home," Stacy told him in a sassy tone.

"She won't be at the event tonight, so it's just you and me, baby," Antonio assured her.

"Maybe we can grab something to eat after the event," Stacy inquired trying to spend more time with the unavailable man who she had fallen in love with.

"If you promise to wear those black lace thongs and high heels I like, I'll think about it," Antonio said, teasing.

No one could ever forget Stacy Scattos because she was the life of the party. She believed in enjoying her life to the fullest and never took anything too seriously. Hair salon owner by day and party animal by night was the life she led.

She had built her career from the ground up and was determined never to work for anyone but herself. She was the proprietor of the most exclusive hair salon in town. If you weren't making over six figures, you wouldn't be sitting in her chair.

Light-skinned with short curly hair, you never knew what her hairstyle was going to look like because she like to changed things up. Her make-up went along with whatever hairstyle she wore. Long lashes and fake nails always completed her look.

Stacy was calm, bubbly and drop-dead gorgeous, and her face resembled the actress Jada Pinkett. Stacy was thick in all the right places and small where it matter the most. With 38D breasts, a 26-inch waist, and a butt that could hold a cup on it, she was any man's ideal woman.

Stacy couldn't wait until she found the perfect rich man of her dreams.

Since she was successful, she didn't want a man living off of her. So, he had to be just as successful as she was or better.

She had no problem getting a man, but she hadn't found a man who was interested in a committed relationship. Dating made her happy, and dating someone else's man strangely turned her on. The thrill of doing something she knew she shouldn't be doing was making her relationship with Antonio stimulating.

"Can I call you back? My girlfriend just got home," Antonio said, rushing off the telephone.

"Sure," Stacy said sadly.

Even though they had an open relationship and Antonio never hid the fact that he was dating another woman, whenever he mentioned his girlfriend, it drove her crazy. She didn't like sharing, and wanted him all to herself.

CHAPTER 6

The rich, mahogany floors complemented Lisa's bi-level, three-bedroom condo. With unique custom-made furniture, it felt like you were in a museum. The house was very warm with a neutral color scheme, which was tranquil. The kitchen was a chef's dream with stainless steel appliances, granite countertops, and dark wooden cabinets. However, the kitchen didn't get much use because Lisa couldn't cook.

The master bedroom was made for a queen, and the oversized closet was the reason Lisa purchased the condo three years ago. One of the bedrooms was converted into an office, and the other bedroom was turned into a mini gym. The two-car garage fit her Jaguar and Mercedes Benz truck perfectly.

Lisa took a lot of time, money, and creativity putting her home together, and she was happy with the results. Her home had to set a great example of the work she could produce since she was an interior designer. She wouldn't settle for anything less. She enjoyed designing her home and making it her own.

"Do you have any more wine?" Stacy asked, holding up the empty bottle.

"You're going to be drunk before you get to the event. Stop drinking so much," Lisa told her.

"I'm happy you guys are ready. Now let's go meet some rich men tonight," Candace said as she applied more lip gloss.

Candace always played the game with her girls, making them think she was on the hunt for a man, but in reality, she only wanted Jarvis. She knew exactly what to do and say so she wouldn't draw attention to her well-kept secret.

"Stop being so eager," Lisa said.

"This is going to be a great charity event," Stacy commented while opening another bottle of wine and pouring a glass.

Stacy had no intention on meeting any men because all she could think about was her planned evening with Antonio. She didn't tell Lisa or Candace about her relationship with him because if they knew he had a girlfriend, she knew they would have tons of their negative comments.

"It's going to be interesting," Candace said, knowing she was going to struggle watching other women bid on Jarvis.

"I'm excited to see Jarvis. I haven't seen him in a while," Lisa said.

Lisa had met Jarvis when she took her clients out for drinks to his club one evening, and Candace had given Lisa's business card to him just in case he was looking for an interior designer. They kept in contact, but there were no real sparks between them, just a lot of flirting whenever they saw each other.

"I'm not going down that road again," Candace said, tired of hearing her talk about Jarvis.

"I still don't understand why you don't want me to date him," Lisa responded as she grabbed her purse.

"I don't think you want to mess around with Jarvis. He's good looking, but I don't think you can handle him," Candace told her.

The truth was, she didn't want Lisa dating the man she was sleeping with, but she couldn't tell her that. She also couldn't let her know he was married, a secret he never told anyone but close friends.

"What do you mean by handle him? He's no different than any other man," Lisa said, trying to get some real answers.

"Jarvis is out of your league. He's not your type," Candace tried to explain.

"Is that any way to talk about your boss? Sometimes opposites attract,"

Lisa said.

"He has no respect for women," Candace responded seriously.

"Let that woman date who she wants," Stacy said, butting in.

"Whatever! Let's go," Lisa said, paying no attention to Candace's remarks.

"I'm just trying to look out for you. You're like a sister to me, and I don't want you to get hurt," Candace said sincerely.

Candace met Lisa and Stacy as soon as she moved to Chicago. They were members of the same elite health club and loved taking Yoga classes together. They hit it off the first day they met and had been close friends ever since.

"He really doesn't seem like the type of guy you're portraying him to be," Stacy voiced, confused.

"The few times I've been around him, he seemed like a respectable man. He has always been a perfect, sexy, fine gentleman," Lisa added.

"Enough talking about Jarvis, I'm ready to get out of here," Candace said, knowing she had already said too many negative things. The last thing she wanted was for her comments to get back to him.

The more Candace was against Lisa and Jarvis dating, the more attractive he became to Lisa. Staying away from something she wanted increased Lisa's feelings for him and made her want to get to know him even more.

They all worked hard to get to where they were in their lives, and they were all successful and doing well financially. The only thing missing from their lives were husbands, but they knew one day they would find Mr. Right. They didn't have a problem finding men; the problem was getting them to commit.

They were used to men going out of their way for them, and they always got what they wanted. They needed to find men who were just as driven and self-motivated as they were. They didn't want anyone riding their coattails to the top.

Lisa was strong and didn't take mess from any man, and if you did her wrong, she would cut you out of her life quickly. She always dominated the relationship and was always too much for most men to handle. She wanted things done her way, and she wanted control. Lisa was fun and outgoing, and she wanted to be with someone who was spontaneous and wealthy. She also wanted them to be over six-feet tall and muscular since she was 5'8" with flats on.

They arrived at the charity event promptly at seven o'clock. After walking into the hotel, they were escorted to the large banquet room. People were already there and more were arriving. They went straight to the bar and ordered apple martinis.

Once they had their drinks, they found the table Jarvis had reserved for them, which was already occupied by four other women. The event was lively and the music made them want to get up and dance, but they decided to wait.

Two drinks later, they were feeling good. By now, they were ready to dance and mingle. Stacy was done drinking for the night because she had reached her limit. They were determined to enjoy themselves since this was such an expensive night for each of them.

Not long after dinner, the auction started. It cost one hundred dollars just to enter the event. Then they wanted you to participate in the auction, which had a starting bid of five hundred dollars.

They were happy the proceeds were going to charity, but they were feeling the dent in their pockets. Lisa wanted to outbid everyone and win the date with Jarvis, but she knew every other woman in the room was going to be bidding on him, as well.

"Make sure you guys don't try to outbid me. You know I'm trying to get that date with Jarvis," Lisa told them.

"Jarvis is all yours. I'm bidding on another man I saw in the program," Stacy replied, knowing her mind was fixated on Antonio. She would only be bidding to give to charity, not to win a date.

"There are so many other men to bid on. Why are you wasting your money on Jarvis?" Candace asked.

"Candace, let it go. I'm bidding on him and winning," Lisa said, determined.

"Be quiet you guys. It's about to start," Stacy told them, trying to stop the argument before it got out of hand.

The men and women being auctioned walked out on stage and paraded around like runway fashion models. The women in the audience were screaming like they were at a strip club, and the men were barking like they were begging for a lap dance.

With the help of an open bar, the once elegant event had quickly turned into a raunchy scene. It became very fun and exciting for everyone, and it didn't seem so stuffy.

Since the attendees came to spend money, they didn't hesitate to place their bids. They were focused on winning dates with the man or woman of their dreams. Stacy put her bid in for a man, but didn't try to outbid a woman who seemed desperate to win the date with him. He was swept away with a high bid of $3,500.

Saving the best for last, Jarvis walked out on the stage, and when he did, the women in the room went wild. They were screaming while waving their money and credit cards high in the air. It's amazing how upscale, classy women loosen up and become wild after having a few cocktails.

Lisa knew it was going to be expensive if she wanted to win a date with him. After about ten minutes of biding on Jarvis, she bowed out gracefully and allowed a woman to win a date with him for the price of $5,000.

"Why did you let that woman take your man?" Stacy teased Lisa.

"I like him, but I'm not going to spend $5,000 on him," Lisa said, defeated.

"Every woman in this room wanted Jarvis. It would have been hard to win a date with him anyway," Stacy commented, amazed.

"He would probably try to date all of the women in the room if he could," Candace voiced hatefully.

"He's single and doing what single men do," Lisa said.

While they continued talking about the auction, Jarvis and Antonio made their way over to their table. When Lisa looked up, she saw a tall, handsome man and quickly stood up to give Jarvis a hug.

Jarvis was dressed impeccable in a tailor-made black tuxedo, Italian black shoes, and simple yet expensive jewelry that consisted of a Rolex watch and a diamond ring. His stride to the table was just as smooth as his hello. You couldn't help but watch this confident man.

There was something about him that made you want to get to know him. Jarvis and Antonio possessed an identical demeanor. They both were handsome, powerful and confident men.

Everyone stood up from the table to acknowledge them.

"What's up, ladies? You all look beautiful," Antonio said as they thanked him.

"You guys bailed out fast on the bidding. What happened?" Jarvis asked, then slowly licked his lips and smiled to show his perfectly straight, white teeth.

"We tried, but these women are desperate," Candace responded, giving him a hug.

"What's up, Stacy? Why didn't you bid on me?" Jarvis asked playfully. He knew she was sleeping with Antonio, but he enjoyed teasing her.

"You're too expensive for my bank account," Stacy said, smiling as Antonio observed her.

"Lisa, you were being cheap," Jarvis said, continuing to joke with them.

"I'm not cheap. I'm just not going to go broke for a date," Lisa said. "I guess you have to go spend time with the big spender," she added, playfully pouting her lips.

"Don't be a sore loser. Maybe you'll win next time. I guess I do need to go meet the winner," Jarvis said, flashing a big smile.

Jarvis hugged each of them, but gave Lisa a longer hug than the others. He looked at her and tried to say something with his eyes, but she couldn't figure it out.

"Maybe we can get a drink later," Jarvis whispered in Lisa's ear.

"Sounds good," she said, flirting back.

He smiled at her as he walked away, while they all watched. His presence was so strong they couldn't resist staring at him and being drawn in. Candace was upset with Jarvis for flirting with Lisa right in front of her, but it was nothing new to her. She was used to this behavior; however, the life she had chosen for herself was wearing thin on her.

After an hour of dancing and drinking, they decided to take a break and rest their feet. After returning to their table, they noticed Candace was nowhere to be found. They figured she had met someone and was talking privately.

They didn't worry about her and continued their conversation. Even though the crowd had dwindled down, they decided to continue enjoying themselves and close the event.

As the evening was coming to an end, Stacy went to retrieve their coats from the coat check room, while Lisa sat at the table talking to a couple about remodeling their home. Lisa was always about business and would never let an opportunity pass her by. The couple knew who she was because she had such a great reputation, and they were excited to meet her and possibly work with her.

Stacy headed to the coat check area, but when she got there, no one was there to assist her. Since everyone had gone home and only a few people were left at the event, the coat check person had left for the night. After waiting five minutes for someone to help her, she took it upon herself to get the coats. She opened the door to the narrow room, knowing it would be easy to find their coats.

When Stacy flicked on the lights, she was shocked to see Jarvis and Candace having sex. He had her bent over a chair while pounding her from behind. The look on Candace's face was memorable because she was mortified, but the look on Jarvis' face was relaxed and unaffected.

The way Jarvis looked at Stacy, she felt as if he was flirting with her. She shook off the feeling she was receiving from him, which made her a little uncomfortable.

"Oh my goodness!" Candace shouted, while jumping to the side to cover her body.

"I'm so sorry. I didn't know anyone was in here," Stacy said, staring at them like she had seen a ghost. Then after thinking for a moment about what she was seeing, she asked, "Candace, what are you doing?"

Candace never responded. Instead, she continued adjusting her clothes.

"I'm leaving," Stacy said in a disgusted tone as she continued to stare.

Stacy walked backwards extremely slow as she looked at the both of them completely speechless. Candace moved around frantically trying to fix her dress, while Jarvis took his time trying to put his erect penis back into his pants. Stacy got the impression that he wanted to finish where they had left off and she was interrupting them.

"What the hell just happened?" Stacy mumbled to herself as soon as she closed the door behind her. "I can't believe Candace is sleeping with Jarvis. Why didn't she tell us? Lisa is going to flip out!" Stacy said, continuing to mumble to herself in utter shock.

So many thoughts ran through her head on the way back to the table. Should I tell Lisa? She doesn't need to be chasing after Jarvis if he's sleeping with Candace. He was flirting with Lisa right in front of Candace. That dog! Candace knows how much Lisa likes Jarvis. I guess that's why she was so against her dating him. She's a dirty dog, too. Damn, this is too much. Stacy took a deep breath and tried to think of something to tell Lisa.

Deciding she wasn't going to ruin the night, she didn't say anything to Lisa about what she had just witnessed. She sat down at the table, but kept looking back at the door to see when Jarvis and Candace were going to walk in.

After ten minutes and still no sign of them, Stacy got the feeling they were finishing what they had started, or maybe they were too embarrassed to show their faces.

"Where are the coats?" Lisa asked.

"Oh my God, I forgot the coats," Stacy said.

"How did you forget the coats? What were you doing?" Lisa asked.

"I stopped and talked to some friends. You know I get forgetful when I've been drinking," Stacy replied, trying to play it off.

"I'll go get the coats," Lisa said, getting up from the table, now ready to go home.

"No!" Stacy shouted as she jumped up from the table.

"What the hell is wrong with you? Why can't I get the coats?" Lisa asked with a confused look on her face.

"I'll get them," Stacy insisted.

"Okay, drunk woman," Lisa said, laughing at her.

"Can you get me some water? I'm thirsty," Stacy said, trying to take the attention off the awkward situation.

Stacy quickly turned around and walked fast to the coatroom. Not saying anything about Stacy's bizarre behavior, Lisa simply went to the bar to get them both some water.

Stacy returned to the bar with their coats on her arm. She was happy she didn't bump into Candace and Jarvis again in the coatroom. A few minutes later, Candace walked up to the bar with her coat on, and Jarvis was following behind her with a stride in his step. Stacy's eyes got wide. She didn't know what was about to happen, but she sat back to see the outcome.

"Where have you been, missy?" Lisa asked Candace.

Candace responded swiftly without hesitation. "I ran into an old boyfriend, and I've been talking to him. I lost track of the time."

Jarvis walked up to the girls with a half-crooked grin on his face. His demeanor showed arrogance, and he didn't look like a person who had just been caught having sex with Lisa's friend.

He walked straight up to Lisa and said, "You're leaving so soon?"

Stacy looked at him and shook her head. She couldn't believe he would still try to get with Lisa.

"It's late, so we're about to leave. Where did you disappear to?" Lisa asked.

"I was talking to the woman who won the date with me," Jarvis said, showing he was a great liar.

"Really!" Stacy said, looking at Jarvis with disgust.

"What's wrong, Stacy?" Lisa asked.

Candace looked at Stacy, wondering if she was going to tell. Candace didn't look nervous, just curious to see what she was going to say.

"Nothing's wrong. I'm just ready to go," Stacy replied as she rolled her eyes at Candace and twisted her lips up at Jarvis.

"Let's go, guys," Candace said, trying to break up the tense moment.

Stacy was eyeing Jarvis, and it showed in her face how appalled she was with him. She really wanted to tell Lisa what was going on. It looked like they were all in an old western movie waiting for the first person to draw their gun. Frowning, Lisa looked at Stacy, and with her eyes, she asked her to tell her what was going on, but Stacy didn't speak.

"What's the problem?" Lisa asked after feeling the tension between them. When Stacy didn't respond, she questioned Candace. "What's up?"

"I'm cool. Let's just go home," Candace said.

"You're really special," Stacy told Candace.

"Stacy, you need to chill out," Candace responded calmly.

"Whatever," Stacy said.

"You guys, stop it. What happened?" Lisa asked again, confused.

No one said a word. They just continued looking at each other. Jarvis, who never broke character, acted like he didn't know the cause of the weird tension between them. Unconcerned about the conversation Candace and Stacy were having, he continued whispering in Lisa's ear about taking her out to dinner.

"I'm going to let the cat out the bag!" Stacy said.

"Stacy, let it go!" Candace shouted, trying to stop her.

"What cat? What are you talking about?" Lisa asked, now totally confused.

"I don't know what's going on with you guys, but it's time to leave. You women are so strange," Jarvis said as he started escorting them out the door.

As they walked out, Jarvis spoke to Lisa, telling her that Candace and Stacy got into a little spat over a man they saw and both wanted. Lisa laughed and couldn't believe they would be that upset over a man, but she knew she would get to the bottom of it later.

While Candace and Stacy walked behind them, Candace whispered to Stacy, "I think you need to keep your mouth shut, because you wouldn't want your dirt to get out."

"What are you talking about?" Stacy asked.

"Antonio," Candace said, feeling like she had hit her with the knockout punch. She had overheard Antonio talking to Jarvis about their relationship, and now was the perfect time to dangle it over her head.

Stacy looked at Candace, shocked that she knew about her secret love affair. She was embarrassed and upset.

"Wow!" Stacy said, stunned.

"Checkmate!" Candace said as she walked away from her.

Valet drove up in Jarvis limited edition, metallic black, CL600 Coupe Mercedes Benz. He gave everyone hugs and kisses before getting into his vehicle. Antonio couldn't wait to get with Stacy later on that night, but remained inconspicuous as he got in the passenger seat. As they drove away, Jarvis smiled and winked at Candace, while Lisa thought his gesture was meant for her.

They all got in Lisa's car and headed home without saying a word, until Candace broke the ice when she started talking about the gorgeous men who were at the event. This opened everyone up, and they all joined in the conversation. Stacy wanted to stay upset, but she realized she didn't want anyone else to know about her relationship with Antonio. So, she brushed off her feelings and continued talking with them.

"Don't think we're not going to discuss what happened tonight between the two of you, but I'll wait until tomorrow," Lisa said, letting them know she hadn't forgotten about their weird behavior.

CHAPTER 7

The next morning, Stacy couldn't wait to call Candace to hear in detail what was going on between her and Jarvis. She wasn't sure if she was going to tell Lisa since Candace was holding her relationship with Antonio over her head. She thought Candace would have been calling her first to make sure she didn't spill the beans, but she hadn't gotten a call from her yet.

Candace was egotistical and thought she had Stacy right where she wanted her. So, she wasn't worried about her. She also was ready to deny anything Stacy told Lisa.

Stacy dialed Candace's number and heard her voice on the second ring.

"Good morning," Candace answered cheerfully.

"You're happy this morning. What's up with you?" Stacy asked.

"Today is just a good day," Candace responded vaguely.

"I was calling to discuss last night," Stacy said, getting right to the point.

"I'm sorry you walked in on us. I don't know what to say," Candace replied.

"Start by telling me when, how, and why you hooked up with Jarvis," Stacy said, wanting some answers. Candace didn't sound like the same person who had been so nonchalant and cruel the night before.

Candace didn't know where to start or how to explain her situation to Stacy. Since Stacy saw her having sex with Jarvis, she couldn't deny it. A part of her wanted to tell someone about her unusual connection to Jarvis, but she knew it could affect her livelihood.

She knew Stacy was waiting for an explanation and she knew she had to tell her something. Luckily for Candace, she was used to thinking quick on her feet.

"You saw how good Jarvis looked last night. Well, I just couldn't resist. I didn't want it to get out like that. This was our first time having sex," Candace told her, trying to sound convincing.

"The way he was banging your back out, I hardly believe it was your first time having sex with him. And in a closet? Really, Candace? You have more class than that," Stacy said, not believing the lie she was hearing.

"That was our first time. I'm telling you the truth. It just happened to be in the closet when we both went to get our coats. We were drunk, and one thing led to another," Candace tried to explain.

"How could you do that to your girl?" Stacy asked.

"I didn't plan it. It just happened. I don't want to hurt Lisa. I love her like a sister. You wouldn't understand. I just can't," Candace started to ramble and sounded a bit uneasy.

At that moment, she wanted to confide in Stacy and tell her what was really going on because she was tired of the situation with Jarvis and wanted out. She knew Jarvis was never going to leave his wife, and she would never have her chance to have him all to herself.

Since Jarvis didn't want her to date anyone, it made her life miserable and kept her yearning after him. She felt herself being weak for a moment, but she quickly regained her composure and kept her feelings hidden.

"You know you're wrong," Stacy said.

"I'm sorry," Candace replied, getting frustrated with the conversation.

"You have to tell Lisa," Stacy demanded.

"I'm not going to tell her something that won't ever happen again," Candace said.

"If you don't tell her, I will. You're dirty," Stacy said.

"Don't judge me."

"This is wrong and you know it."

"Did you tell Antonio's girlfriend that you're sleeping with her man?" Candace asked then said, "You need to leave this alone. I told you it won't happen again. It was a one-time thing. Let it go."

Stacy was furious because she knew she couldn't judge Candace, especially since she was no better than her. As much as she enjoyed being with Antonio, the shame was the bad part of dating someone else's man. It didn't feel good when it was thrown in her face and humiliated her.

She didn't want to share Antonio. However, it was taking longer than she expected, and she wasn't sure how long she could deal with sharing him.

"So that's your strategy, to hold that over my head so you can feel better about your own dirt?" Stacy asked.

"I'm not holding anything over your head. I'm simply stating the truth. I'm just telling you to stop making a big deal out of it. You don't want to hurt Lisa by telling her, do you?" Candace asked.

"Fine, I'll leave it alone," Stacy replied, giving in.

Feeling relieved, Candace let out a quiet breath, but she knew she still had to watch her.

"I'm still in shock. I can't get the mental picture out of my mind of you two having sex in the coatroom. Damn, girl, you couldn't wait until you got home?" Stacy said, trying to take the attention off of her exposed relationship with Antonio.

"We were both drunk and horny, so the coatroom worked out just fine," Candace replied with a laugh.

"You slut," Stacy said, laughing with her. "Well, how was it?"

"It was the best I've ever had," Candace said, as she got a tingling sensation between her legs.

"I guess the rumor is true about him being good in bed."

"I can confirm that it's definitely true."

"Can I ask you a question?"

"Sure," Candace said curiously.

"Did you guys finish having sex when I left the coatroom?"

"Yes. We were already caught, so why waste the moment."

"Damn, you're scandalous," Stacy said.

"Are we still having our girls' night out this weekend?" Candace asked, trying to change the conversation.

"Yes, we're definitely going to hang out for dinner, drinks and trash talking," Stacy responded, smiling. They always enjoyed their nights out together.

"Cool."

"I'll call Lisa to remind her," Stacy said.

"Thanks for not telling her."

"No problem. We all have some skeletons in our closet that we don't want anyone to know about."

"See you guys this weekend," Candace said before hanging up.

CHAPTER 8

"Stacy, we're just going to dinner," Lisa shouted in the telephone receiver, trying to explain to her while she got dressed for her date with Jarvis.

He had finally made an effort and was taking her out to dinner, and she was anxious to go. She didn't know why it took him so long to ask her out, but she didn't care.

"I thought you weren't going to get involved with him?" Stacy asked.

"I changed my mind and decided to see what he's about. You're starting to sound like Candace," Lisa told her.

"I'm just giving you a hard time," Stacy replied, knowing she was hoping she would change her mind.

"You know how long I've been trying to get with this man. He's the most available bachelor in town right now. He's really the whole package."

"Maybe he's not the man for you," Stacy said, wanting to tell her about him and Candace.

"Well, I'll let you know after tonight," Lisa responded with a laugh.

Trying not to sound suspicious, Stacy told her, "He's single, smart, cute and rich. Get that man before someone else snatches him up."

She knew this would make Candace upset. She also knew that no matter what she said, Lisa was still going out to dinner with him.

"I guess I'm wondering why he is single if he's such a good catch," Lisa admitted.

"The same reason you're single. You do remember you're also single, right? Stop questioning it and just go with the flow," Stacy advised.

Lisa looked stunning in a fitted, soft grey knit dress that stopped right at her knees and exposed her back. Knowing the person Jarvis was she knew she had to dress up. Her hair was flowing and bouncing, and her make-up was flawless with the help of a make-up artist at the cosmetic counter at the mall.

She wanted everything to be perfect, and she wanted to look beautiful. Satisfied with her reflection in the mirror, she felt she had accomplished her mission.

Lisa moved around her house quickly, trying to make sure she would be ready by the time Jarvis arrived. They were going to dinner, and she was sure it would be a five-star restaurant. She knew Jarvis would be dressed up, so it was appropriate for her to wear a dress and heels.

"I'm going to finish getting ready. I'll call you after my date," Lisa said eagerly.

"I can't wait to hear all the details. Have fun," Stacy replied.

She knew she should have told her, but hearing how excited she was about their date, she couldn't break her heart, at least not tonight.

Twenty minutes later, Lisa's doorbell rang and she became nervous. She tried to take a moment to compose herself, but her nerves were out of control. Mr. Jarvis Denttin was at her house, and she was overly excited.

Trying not to seem too anxious, she took her time walking to the door. She wasn't sure what she would do when she saw him, but she was going to do what came naturally.

She opened the door and their eyes met. When she finally looked down, she was surprised at the enormous bouquet of yellow roses he was holding.

Jarvis looked gorgeous even though he was dressed casual in dark blue jeans that hugged his firm butt and a white button-down shirt.

"The flowers are beautiful."

"You deserve them," Jarvis said as she escorted him into her home.

"Thank you. Let me put these in some water."

"You look so beautiful," Jarvis said, admiring her from head to toe.

"Thank you. You're dressed casual. I thought we were going out to dinner?" Lisa asked as she played in the flowers.

"We are. I just didn't have time to change. I hope you don't mind."

"Where are we going to eat, McDonald's?" Lisa asked jokingly and smiled, even though she was a bit annoyed by his attire.

"I'm sorry. I can go home and change," he told her.

"It's no problem. I just feel overdressed."

"A woman can never be overdressed," Jarvis said staring at her. "Your home is beautiful," he commented while looking around.

Blushing, Lisa replied, "Thanks."

Neither of them could ignore the attraction they had for each other.

"I know you decorated your own place since you're the famous interior designer," Jarvis said, admiring her home.

"I designed every inch of my home."

"It looks wonderful."

"Thanks," Lisa said modestly.

"May I look around?"

"Sure."

When Jarvis returned from his quick tour of her home, he walked up to her, hugged her from behind, and kissed the back of her neck softly. This sent chills down her spine and made her tremble. He pressed his body against her hard enough for her to feel the bulge in his pants.

Lisa turned around and gently pushed him away as he softly kissed her neck again. He caught her off guard when he suddenly picked her up and put her on the kitchen counter, sucking and licking her lips before he kissed her.

"We can't do this," Lisa protested, trying to get off the countertop, but he stopped her.

"Do you still want to go out to eat?" Jarvis asked as he continued caressing her body.

"Yes, that was the plan, and we're going to be late for our dinner reservations if we don't leave soon," Lisa said, knowing things were moving too fast.

"Do you really want to go to dinner?" Jarvis asked, hoping she would change her mind.

Lisa was disturbed that he was moving so fast on their first date. He was coming on extremely strong, and this made her a little leery of him. She started thinking that maybe he just came over to have sex with her, especially since he wasn't dressed for the occasion.

"I'm ready to eat," Lisa responded, as she started getting turned on by him touching her body.

"Okay, let's go," Jarvis said in a tone that sounded like he was no longer interested in her.

The restaurant was exquisite, just like Lisa thought it would be. Jarvis was a perfect gentleman and spoiled her the entire time. They talked the night away and nothing was off limits.

Jarvis told her about his last relationship and how he was in love but his girlfriend left him for another man. He said it tore him up, and it had been so hard for him to get over the heartbreak.

Lisa talked about her past relationships and how hard it had been for her to be committed to someone because she had thrown herself into her work. This was something they both could relate to. They shared their dreams and ambitions over dinner.

The more Lisa talked to Jarvis, the more she became attracted to him. Jarvis was enjoying the conversation and didn't want it to end. Although he was ready to tear her clothes off, he was willing to wait.

"It seems like you need to be in charge at all times," Jarvis said, smiling.

"I guess I do have a control problem, but I do know how to be submissive. Well, not too submissive," Lisa replied, smiling back.

"Being submissive can be good," Jarvis said, trying to get her on his team. If she was going to be with him, she had to be a team player.

"I guess it's good for men, but I want a man that can be submissive to me," Lisa divulged.

"I'll be submissive to you," Jarvis said.

"Yeah, right. You're too dominant and successful to be submissive to anyone," she told him.

"True, I like to be in control at all times. It takes a strong woman to handle me," Jarvis said.

"It takes a stupid woman to deal with that."

"Why she got to be stupid? She could just be trying to satisfy her man. There's nothing wrong with that."

"I'm sure you have tons of women who want to be with you that would be surprised to know you're so crazy," Lisa said, laughing.

"Now I'm crazy? I'm just telling you what I like," Jarvis responded.

"With the type of business you're in, I'm sure you can have any woman you want."

"Most of the women I meet come to my clubs every weekend, and I'm not looking for a club hopper. Just because I'm a club owner doesn't mean I want to date a woman who frequents nightclubs. That's not my type of woman. I want a woman who is smart, beautiful, and has her own career and money."

"I understand," Lisa said, staring at him. He was so handsome she could barely concentrate.

"So do you want to know why I'm interested in you," Jarvis said.

"I wasn't going to ask you that, but feel free to answer the question," Lisa said, grinning.

"You have everything I'm looking for in a woman, and you didn't track me down to date me. Men like to be the chaser, and you allowed me to chase you. Also, you're beautiful, smart and sexy."

"Thank you," Lisa said, blushing.

"I'm going to make you fall in love with me," Jarvis told her, knowing she was going to be more work than he expected.

He knew she was not like the other women he had dated. She was a challenge, and he was ready to take on the task.

"You think I'm going to fall in love with you?"

"You'll see," Jarvis said confidently.

Before they could continue their conversation, a beautiful, tall, model-type woman walked up to the table. Jarvis looked a little surprise but didn't show his true feelings, while Lisa sat there wondering who she was.

"Hello, Mr. Jarvis Denttin. It's nice to see you," the well-dressed, poised woman said.

"Hello, Rosa," Jarvis replied as he stood up and kissed her on the cheek.

"You still look good. I see you're taking a break from working so hard," Rosa said, winking at him.

"Even I need a break sometimes," Jarvis told her. "Let me introduce you to my girlfriend, Lisa," he said, surprising Lisa by the title.

"Hello, I'm Lisa Cotus. It's nice to meet you," Lisa said, cordially extending her hand.

"I'm Jarvis' ex-girlfriend. I see you still date beautiful women. You did a good job with this one. She's pretty," Rosa complimented as she smiled at Lisa.

"It's nice to meet you, Rosa," Lisa said as she continued to eat her food, trying to give her the hint to leave.

"You should call me, Jarvis." Rosa said, boldly flirting right in front of Lisa. Then she put her hand on Jarvis' shoulder, rubbed his arm, and rested her hand on his hand.

"Goodbye, Rosa," Jarvis said.

It appeared that he gently took Rosa's hand off of his, but he actually squeezed her hand tight enough to make Rosa remove it quickly. He never looked at her while putting a piece of filet mignon in his mouth.

"I see you still like it rough," she commented, referring to the sexual encounters they once had.

"Rosa, I'm trying to have dinner. Can you please give us some privacy?"

Jarvis still did not look fazed by her. Lisa was actually impressed by how he was handling the situation and not letting Rosa get under his skin. Rosa was disrespectful, and Lisa wasn't going to give her any ammunition to start trouble, so she let Jarvis handle it.

Rosa stood at the table for a moment, and after realizing they were not paying attention to her, she eventually walked away. Lisa looked up at Jarvis to see his facial expression, but she couldn't read him. So, she immediately started asking questions about Rosa.

Jarvis told her that they dated briefly before breaking up. However, he started dating her again, but soon realized he shouldn't have rekindled their relationship. So, he broke it off with her again, but Rosa had never gotten over him. He said she stopped by his office and had been calling, but he wasn't interested in her.

Lisa knew she couldn't control Rosa's actions, but it was important how Jarvis handled the situation, and he passed with flying colors. Still, she would keep her eyes open just to make sure he wasn't messing around with Rosa.

Jarvis continued to tell Lisa that he was not interested in Rosa and how she was the only woman who had his attention right now. So, Lisa decided to enjoy the night and not let Rosa ruin it.

The night was wonderful, and it ended with them talking so long that the manager had to ask them to leave because the restaurant was closing. Jarvis dropped Lisa off at home and tried to come inside, but she refused to let him.

She knew if he came inside their relationship would fast forward quickly, and she wasn't ready for that. So, she gave him a peck on the lips and walked inside her house feeling happy.

CHAPTER 9

It was the weekend and time for girls' night out. So, Candace, Lisa, and Stacy went to their favorite authentic Mexican restaurant that made them feel like they were in Mexico. Dinner was just like old times, full of fun and laughter. They ate all the guacamole and tortilla chips they could handle, and they also drank as many margaritas as they could.

As always, they talked about their friendship, their futures and men. They had grown so close together that they loved each other like sisters. They always promised to have each other's back and never keep any secrets. Up until Candace was caught with Jarvis, this was the first time there was betrayal within the group.

The discussion of men usually dominated the entire conversation. They were three different women with different taste in men and tons of opinions. They laughed about old boyfriends and the new men they wanted to get close to. They laughed and cried and cried some more. This was an evening of releasing everything they had held inside and leaning on each other for support.

"Why do women think they are doing something when they get in the car first and lean over to open the door for a man?" Lisa asked.

"Men think they have a good woman when she opens the door for them," Candace replied.

"I'm not opening the door for a man who doesn't open the door for me first. What happened to the men opening the doors for women? We have it backwards," Stacy said as she gave Lisa a high-five.

"If a man doesn't open the car door for me and expect me to lean over and open the door for him, he will be waiting, because I'm not doing it," Lisa said.

Candace laughed with them, but she never looked at it that way. She had always opened the door for Jarvis, and if she didn't, he got upset. Now that she thought about it, Jarvis had never opened the car door or any door for her, but he always opened doors for Kora. Every time she had dinner with her friends, she learned something new.

The more she was around Jarvis; the more she started hating him. He was no longer a good catch, and she needed to move on. She was wasting her life on Jarvis and it was rotting away before her eyes.

"Are you still seeing Tony?" Lisa asked.

"We still hang out, but I told him that I needed some space," Candace responded.

"Why? I thought he was perfect for you," Stacy asked.

"He wine and dines me, and he's handsome, but I just don't see myself with him. He drinks too much and I hate when he gets drunk," Candace told them.

"Yes, we've seen how he acts when he's drunk. I really thought you guys made a cute couple," Lisa said.

"We see each other once in a while, but he wants more."

"Well, another one bites the dust," Stacy voiced.

"You better hold on to him until you find someone else. You don't want lonely nights," Lisa said.

"I'm going to hang on to him for now, because he's good in the bed," Candace said.

Actually, Tony was getting on her nerves, and she couldn't focus her attention on him because her mind was on Jarvis.

Bringing up the subject from the other night, Lisa inquired about Stacy acting weird. Lisa wanted to know what was going on. She knew it was more than Stacy having too many drinks or them fighting over the same man.

Stacy glanced at Candace and wanted to tell Lisa what really happened, but she couldn't. Instead, Stacy did what she knew would bother Candace the most. She started talking about how great Jarvis looked the night of the charity event.

Lisa quickly joined in and started talking about how he was flirting with her at the event. Candace looked at Stacy, knowing what she was trying to do, but she didn't let it worry her. Lisa talked about her date with Jarvis and how his ex-girlfriend showed up. While they were talking and laughing, Jarvis and Antonio walked up to the table.

"What's up, ladies?" Jarvis greeted.

"Hello," the women said in unison.

"I'm surprised to see you guys here tonight," Jarvis said, while looking at Lisa and then quickly at Candace.

"This is our favorite restaurant. We try to come here once a week for girl talk and drinks," Lisa told him.

"Oh, this is men bashing night," Antonio said.

"It's not like that. This is women releasing their stress night," Stacy informed them, smiling at Antonio.

"You look nice," Jarvis said, flirting with Lisa as Candace pretended not to care.

Candace was trying to downplay her feelings, but she was burning up inside. She was hurt that Jarvis would continue to seduce Lisa in front of her.

Jarvis looked at Candace wondering why she didn't tell him that she was going out tonight. He wanted to know her every move and seeing her out made him suddenly angry. Candace was a little uneasy, but had to keep her composure. She hated hiding her feelings for him around people, and couldn't wait for the day she could walk into a room on his arm.

"Thanks, Jarvis. You look good yourself," Lisa complimented.

"Don't eat too much guacamole because it's fattening," Antonio joked.

Stacy didn't laugh and was a little disappointed that Candace knew about their relationship. She knew Antonio was talking too much, which made her feel cheap.

"What's wrong with you, Stacy?" Antonio curiously asked.

He figured she was still upset that he wasn't able to spend the night with her after the charity event, but he planned on making it up to her.

"I'm just tired," Stacy replied.

"You have to make sure you get your beauty rest," Antonio said, looking at her.

"Enjoy the night, and I'll take care of your bill," Jarvis told them as he looked strangely at Candace.

"Thanks, Jarvis," Lisa and Stacy said.

"Make sure you guys stop by the club because we're having a couple of big events next week," Antonio informed them.

"What type of events?" Stacy asked.

"One is a party with some celebrities stopping by, and the other is a charity event for stray dogs. That event will be at another location," Jarvis said before Stacy interrupted him.

"Do we look like we want to go and play with some damn dogs," Stacy voiced, shaking her head.

"Well, the dog owners will be wealthy athletes and business owners, so I know you will be interested now," Jarvis said sarcastically.

Stacy rolled her eyes at Jarvis. "Well, you didn't say rich men would be there." She knew her comment would also piss Antonio off.

"It's for charity, so you guys should stop by," Jarvis said, ignoring Stacy.

"What is with all these charity events?" Lisa asked.

"You have to give in order to receive. Besides, you know how I love dogs. So, I'm really excited about this event. It will help homeless dogs find owners," Jarvis said.

"Yes, we all know how you love dogs. You have too many of them," Candace expressed.

"I only have three dogs," Jarvis retorted. "Who knows, I might get another one."

"What types of dogs do you have?" Lisa inquired.

"I have a Maso Mastiff, a Great Dane and a Rottweiler," Jarvis answered.

"Wow, those are huge killer dogs," Lisa said.

"They are friendly dogs. I keep them locked in cages, and they have their own room. That's why I'm happy I found a home to keep my dogs. The condo I stayed in didn't allow pets."

"No one wants to visit you with those dogs running around," Stacy said.

"I definitely won't be coming to your house, because I'm terrified of dogs," Lisa told him.

"I wouldn't let the dogs hurt you. You should come over and see," Jarvis said with a sexy, inviting look on his face.

Stacy looked at Candace to see if she was going to say something about Jarvis flirting with Lisa, but she never said a word and appeared unaffected by his comments. Stacy wondered what really was going on between them.

Even though Jarvis flirted with Lisa every time he saw her, and tried to sleep with her on their first date, he never made any real efforts to make a connection with her. She definitely wasn't going to throw herself at him, although she wanted to. She wanted him to come after her, and if he weren't going to make the next move, she would have to move on.

"I wouldn't want to get bitten by your dogs," Lisa said, then looked at Stacy who was scowling at Candace. She knew something was wrong with Stacy. Also, Candace hadn't said a word since Jarvis came to the table.

Before she could comment, Jarvis and Antonio were escorted by a waitress to their table in the back of the restaurant.

"Let's make sure we go to both events next week," Lisa said.

Stacy nodded her head. "It actually sounds like fun."

"You're just happy there's going to be rich men there," Lisa laughed.

"I just want to get out of the house," Stacy responded.

"What's wrong with you? Why are you so quiet?" Lisa asked Candace.

"I'm just getting tired," Candace replied.

"It seemed like you had a problem with Jarvis," Stacy instigated.

"I'm just thinking about the work I'm going to have to do to coordinate these events," Candace said, knowing what Stacy was trying to do. "I wonder why Antonio didn't bring his girlfriend with him. They go everywhere together," she said, shooting back at Stacy.

"I guess he's riding solo tonight," Stacy replied as she took a sip of her margarita, unaffected by her comment. "But, it looks like Jarvis wants to go home with Lisa," she added, smiling.

After several more sips of their drinks and ordering more guacamole and tortilla chips, they went back to laughing and talking about old times. Lisa's ego was a little bruised because she expected Jarvis to call her after their date, but since he was only interested in flirting with her in public, she decided it was time to leave him alone.

Jarvis sent them another round of margaritas, and they continued to drink and eat all night long. Lisa stole glances at Jarvis, but sucked it up and started looking at the other men in the restaurant.

As the margaritas started settling in and controlling their thoughts, they started getting deep with their conversation, talking about their childhood and struggles through life. Lisa started talking about being adopted as a child and not feeling like she belonged for a long time in her life. Although Candace and Stacy knew Lisa was adopted, they never really felt the pain in her voice as they did this night.

Having Lisa show her true feelings made Candace want to share her pain with them. She wanted to tell her about Jarvis and hoping to find peace. She wanted to feel normal and move on with her life, but she just couldn't bring herself to tell. As Lisa continued to talk about her life, Stacy and Candace sat quietly and listened. They both wanted to release their hidden secrets, also. Candace had tears in her eyes that she tried to hide.

"Are you about to cry, Candace?" Lisa asked, baffled.

"No!" Candace quickly responded.

"I know when something is wrong. We've been friends for too long now, and I know when something is bothering you. You know you can talk to us," Lisa said.

"I just need time," Candace said, confusing Stacy, who didn't know if she was being sincere or if she was playing a game.

"What's wrong with you?" Stacy asked.

"I wish I could tell you. I'm just not ready to talk about it," Candace said, desperately wanting to tell them.

"What is it concerning?" Lisa asked.

"Jarvis," Stacy blurted out, shocking herself.

"What happened?" Lisa asked, now really interested in what was going on since it had something to do with him.

"Nothing. Let's talk about it later," Candace said.

"Is there something wrong with him?" Lisa asked.

"No, it's not that," Candace replied.

"Because you know I'm done with him," Lisa told her.

"That's good, because you really should stay away from him. He's no good," Candace said.

"Thanks for warning me for the hundredth time," Lisa sighed.

"Well, maybe you should listen," Candace said, irritated.

"Okay, okay. If something is bothering you, then it's worth talking about," Stacy said, trying to be serious.

"Let's talk about it later," Candace responded, quickly realizing she was going to take her secret to her grave.

Candace glanced over at Jarvis, who was sitting at the back of the restaurant, and knew it was going to be hard to break the ties she had with him. She had to get back to her purpose, which was keeping her bank account full. She didn't want to get her heart involved, but she couldn't resist him, which sidetracked her. She soon would be back on the right path. She just needed to shake it off.

Candace didn't look at herself as a gold-digger because gold wasn't enough for her. She just wanted to be with a man who had his life together and was going places. She wanted him to love her and take care of her like she was going to do for him.

She never understood why people labeled women as gold-diggers when they wanted a man who had money. Most men have certain criteria for women, so she didn't feel guilty about her request. She always had plans on working and living her life.

CHAPTER 10

It was late when Candace pulled up in front of Jarvis' house the next day. Sitting on top of a hill and surrounded by four acres of land, Jarvis home was enormously impressive. It was warm and elegant with a four-car garage and oval driveway. Candace always enjoyed visiting because it made her dream of how she wanted to live. She felt like royalty whenever she was there.

She grabbed her briefcase out of the trunk and walked up to the front door. She had some paperwork he needed to sign off on for some projects he had lined up. She didn't have time to wait until the next day because the information needed to be faxed immediately.

Jarvis opened the door before she could ring the doorbell. Appearing happy to see her, he quickly grabbed her and kissed her. Even though they were keeping their relationship a secret, Candace was still happy to have him in her life. She didn't like the arrangements, but she enjoyed the time they spent together. She still couldn't get used to their open affection while she was in his house, because his wife, Kora, was always in the bedroom.

Candace walked into the house that she wanted to call her own. She wanted them to get married, have kids, and live happily ever after. She enjoyed the finer things in life, and visiting his house allowed her to experience the luxury for a short time.

Jarvis' house was beautiful with custom-made furniture and accent pieces. The foyer color scheme was beige, brown, and white, with a large chandelier that hung low enough from the high ceiling for you to see the intricate details. This was no ordinary home; his taste was unique and striking.

Jarvis escorted her to the family room that was equally stunning with a black and white theme. The large custom-made black leather sectional and uniquely shaped chairs had black and white printed pillows that were incredible. On one side of the room were floor-to-ceiling windows that allowed you to see directly into his beautiful, spacious backyard.

The flat screen television, fully stocked bar, and distinctive desk made the room even more impressive. The beautiful artwork hanging on the wall was colorful and added the finishing touches to the room decor.

Jarvis was very attentive to Candace, offering her a glass of wine and taking her briefcase. He signed the important documents and watched as she faxed them. Once she was done, she sat on the couch, sipped her wine and relaxed.

He turned the eighty-inch projection television on, poured himself a shot of liquor and sat next to her. They didn't talk much and appeared to be interested in watching the news that was showing on the television.

After Jarvis finished two more shots of Hennessy, he pulled her closer to him, then took her wine glass and put it on the table. He immediately started sucking on her nipples through her expensive silk blouse. She allowed the pleasure and opened her shirt for him to get full access. He swiftly removed her bra, than continued to suck and lick her breasts.

When Candace tried to adjust herself, he sternly said, "Don't move."

He continued to kiss her breasts as he pulled her skirt up. He always wanted her to wear a dress or skirt so he can have easy access to her.

"Where's Kora?" Candace asked.

"Don't worry about her," he told her.

"You know how uncomfortable I feel doing this in your house. Can we go to my place or a hotel?"

Growing angry, Jarvis replied, "If you were so uncomfortable, you wouldn't have come over here. You knew what was going to happen. You can go to a hotel without me. So are you staying or going?"

"I'm staying," Candace answered.

She knew he was upset with her, and she didn't like it. So, she dropped to her knees and filled her mouth with him. While giving him the best deep-throat blowjob, she started shaking her butt better than any stripper, just the way Jarvis liked it.

He gripped her neck and guided her down on the floor, where he removed her clothes and forcefully went inside her. She tried to cover her mouth so she wouldn't make too much noise. She liked it rough and loved to express herself vocally, but tonight, she was muted.

She got on top of him and rode him slowly, then faster and harder. He grabbed her neck again and squeezed it hard, making her wheeze for air. She opened her eyes and looked at him oddly, but she never stopped enjoying the ride as he continued to squeeze her neck harder.

Candace started to panic as Jarvis looked in her eyes while squeezing her neck a little tighter, choking her until she couldn't breathe. This time, she stopped moving and grabbed his hand, trying to remove it.

"Don't stop. I won't hurt you."

She trusted him and was a good servant doing what she was told. Again, she moved her hips slowly and started to go faster as he moaned. The faster she moved her hips, the harder he pumped and the harder he continued to choke her.

They never took their eyes off each other. It was like a game of trust while they fell further into a trance. Feeling herself about to have an orgasm, she moved wildly. Jarvis added more pressure to the grip he had around her neck, making her struggle to breathe as she had the best orgasm of her life. She almost felt like her head was about to burst wide open.

She collapsed on top of his sweaty body. He immediately pushed her off of him and got on top of her, entering her again. Minutes later, he exploded. After he finished having his way with her, he kissed her, making her melt. In public, he never showed that he cared about her, but behind closed doors, she felt like he was deeply in love with her.

At first, she was flattered by his controlling personality and the way he boosted her ego. As time passed, his controlling ways became unbearable and made it very hard for her to accept. By that time, she had allowed him to manipulate and control her life. He told her what to wear, where to go, and how to act. Since she was working with him, he had control over her career, too.

It happened so fast that she didn't know when it got out of control. She tried to stop him from controlling her, but he wasn't going to allow that, and he always threatened to leave her if she didn't obey him.

She didn't want to end up like Kora, on permanent lockdown. The only thing that helped her was being able to leave his house and return to her home. Kora never could leave the house without his permission.

The thing Candace missed from her childhood was her father's presence and love. She hadn't seen or talked to her father since she was five years old, and she had never forgiven him for not being a part of her life. Her mother divorced her father, but she still expected him to keep in contact. Yet, he never did. She longed for a father figure and searched her whole life for someone to fill that position.

That is why it was so easy for Jarvis to move into her life and take over. In her eyes, he was the father figure she had always been looking for. Jarvis knew about her childhood and absent father, and he used that to get what he wanted from her. In some strange way, when Jarvis treated her like a child, she embraced it and felt love from him.

Jarvis rubbed her stomach while she caressed him. The beads of sweat rolled off their naked bodies and merged into one puddle. Disturbing his peaceful mood, Jarvis could hear his dogs barking. They continued to bark, and it sounded like they were destroying something.

He grabbed his cell phone and called Antonio and John, who were in his office handling some business. He asked Antonio to go and check on the dogs to see what was going on. Then he immediately returned his attention back to Candace as he stroked her face. He couldn't resist her perfectly shaped body, and he admired it with his eyes and hands.

Jarvis moved down between her legs and started licking her slowly. Candace moaned while opening her legs wider. He licked faster as she moaned louder and moved her hips to the motion of his tongue. Right when she thought she was going to explode, she slowly opened her eyes with an eerie feeling that someone was watching her.

She looked towards the door, and the familiar eyes disappeared. Hoping she was just imagining things, she blinked a few times, but she was almost sure Kora was peeking in the door at them. Just like the person Jarvis had created, she ignored the thought of Kora seeing them and continued receiving pleasure from his tongue. When she returned her attention back to Jarvis to experience her second orgasm of the night, he instantly stopped and looked up at her.

"What's wrong, baby? Why did you stop?"

"Why didn't you tell me you were going out to eat with your girls last night?" Jarvis asked.

"What?" Candace said while trying to push his head back down between her legs to finish what he had started.

"I want to know why you were out to dinner with your friends without telling me," Jarvis said, now sounding heated.

By the sound of his voice, she knew he was serious, but she didn't understand why he chose this moment to discuss it. She gradually took her hands off his head.

"I tried to call you, but you didn't answer. So, I just left."

"You know not to go anywhere without telling me. What's wrong with you?"

"I'm sorry. I didn't think you would mind," Candace said, becoming worried.

She was upset that they were discussing this so loudly and changing the mood. She always tried to whisper when she was in his house because she didn't want Kora to hear them, but he never cared how loud he was. The silence was broken when his cell phone started ringing.

He continued looking at her while he grabbed the phone to answer it. It was Antonio telling him that he needed help with the dogs. Jarvis told him he would be right there. He got up, put his pants on, and walked out of the room without saying a word. Candace listened to him in the hallway talking to Antonio.

"Sorry to disturb you. I didn't know you were with Candace," Antonio said.

"No worries. It's cool," Jarvis replied casually.

"You're cold-blooded having both of your women in the same house. You're the man," Antonio said, stroking Jarvis' ego.

"That's how I like it. Keep them all together for easy access."

"I see you like living dangerously. You're not worried that they might run into each other in the house?" Antonio asked, perplexed.

"They're both like dogs; they obey their master. No matter what I do, who I've been with, or how long I've been gone, they are always happy to see me," Jarvis replied, laughing.

"You're crazy, man. I need to be more like you," Antonio said.

"To be like me, you got to learn how to keep your women on a tight leash," Jarvis told him.

"I'm still working on Stacy to do as she's told, but she's a stubborn woman," Antonio said.

Candace didn't know Jarvis felt that way about her. It was difficult for her to listen to him disrespect her.

"Either she does what you say or you should leave her alone. As long as you have money, you can get women to do whatever you want them to, and you don't have to beg a woman to stay."

"You know how women are. They get their feelings involved and then you can't get rid of them," Antonio said.

"Who cares how these women feel. As long as they're good in bed and beautiful, you should be content. When you get tired of them, kick them to the curb and find a new woman. They will be waiting in line for you," Jarvis said, schooling him.

"Have you ever cared about any woman you've dated?" Antonio asked, amazed at Jarvis' cold-hearted attitude.

"Not really. All these women care about is how much cash you have, and all I care about is making money. So, we work well together. Money rules the world. A man isn't worth anything if he doesn't have money in his pockets. I would kill myself if I was broke," Jarvis said, laughing.

"The way you carry yourself, people would never know you're really a piece of shit," Antonio said, joining him in laughter. "I'm learning to be deceiving like you."

"I'm just giving these women what they need," Jarvis replied while still laughing.

"You're misleading them," Antonio said.

"I'm just creating the fantasy that every woman dreams of, but in the process, I have to train them to please me."

"Come on so you can help get these damn dogs," Antonio said, laughing as they walked away.

Jarvis stopped him with sincerity in his voice, and told him, "You know you're my man and I trust you."

"You know I will always hold you down," Antonio replied.

"You have proven that, and I appreciate your loyalty."

"Well, you've taken care of me and I appreciate you. Now, let's get these dogs before they tear up your house. John can't control them by himself," Antonio said.

Antonio was Jarvis' right-hand man, and he knew Jarvis trusted him with his businesses and life. He had followed all his rules from day one and had never done anything to have Jarvis distrust him. Jarvis taught him everything he knew about being an entrepreneur, and he was working toward opening up his own restaurant one day.

Due to Antonio's loyalty, Jarvis planned on helping him start his own business. Antonio didn't like the way Jarvis treated women, but it wasn't his business to say anything. Being so close to Jarvis made his womanizing ways rub off on him.

As soon as Candace heard them walk away, she put her clothes and shoes on, and went into the bathroom in the hallway. She was still hurt thinking about the comment Jarvis made about her. She had made up her mind that she was not going to continue taking this abuse from him.

She couldn't handle hearing him talk about her and referring to her as a dog. She knew it was time to let go of her feelings for him. It was time to walk away.

As soon as she walked back into the room, Jarvis was standing by the window throwing another shot of Hennessy down his throat.

"That was fast. Are the dogs okay?" Candace asked.

"The dogs are fine. Antonio and John are scared to take three dogs out of their cages and put them into the backyard. That's pitiful."

"I'm glad they're outside so I don't have to worry about them biting me," Candace jokingly said.

"Where were you?" Jarvis asked, changing the conversation from pleasant to tense.

"I went to the bathroom," Candace said in a carefree tone.

Jarvis became irritated. "We just had this conversation about you leaving without telling me."

"I just went to the bathroom," Candace replied, not knowing he was really upset.

"You shouldn't have left this room," he told her.

"Kora didn't hear or see me. I was very quiet," she said, trying to explain.

"I'm not worried about Kora seeing you. She does what she's told, and it's obvious you don't. That's why she's my wife and you're just a good piece of ass," Jarvis said.

"I'm sorry."

"Why is it so hard for you to do what you're told?" He asked.

Candace couldn't say a word. She was still shocked by his behavior. She knew he was controlling, and had been since the first day they were together, but now he had taken it to another level.

What have I gotten myself into? She asked herself over and over in her head.

"Come with me," Jarvis said, grabbing her hand and leading her out of the room.

They walked down the hallway and into the room where the dogs stayed. The dogs were outside in the backyard, and she was glad because she was scared of them. The room was empty except for the two huge dog cages that were in the middle of the floor. The largest dog had his own room because he didn't get along with the other two.

There were blinds on the windows, a flat-screen television on the wall, and a food and water tray inside each cage. The room reeked of wet dogs, feces and dog food. She wasn't sure why he was bringing her into the room, and she never questioned him.

"How do you like this room?" Jarvis asked while turning on the television.

"It's a nice room for dogs, but you need to open a window and air it out. Do the dogs really need a television?" Candace asked as she covered her nose because of the strong, disgusting odor in the room.

"I like for them to be comfortable. They are a part of the family," Jarvis said as he closed the blinds.

"Those are really large dog cages."

"I got them custom made so they can move around freely. Go ahead. Step inside and check it out."

"I don't want to go inside the dog cage. I can see it from here."

The look on Jarvis' face had her feeling like a little girl, and she became apprehensive. He had a way of looking at her that made her do whatever he told her to. She stepped inside the cage and was actually impressed at how large it was.

She wasn't able to stand up, but it was roomy enough for her to walk around in a bended position. There wasn't much to see inside the cage but the dog food tray, newspaper, and feces on the floor.

"This is a cool cage. Very spacious," she commented.

As she turned around and began to walk out of the cage, Jarvis quickly closed it and secured it with a padlock.

"What are you doing?" Candace said as she rushed to the cage door.

"I don't like you leaving without my permission. So, I guess I have to cage you up like a dog for you to understand that."

Candace was livid. "Open this door, Jarvis!"

"No! I'm going to let you think about it for a while. I'll be back."

"Jarvis, don't you leave me in this dog cage!" she yelled, not caring who heard her.

She couldn't believe he walked out of the room without responding. Continuing to panic, she started yelling and screaming louder, but after five minutes, her voice was tired. She sat down hoping he would come back if she stopped screaming, but she had a feeling he wouldn't. Jarvis was stubborn and always wanted his way, and she knew she would have to stay in the cage quietly before he let her out.

An hour later, she was still sitting on the floor staring at the wall in shock, when she remembered she had her cell phone in her pocket. She didn't know who to call, and she didn't want to cause a scene by calling the police. She also knew not to call Jarvis because he would come and take her phone.

After five minutes of contemplating what to do, she thought about calling Kora since she knew she was upstairs in the bedroom, but she wouldn't be able to explain why she was in the dog cage.

Three hours later, she jumped up and started shaking the cage while screaming like a wild animal. She felt so humiliated. After a few minutes of going insane, she sat back down on the floor with her skirt, blouse and heels on, as she cried herself to sleep in a fetal position.

CHAPTER 11

Candace slept the night away into the morning in the dog cage. The sun was beaming through the blinds, poking her right in the face and waking her up. She didn't have the remote to change the television station that continuously played cartoons, which was driving her insane. She was so hungry and thirsty that she could have eaten the food and drank the water left in the dog tray.

She pulled the cell phone from her pocket to see the time and was surprised to see the clock showing twelve noon. She jumped up furious and devastated that he would leave her in the cage for such a long time. What is wrong with this man? She thought to herself.

She was outdone and going crazy being locked up, and was furious that she was sitting on the floor in her designer clothing. She decided to call Stacy, hoping she could get her out of the situation. If not, she was calling the police. She wasn't sure why she was calling her, but since Stacy already knew she was sleeping with Jarvis, she was the only one she could call.

When Stacy didn't answer her telephone, she hesitated for a moment before she made the call to the police. She quickly changed her mind and decided to call Jarvis, who picked up on the first ring.

"Let me out of this damn cage!" Candace shouted, sounding like a deranged woman.

Silence was all she heard because Jarvis hung up the telephone. She redialed his number, but this time, he didn't answer. Frustrated, she screamed and threw a tantrum like a child. A few hours later, she noticed the sun was starting to go down. There were no more tears left in her eyes, and she was now hoarse from screaming and yelling. She felt overpowered. She felt like killing him.

The hunger pains were stabbing her stomach. Starving, she picked up the dog tray, drank some water, and nibbled on the dog food, which wasn't as bad as she thought it would be. She also had to go to the bathroom and couldn't hold it any longer. So, she squatted in the corner of the cage and urinated. She had no more dignity left, and the only way to deal with the situation was to sleep. With closed eyes again, she drifted off devastated.

When she woke up hours later, the cage door was open. After looking around the room and not seeing anyone, she didn't waste any time running out of the cage. She ran to the family room to get her purse and head for the front door. To her surprise, Jarvis was in the room on the telephone. When he saw her, he was startled and quickly hung up. She immediately stopped. Jarvis rushed over and tried to grab her, but she snatched away from him.

"How did you get out of the cage?" Jarvis asked, puzzled.

"Don't touch me!" she yelled.

"Who are you talking to?"

"I'm so mad I can kill you!"

"I just wanted to make a point," Jarvis said, laughing as he continued to wonder who opened the cage.

"What point? You think this is funny? I'm going to kill you," she said as she swung, hitting him in the head.

Jarvis looked at her, and she knew she had gone overboard, but she didn't care. She kept swinging and kicking until he restrained her.

"I don't want you to leave without telling me where you're going. Now calm down!"

"I'm sorry I ever got involved with you! I hate you!" She yelled, while trying to get out of the house.

"I think you got the point."

"Get out of my way!"

"I'm not going to try to stop you. If you want to leave, then get the hell out! Just know you can never come back to me or your job if you walk out that door. No one will take care of you the way I have. So, do what you want."

Candace stood still, wanting the love from him to replace the love from her absent father. She had done everything he told her to, and she didn't understand why he would treat her this way. She realized she was no different than any other woman he slept with and kicked to the curb. She allowed him to mistreat her.

"Are you leaving or staying?" Jarvis asked.

She thought about her job, her salary, their great sex life, and also the pain, humiliation, and disrespect that came along with being involved with him. She was tired, but not ready to walk away.

"I'm staying," Candace replied softly.

"That was a smart choice. Now go make dinner reservations for Kora and me. Help pick her out something nice to wear. She has such a great body. I want to see her dressed sexy tonight," Jarvis said, sounding like a pompous jerk.

She hung her head low and did what she was told. Smiling, Jarvis looked at her. He knew he could do whatever he wanted to do to her, and she would accept it and continue to serve him. He knew how to break women down. As long as Candace had a love for money, he knew he could control her. When a woman chases money, she loses her dignity.

Candace was nervous about going into Kora's bedroom because she thought she saw her and Jarvis having sex, and wasn't sure if she had opened up the dog cage. Like she had done so many times, she swallowed her pride and knocked on Kora's door to prepare her for a night out with her husband.

Kora was special to Jarvis and he continued to prove that to Candace, which drove her crazy. She once wanted Kora out of the picture, but now she didn't want to be in her shoes. When Kora made an impromptu visit meeting Candace for the first time, Jarvis has kept her on lock down ever since. He didn't want her showing up anywhere else unexpected and telling the world they were married.

Kora opened the bedroom door, and as always, she welcomed Candace in. She was excited to see her and couldn't wait to talk to someone.

"Hey, girl, where have you been?" Kora asked.

"Jarvis has been working me to death. You know how your husband is," Candace responded, trying to read her face.

"You know he's a hard worker and demands a lot from his employees."

"He's taking you out tonight, and he wants me to help you get ready. He wants you to look sexy."

"Where are we going?" Kora asked, happy to be getting out of the house. She knew the night was going to be something extravagant.

"I'm not sure, but you know whatever he has planned will be unforgettable," Candace said.

Since Jarvis didn't take Kora out on a regular, whenever he did, he made up for lost time. He made sure their outing was enjoyable and would hold her over until the next time.

"When is the last time you've been on a date? It's time to get you a boyfriend. You don't want to be old and lonely," Kora said.

"I've been looking. It's not a big selection out there. I have this guy in mind, but it's going to take some time to work my magic on him," Candace replied, referring to Jarvis.

"You need someone in your life. I know you have sexual needs," Kora pressed.

"I'm dating this one guy, but it's not serious. It's just sex and something for me to do," Candace said, shocking herself that she was telling Kora about dating Tony.

"I'm going to find a man for you," Kora told her.

"You never leave the house, so how are you going to find a man for me?"

Sadly, Kora replied, "You're right. What was I thinking?"

She knew she had been locked down for too long. She felt depressed that she couldn't go out of the house when she wanted to. She was tired of the isolation.

"I wish you could get out more. I'm sorry you are locked in this house every day," Candace said in a lowered voice.

"I'm so tired of this. He treats me like a queen, but keeps me locked up like one of his dogs," Kora expressed.

"Whenever you're ready to get out of this hellhole, you know I'll be right here to break you out."

"You're such a good friend. I wish I could," Kora stopped in mid-sentence.

"Finish your sentence. You wish you could what?" Candace asked, hanging on to her every word.

"It's not important."

"Kora, do you have any friends?"

"I used to have friends, but I've lost touch with them. You're my only friend now. My life is pretty depressing."

"You didn't know your life would be like this. You did have a life before Jarvis, right?"

"My life was great. My modeling career was really taking off, and everyone wanted to hire me. I met Jarvis at a private party for a magazine. He was so charming and professional. I didn't want the street type of guy. I wanted someone who was hardworking and just a good person. I focused on my career and traveled the world, before he swept me off my feet by sending me flowers daily, giving me diamonds, taking me on shopping sprees, and putting it down in the bedroom," Kora said, thinking about how great it was in the beginning.

"Wow!" Candace said, trying to sound excited. She recited the entire courting ritual to herself because those were the same things Jarvis did to win her over.

"Girl, did I say the sex is amazing! I think that's what won me over," Kora said, laughing.

"I don't want to hear about your sex life," Candace said with a forced smile, knowing she truly didn't want to hear about it.

"He knew money and fame was what I wanted, so he used that to lure me in. We used to do everything together, but once we got married, things changed and I became locked down in this house," Kora said as her story became gloomy.

"Why didn't you continue your modeling career?" Candace asked.

"Jarvis said there could only be one star in the family and that was going to be him. He couldn't allow me to be out in the public eye with men lusting after me. He couldn't handle all of the attention I was getting from men and women."

"That's so selfish. I saw some of your pictures in several magazines, and you looked so beautiful. Never give up your dreams for anyone."

"My modeling days are over," Kora said solemnly. "I knew Jarvis was wealthy and had his own businesses, and I was impressed. Just like any other woman, I wanted to lock him down. So, I went after him and did whatever he wanted me to do, so I could get my man. I just didn't know it would backfire on me. I never thought my career would be over."

"You are very beautiful, and you have a great body. You need to be modeling."

"I gave up my career for Jarvis. I love him," Kora said, staring at the wall.

"Was it worth it?"

"No. Yes," Kora stuttered.

"You sound like you have hesitation about this marriage. Just make sure you're happy. Even though you're rich, you can't enjoy it the way you want to because he controls your every move. People don't even know he's married. People don't know you exist," Candace told her.

"I know I'm nonexistent to people, but I love him so much."

Kora broke down and cried. She knew she was not happy; her life would have been different if she wasn't married to Jarvis. It was hard for her to break away from him. He stripped her away from her friends and family, and she didn't have anyone to turn to.

Candace was her only friend, and she was just getting to know her. She knew Candace was Jarvis' eyes and ears, so she didn't really trust her. But, she didn't have anyone else to talk to. She wanted out of her marriage and was trying to muster up the strength to get out of captivity.

"I'm sorry. I went too far," Candace said.

"No, you just told the truth," Kora told her.

"You don't have to live this way."

"You don't have to live the way you're living, either."

"What do you mean by that?" Candace asked nervously.

She was afraid Kora knew about her and Jarvis, although she always felt like she knew but just didn't say anything. Kora couldn't possibly think Jarvis was a faithful man.

"I better get ready before I'm late," Kora quickly said without answering her question. After giving Candace a hug, she started to get dressed. Candace knew not to push the issue, but her comment sent chills through her body.

"You know you're my only friend," Kora said while slipping on her dress.

"I know, and I'm happy to be your friend," Candace responded, feeling horrible inside because she knew she was the worst friend in the world.

"You can talk to me about anything. I'm here for you."

"Thanks, Kora. I'm always here if you need me. I want you to be happy, and no matter what, you shouldn't live this way. Try to take back control of your life," Candace said, feeling terrible.

She really liked Kora as a friend, but knew she would be hurt if she knew the truth. How could she be friends with her and sleeping with her husband? She smiled in her face, assisted her, and screwed her husband on a regular.

Once Kora was dressed, looking beautiful and sexy, Candace walked her downstairs to where Jarvis was. The sexy dress fit her body like a glove. Kora was a beautiful woman, and her chiseled features made you take a double look at her. She had the perfect body that most women worked out every day to get.

Because of her beauty and Jarvis' insecurities, Kora realized why he wanted to keep her hidden from the world. As tough as he appeared to be, he was an insecure man who was afraid someone would take his precious wife away from him. Therefore, he kept her on lockdown.

When Jarvis saw Kora walking down the stairs, the look in his eyes told Candace that he was in love with her. He had never looked at Candace that way, and she knew he never would. He told Kora how beautiful she looked and gave her a soft kiss. He then reached in his pocket and put a diamond necklace around her neck. He was so gentle to Kora, and Candace always knew she was not on the same level as her.

"I forgot to put some perfume on," Kora said.

Jarvis looked at Candace, annoyed that she had forgotten to make his wife smell good.

"Candace, you're not on your job. Go get her perfume," Jarvis instructed.

With tears in her eyes, Candace ran back up the stairs and grabbed an expensive bottle of perfume from off of the dresser. She ran back downstairs and handed the bottle to Kora.

Jarvis quickly stopped her and said, "Spray it on her."

Candace smiled, gritted her teeth, and sprayed the perfume on Kora.

"Now you smell wonderful. Have fun tonight," Candace said.

"Thanks, Candace. You should go with us next time," Kora suggested.

"A threesome, that sounds great," Jarvis said grinning.

"Stop being so nasty," Kora told him as she playfully hit him.

"You know I would never share you with anyone," Jarvis said, giving her a soft, sweet kiss on the lips.

Jarvis was serious, and Candace knew it. She knew it was only a matter of time before he planned a threesome between them. First, he needed to work on Kora a little because she was not that type of woman.

Candace watched them walk out the house looking like a couple in love. Even though she was upset with him, jealousy filled her body. First, she wanted him, and then she didn't, but when she saw him with Kora, she wanted to be in her place.

Before Jarvis closed the door, he stuck his head back in and said, "Be here when I get back."

"I'm not going anywhere," Candace said, obedient.

CHAPTER 12

A week later, Candace, Stacy, and Lisa arrived at Jarvis nightclub for one of his big celebrity party. The club was already overflowing with people and expensive cars flooded the streets. Valet escorted them out of Candace's brand-new white CLS550 Mercedes Benz, and they walked into the club looking like superstars and feeling like millionaires. Once inside, they headed to the VIP section.

The club was elegant with a rich décor. With luscious dark hardwood floors, two large bars, huge flat-screen televisions throughout the club, and a distinctive glass VIP section, this was definitely not an ordinary nightclub. This was an elite place, and the people that attended had expensive taste and were ready to let loose and party.

The staff was well-dressed in black suits and black sexy dresses, and they always seemed to stand out in the crowd. You had to come in your best outfit and most expensive jewelry to even feel like you belonged there.

They quickly ordered drinks, invited a few of their friends to their table in the VIP section, and started enjoying the night. In a good mood, Lisa got up and danced to the music at the table. Her friends joined in, and instantly, they had an audience of men watching them.

Candace ordered a bottle of champagne, and they raised their glasses and toasted to friendship. Although Stacy wanted to enjoy the night with Antonio, she had to pretend like nothing was going on between them, so she kept her distance from him.

"I have to go to the ladies' room. Does anyone else need to go?" Lisa asked Stacy and Candace.

"I'll go," Candace replied.

"I'll pass," Stacy said.

She stayed behind and continued enjoying the night. Stacy had met a guy that caught her interest, and she didn't want to leave him so soon. She knew Antonio was watching her, but she was tired of being faithful to an unavailable man. She wanted to have fun even if it wasn't with Antonio. So, she continued to flirt with her new male friend.

"It's really crowded," Lisa said as she held on to her drink tightly while making her way through the crowd on her way to the bathroom.

"It's jam-packed in here," Candace shouted over the music as she pushed through the crowd, as well.

It seemed like it took them forever to make it to the bathroom, and as always, the women's bathroom had a line out the door. Irritated that they had to wait, Lisa and Candace took their place in line.

"This is ridiculous! Why is the women's bathroom always so congested? As nice as this club is, you would think they would have more bathrooms for the ladies," Lisa voiced, frustrated.

"Jarvis owns this club and he's a man. So, you know he doesn't care about women having to pee," Candace said, laughing.

"It's obvious they don't care because all clubs are like this, and we're always the ones waiting. It's so tacky standing in line to go to the bath-room," Lisa griped.

"I really have to go," Candace expressed, struggling to squeeze her thighs together.

Annoyed, Lisa said, "I'm not waiting. Come with me." Without hesitating, they headed for the men's bathroom.

"Lisa, we can't go in there," Candace protested, shocked.

"They have toilets, don't they?" Lisa said as she grabbed Candace's arm and pulled her towards the men's bathroom.

"That's my girl," Candace said, laughing.

Lisa walked right into the men's bathroom, dragging Candace behind her. There were five men in the bathroom, and as soon as the door opened, all the men turned around surprised. A few men didn't care and continued using the urinal, while some of them started cracking up laughing. The rest looked annoyed that the ladies were in the restroom and shook their heads as they walked out.

Lisa and Candace went straight to the handicap stall and closed the door.

Realizing what they were doing, Lisa laughed. "Hurry up so we can get out of here."

"You are really silly," Candace said.

Once they finished, they walked out of the stall, washed their hands, and winked at the men as they strolled out, knowing all the men were watching. The women who were still waiting in line for the bathroom started applauding them for taking a stand. Their actions encouraged other women to go into the men's bathroom, also. Soon, the men's bathroom became co-ed.

While Candace and Lisa were rushing out of the bathroom, Lisa bumped right into a man who was standing outside the door. She hit him so hard that she stumbled right before he caught her.

"Slow down, baby. You're going to hurt yourself." Jarvis stood there with a smirk on his face.

"I'm so sorry," Lisa said, looking up at him as butterflies started forming in her stomach. When she looked at him, she saw a strong, mysterious, composed man who she was still attracted to.

"Were you just coming out of the men's bathroom?" Jarvis asked.

"The line for the women's bathroom was too long. We couldn't wait," Lisa said, now seeming embarrassed.

"You know there's two women's bathroom in the club," Jarvis informed her as a smile came across his face.

Feisty, Lisa replied, "You need to make larger bathrooms for the women."

"You guys look beautiful," Jarvis complimented.

Seductively staring at the black, strapless, short dress Lisa was wearing, her muscular arms were a turn-on for him, and her shape made him keep looking at her entire body. Jarvis gave Candace a slight frown, wondering why she was coming out of the men's bathroom, too. He didn't like it.

"Thank you," Lisa said, blushing as she stared at him.

Jarvis look was well put together with a grey designer suit.

"Can I buy you a drink?" Jarvis asked in a low, smooth tone.

"Sure," Lisa quickly responded.

"I'm thirsty, too," Candace said playfully, even though she was upset from the lack of attention.

"You know I will take care of you," Jarvis said, never taking his eyes off of Lisa.

"Will you save me a dance?" he asked Lisa as he ignored Candace.

"Of course," Lisa replied, trying to control the huge smile coming across her face.

"Let me mingle with my guests, and I will see you in a few minutes."

As he walked away, Lisa admired his body, while Candace stared at him with hatred in her eyes.

"Damn, he's fine," Lisa commented.

"I've told you to leave him alone," Candace said.

"What's wrong with us hooking up?" Lisa asked, irritated.

"I just don't want you to get hurt. Jarvis is a hand full."

"I can handle myself. I'm a big girl," Lisa said with a cocky attitude.

Candace kept her comments to herself as they walked back to the table where their friends were still partying and now entertaining more men. Lisa sat down and filled her glass up with more champagne.

She was feeling good after seeing Jarvis and getting such a warm greeting from him. Candace was now annoyed that Jarvis had messed up her happy mood.

About an hour later, Lisa searched the room looking for Jarvis. Unable to find him, she started feeling disappointed at the thought of him hooking up with another woman, but then she assumed he was busy entertaining his guests. He had a club to run, and she knew he had probably forgotten all about her. She turned every guy's invitation down for a drink or dance because she was waiting on him.

Four hours later, the crowd was dwindling, and they were now tired and ready to leave. They laughed reminiscing about old times, when the DJ played a slow tempo song and everyone started singing along. Someone tapped Lisa on her shoulder, interrupting her groove, but when she turned around, she was pleasantly surprised to see it was Jarvis.

Candace gritted her teeth and held back tears. Sure, this was the arrangement she had agreed to, but it was getting harder to digest. She knew Jarvis was a dog and wasn't going to change.

"Do you want to dance?" Jarvis asked while licking his lips slowly.

"I thought you forgot about me," Lisa responded as she got up, trying to act like she wasn't waiting on him.

"I couldn't forget about you. You're too pretty," Jarvis said as he grabbed her hand and led her to the dance floor. He immediately grabbed her by her waist and pulled her close to him as they slow danced.

"I thought you had given my dance away to another woman," Lisa whispered in his ear.

"I had to make sure my guests were having a good time and that my event was a success," he whispered back as he held her tighter.

"It was a nice party. I had fun," Lisa told him as she laid her head on his shoulder.

"You've been on my mind lately," Jarvis said.

"We haven't spoken since our last dinner date, so I find that hard to believe."

"I'm sorry. I've been so busy. It had nothing to do with you."

"No problem."

"Now that things have slowed down, nothing is stopping us from hooking up."

"Candace doesn't want that to happen."

"Why?" he asked.

"I don't know," Lisa lied, realizing he didn't have a clue Candace told her all about his cheating ways.

"We're going to have to do something about that because I want you," Jarvis said like he wasn't going to take no for an answer.

Stacy and Candace walked on the dance floor and interrupted them right before Jarvis was about to kiss Lisa. They grabbed Lisa's arm and quickly pulled her away from Jarvis, leaving him standing there in awe. Candace looked at Jarvis in disgust, knowing he had broken her down to accept his demeaning behavior towards her.

With a serious look on her face, Stacy said, "Candace's boyfriend Tony is here!"

"Tony is not my boyfriend," Candace shouted while heading to the bathroom.

"You guys interrupted my dance for this nonsense?" Lisa said, annoyed.

"He's looking for Candace, and he doesn't look happy. You know how he makes a scene. I think we should leave," Stacy said, sounding worried.

"It's over between us. I don't want his cheating ass. He still can't get over me. I know I'm fine, but damn, he needs to move on," Candace said while fixing her hair in the bathroom mirror.

Lisa grew concerned. "Jarvis is going to be upset if Tony causes a scene at his club. Maybe we should tell him what's going on."

"I'm not going to involve Jarvis in this petty mess," Candace said, unconcerned.

"Do you want to go home?" Lisa asked Candace.

"No! I'm not going to let him stop me from enjoying my night. I know how to handle Tony," Candace responded as she put the final touches on her make-up.

"That's what you get for dating his dumb ass," Lisa commented.

As soon as they walked out of the bathroom, Tony quickly grabbed Candace's arm.

"What's up, baby? I've been looking for you," Tony said with a smile on his face as he tried to hug her.

"What do you want, Tony?" Candace asked, irritated as she pulled away from him.

"Can we go somewhere and talk?"

"There is nothing to talk about," Candace said, frowning.

"Don't do this, baby. I still care about you. I love you," Tony pleaded.

"Love! Where was the love when you were dating those other women? Cheater! We're done, so leave me alone!" Candace turned around and walked away.

"I've spent too much money on you just to let you go. Now, let's go somewhere in private and talk," Tony said, appearing to be getting angry.

"It's over between you two," Stacy said.

"Shut up and stay the hell out of this!" Tony said, fuming.

"You shut up!" Stacy and Lisa shouted back, while Candace scowled at him.

Tony quickly snatched Candace's arm and pulled her towards him. Lisa and Stacy helped release her arm from his tight grip. He came to the club determined to get Candace back, but things were not going his way. Tony kept pulling on Candace as they argued with each other. They looked like they were having a tug of war contest.

Jarvis, John, and Antonio saw the commotion and were concerned as they walked over to them.

"I can't have this type of shit at my club. Now, what's the problem?" Jarvis questioned in a low, calm voice.

"There's no problem," Tony responded, heated.

"Candace, what's going on?" Jarvis asked.

"Nothing," Candace said.

"You screwing this man and bringing him up in my club. What the hell is wrong with you?" Jarvis whispered in Candace's ear. Although furious, he kept a smile on his face.

"He was just leaving," Candace nervously told him.

"Good. Now let's go finish our dance," Jarvis said while he softly grabbed Lisa's lower back and signaled for Stacy and Candace to follow him as they walked back to the VIP section.

Antonio looked at Tony like he could rip his head off, but with a mild manner, he followed Jarvis.

Jarvis looked back at Tony and said, "Man, go get a drink on me and cool off. I don't need any problems tonight."

Jarvis quickly looked away without showing any emotions. Tony didn't know how to take him and didn't know what to do next, but he decided to go have the complimentary drink.

"Go make sure he gets his drink and leaves," Jarvis told Antonio and John. He wanted to make sure Tony didn't cause another scene.

"We'll take care of it," John told him.

"We don't need any unnecessary drama," Jarvis warned them, not wanting them to embarrass him or his business.

"I'll handle it," Antonio said, assuring him that things would be handled smoothly and professionally.

"Antonio, I'm serious. Let him get his drink and leave with no problems. You understand?" Jarvis cut his eyes at him to let him know he wasn't playing.

He always referred to Antonio as 'The Quiet Storm' because he appeared to be calm and cool, but when you pissed him off or when Jarvis needed him to rough someone up, Antonio was his go to guy. John was the opposite; he was always ready to set it off any chance he got. Jarvis always needed Antonio to keep the peace and didn't want John's ghetto ways to reflect on his business.

Jarvis and Lisa talked while he caressed her hand. They had a lot in common, like working out, cooking, and enjoying a good bottle of wine. Lisa knew they would make a good couple, but she didn't want to move too soon and was struggling to control her feelings.

Even though Jarvis didn't want Candace dating other men, he had no problem dating other women. She didn't know how to feel, but always seemed to feel jealous and instantly confused by her emotions. The night became more and more draining for her, and she was now ready to leave.

Twenty minutes later, Antonio and John returned to the table to give Jarvis an update.

"Tony had his drink and he has left. Everything is cool," Antonio informed him.

Jarvis leaned over and whispered in Candace's ear while smiling, "I know you didn't have this man come up in my club looking for you, did you?"

"I didn't know he was coming," Candace whispered back, trying to pretend nothing was going on between her and Tony.

"You must be sleeping with him if he's here looking for you," Jarvis said. Although upset, he continued smiling.

"I'm not sleeping with him. He just won't leave me alone," Candace replied as she looked around the room, knowing she wasn't telling the truth.

"If you want to act like a dog, then you know where I keep my dogs," Jarvis said, reminding her of her overnight stay in his dog cage. "Don't let that happen again. No one should taste you but me," Jarvis told her while rubbing his chin.

Not saying a word, Candace just clenched her teeth tightly.

As the evening came to an end, they decided to call it a night and go home. Jarvis was determined not to let Lisa get away this time. He gave her a kiss on the cheek and whispered in her ear that he was going to call her in the morning for breakfast. Lisa agreed by returning a kiss on his cheek.

"Be careful going home," Jarvis told them as he walked them to the front door of the club.

"We'll be fine," Stacy said.

They walked outside the club and waited for the valet to get their vehicle. John escorted them to the car, while Jarvis and Antonio walked back into the club laughing and talking. Lisa jumped in the passenger seat and Stacy got in the backseat. John walked around the car and opened the door for Candace, helping her into the driver seat. He held her door open as he talked to them for a few minutes.

Out of nowhere, a black shiny 750Li BMW drove at full speed right towards Candace's vehicle. Candace had just gotten into the car, and John, who was facing the opposite direction, never saw the car coming.

The car hit him so hard that he went flying in the air along with the car door. Lisa and Stacy jumped out of the car, and everyone started running and screaming. The car never stopped. It drove away from the scene at full speed.

They ran over to John, who was laying three feet from the car in the middle of the street. Lisa immediately started talking to him, but he was unconscious. Stacy quickly grabbed her cell phone and dialed 911.

"Don't touch him!" Candace yelled at the crowd of people who were trying to help.

"Oh my God!" Stacy and Lisa kept repeating.

One of his legs appeared to be broken and the other one was hanging off. His body was full of scrapes and bruises, and his head was bleeding profusely. Jarvis and Antonio came running out of the club after word got back to them that someone had been hit by a car. They immediately ran over to John.

"What happened?" Jarvis asked frantically.

"A car hit him," Stacy said.

"Call the ambulance!" Jarvis shouted.

"They're on the way!" Candace told him.

"Who did this?" Antonio asked.

"It happened so fast. All I saw was a black car driving away," Lisa replied.

"A hit and run! Damn!" Jarvis said.

Antonio immediately took action and walked away to find some answers. He quickly returned, leaned over, and whispered in Jarvis' ear that a few people who were standing outside saw the whole incident and said Tony, Candace's ex-boyfriend, was the one driving the car.

Jarvis closed his eyes and slammed his hands against his head repeatedly. Lisa grabbed him and held him tightly while they waited for the paramedics to arrive.

The ambulance and police made it to the club within five minutes, and they immediately started questioning Jarvis about what happened. Unable to speak, Antonio took over for Jarvis and explained to them what happened based on what the crowd said. He gave a full description of Tony and was willing to answer any questions they had.

If she wasn't sleeping with another man, none of this would have happened. This was the only thing Jarvis kept thinking to himself. The more he thought about it, the more he became irate. He was furious that he wasn't the only man in her life, and now his friend was lying on the ground fighting for his life because of her. He thought he had her on a tight leash and knew everything she was doing, but this relationship slipped under the radar.

"Slick bitch," Jarvis mumbled to himself as he looked at Candace sitting on the curb.

Jarvis nervously observed the paramedics while they worked on John. The expression on the paramedics' faces told him that it didn't look good. John was not moving, and the pool of blood surrounded his body and cradled it.

Jarvis walked away for a moment to register everything, and Antonio was right by his side. One moment, they were having a great time, and the next moment, all hell had broken loose. Jarvis couldn't believe what was going on; he felt like he was dreaming.

Antonio bowed his head and said a silent prayer that John would recover. Jarvis was fuming because he didn't need this type of tragedy happening in front of his club. He was also becoming more fearful because his friend didn't look so good.

Walking over to where Candace was sitting on the curb with Stacy and Lisa, who were all shaken up, Jarvis asked, "Are you guys okay?"

"Yeah, we're fine," Candace responded while looking around in a daze.

"I'll have someone drive you guy's home," Jarvis told them. Then he leaned over and whispered in Candace's ear, "All of this happened because you can't keep your damn legs closed."

Candace didn't respond as she started to cry while staring at John's limp body lying on the ground. Even though he shouldn't have been saying anything to her about who she was sleeping with, he thought he had every right to since he felt like he owned her. In his mind, she had disobeyed him.

Candace, Stacy, and Lisa sat on the curb stunned by what was going on and unable to accept what was happening. John was clinging to his life as everyone observed. Jarvis, who had tears in his eyes, tried to walk away to avoid looking at John, but he was getting anxious and started to worry. Antonio kept walking back and forth, obviously nervous but trying to show a tough exterior.

Jarvis tried to compose himself and be optimistic. However when he witnessed the slow shake of the paramedics' head, it was confirmed. John was dead. Jarvis watched his friend's life come to an end, but he was never going to have closure.

"You got my boy killed!" Jarvis shouted at Candace as tears ran down his face.

"I'm so sorry," Candace said while tears continuously fell from her eyes despite Lisa trying to console her.

"If he wasn't here looking for your ass, John would be alive."

"It's not her fault," Stacy said, trying to put out the fire that was in Jarvis' eyes.

"Stay out of this," Jarvis told her as he walked away trying to hide his emotions from everyone.

Antonio looked at Candace, shook his head and followed Jarvis.

The ladies didn't try to go after him because they knew he was beyond upset. Stacy and Lisa tried to console Candace as one of Jarvis' friends instructed them to get in the car so he could take them home.

One week later, they were in Atlanta at John's funeral. Jarvis paid for everything and didn't spare any cost. He wanted his best friend to rest in peace and go out in style. He flew in any family members or friends that wanted to attend his funeral.

Jarvis was taking his death very hard and was still traumatized. The world had stopped moving, and Jarvis found it hard to function without his friend.

After John's funeral, things went downhill for Candace, and she didn't get out of bed for days. She was taking John's death hard and kept her distance from everyone because she felt like it was her fault. She spent most of her time at the office. Even though Jarvis was upset with Candace, he still needed her to help run his businesses.

Jarvis hated Candace at that moment, and took a vacation with Kora to get his mind off of things. When he returned from Cancun, he was hardly ever in the office and remained distant from everyone. His absence gave him time to mourn in peace and avoid hearing Candace apologize every day. Candace was paranoid that he was going to fire her, but he never did.

It was strictly professional between Candace and Jarvis; he no longer showed her any love. Jarvis ceased all contact with people, and everyone was panicking trying to figure out how he was doing. When Jarvis reappeared after months of hiding, everyone was happy to know he was alive.

Once he resurfaced, it was back to business as usual. Antonio handled his business while he was in seclusion, making sure everything ran smoothly and would be ready for his return.

CHAPTER 13

Eight Months Later...

"Hi, I'm Lisa Cotus, and I have a one o'clock appointment with Mr. Jarvis Denttin," Lisa jokingly told Candace as she adjusted her suit jacket.

"Please have a seat, Ms. Cotus, and he will be with you in a moment," Candace said, laughing, playing along with her.

Jarvis was looking for someone to remodel his new office, and he wanted to hire Lisa. However, another tall, beautiful interior designer had caught his eye, and he was interested in her, as well. Candace wasn't going to compete for his attention with a new woman, so she did everything she could to get him to hire Lisa instead.

Because of Lisa's reputation and long impressive resume, the other woman couldn't compare to her experience, so Jarvis hired Lisa. Although Candace recommended Lisa for the job, she wasn't sure she wanted her to work so closely with Jarvis because of the way he felt about her.

Since Lisa hadn't had any contact with Jarvis since John's funeral, Candace thought maybe the attraction had dissolved between them.

"Thanks for recommending me to Jarvis," Lisa said appreciatively.

"Now you know I wasn't going to let anyone but you come in this office to decorate. Jarvis had totally forgotten that you were an interior designer, so I had to remind him. It wasn't hard getting you the job. He seemed very interested in you," Candace told her.

"I might owe you a commission check," Lisa said, laughing.

"I want twenty percent," Candace replied, smiling.

Lisa frowned. "That's steep!"

"Well, I did hook this job up for you."

"When are we going to lunch? It's my treat."

"Let's get together one day this week, because today is hectic for me. The receptionist is out sick, and I'm filling in for her. I'm his executive assistant, but it seems like I do everything around this office," Candace said, snickering.

"You know he is serious about his work."

"I'm happy you're going to change the décor in here. This place really needs a makeover."

"I'm going to hook this place up," Lisa responded, looking at the bare walls as her imagination started creating a plan for the room.

Looking around, she could tell Jarvis didn't put any effort into beautifying the office. It was plain with no color, and the room felt cold and boring.

"Let me tell Jarvis you're here," Candace picked up the telephone to let him know his appointment had arrived.

"Thanks," Lisa said as she took a seat on the black leather couch.

She looked around at the large space and knew Jarvis really needed her help remodeling. She started generating and writing down ideas as she waited. Candace set up the arrangements for Lisa to meet with Jarvis, and one week later, Antonio called her and asked to meet about remodeling his new restaurant and office. Lisa jumped at the chance to take on both projects.

"Jarvis is ready to see you," Candace told Lisa.

"Hey, Lisa, it's so good to see you," Jarvis said, quickly jumping up from his desk and hugging her when she walked into his office.

"I'm glad to see you're okay. Everyone was worried about you," Lisa said as they continued to hug each other.

"I just needed time to myself to get over things. John's death was really hard for me. I really miss my friend. We had some good times together," Jarvis sadly replied.

"I understand. It's been hard on everyone," Lisa said as she released her arms from around him.

"I'm good now, just getting back to business. Work keeps my mind off of things," Jarvis said, smiling as he gestured for her to have a seat.

"I heard that Tony was arrested and will spend a long time in jail," Lisa stated.

"He was dumb enough to run my boy down in front of a crowd of people. I hope his ass rots in jail," Jarvis said, staring at the floor.

"He deserves to die. We were all scared that you would kill him before the police got to him."

"I thought about killing him, but decided I'm not meant to live my life in jail for that punk. So, I made sure he would never hurt anyone again. I hope he enjoys his new home for the rest of his life." Jarvis gritted his teeth as he tried to compose himself.

Although Tony was in jail for life, Lisa could tell Jarvis was still very livid about it.

"I can't believe he killed John," Lisa said.

"He's going to rethink his decision now. My friends in jail will be keeping him company," Jarvis informed her while staring in space.

He was never going to get over John's death and didn't think he could ever forgive Candace. He still blamed her. Candace walked around on edge daily, wondering what he was going to do to her. Since he hadn't done anything yet, it had her scared the most.

"Let's talk about your projects," Lisa said, switching the conversation. She was excited and smiling from ear to ear.

"I've been putting off doing something to this office. However, with all the meetings I have here, I really need something done fast. I'm also partnering with Antonio to open a restaurant, but I will allow him to take the lead on the project," Jarvis told her.

"Wow, that sounds great," Lisa said.

"I'm happy you agreed to take on both projects."

"I'm happy you're able to pay my fee for both projects," Lisa responded, laughing.

"Now you know I can afford you. I will pay you double if you really impress me with your work," Jarvis said, showing his cockiness.

"Don't say things you're not going to do," Lisa replied, sounding interested in his proposition.

"I'm serious. I will double your salary if I love what you do with my office and the restaurant," Jarvis said.

"It's a deal. When do we get started?" Lisa asked eager to impress him.

"Let's start by going out to lunch," Jarvis answered as he sat up in his chair.

"I take my business seriously. I don't mix business with pleasure," she said, sounding slightly peeved.

"I'm sorry you took it that way. I just wanted to go to lunch to discuss the details of your job. I'm actually hungry," Jarvis said laughing as if he was appalled that she thought he was being unprofessional.

"I'm so sorry, Jarvis. I just wanted to make sure you understood that I want to keep this strictly professional."

"Lisa, you're beautiful, but not that gorgeous that I can't stay professional. It's always business first with me," he said.

"Forgive me," Lisa responded apologetically.

"Let's just skip lunch and take care of the contracts and paperwork now. You'll be working with Antonio to help you with the projects. I wouldn't want you to think I'm trying to play some type of game with you," Jarvis said, sounding irritated.

"I'm sorry, Jarvis. Can we start over?" Lisa asked as she smiled, trying to lighten the mood.

"Let's just review the contracts."

"Okay." Not wanting to further irritate him, she bowed her head and read over the paperwork.

"Here is a credit card for you to purchase anything you need. Please make sure you give all receipts to Antonio," Jarvis instructed, sounding like she was now a stranger to him.

Lisa knew she had annoyed Jarvis, but she didn't know how to fix it. It was obvious they had started off on the wrong foot, and she was kicking herself for speaking too soon.

She didn't know how to smooth out the situation, but was happy he didn't fire her. The money she would be making for this job would increase her bank account, and she had almost blown the deal with her big mouth.

"Jarvis, I'm really sorry. I didn't mean anything by my statement. I was just joking," Lisa said, trying to fix things.

"Lisa, everything is fine. No worries. Just do a great job and we won't have any problems." He stood up from his desk and walked to the door to escort her out.

Lisa felt so bad that she couldn't do anything but follow him to the door. She gave him a handshake since it appeared that hugging was out of the question. He was treating her how she suggested she wanted to be treated, strictly professional, and she didn't like it at all.

"All I ask is that you update me once a week on your spending," he requested.

"Of course, I will talk to you next week. Thank you again for this opportunity," Lisa said as she went along with the professional relationship. She then walked out of the office with her head hung low and her foot in her mouth.

"Damn," she mumbled to herself on the way out of the office.

She said goodbye to Candace and walked out of the office. Before she got into her car, her cell phone started ringing. Hoping it was Jarvis calling her to tell her that he wasn't upset with her any longer, a large smile came across her face.

"Hello," Lisa answered.

"Ms. Cotus," the man's voice said.

"Yes, how can I help you?" Lisa asked curiously.

"This is Antonio."

"Hey Antonio. How are you?" She asked, trying to sound excited.

"I was calling to see when you wanted to get together so you could tell me your ideas for the restaurant," Antonio said.

"We can meet tomorrow if your schedule is open."

"I have time now if you haven't left the office yet," he told her.

"Sure, I'm on my way back in," Lisa said, gritting her teeth as she smiled.

She didn't want to go back into the office because she was still embarrassed and didn't want to see Jarvis again, but she sucked it up and walked back in to handle her business and make her money.

As soon as she walked into the building, Jarvis was leaving. He looked at her, nodded his head and walked out the door without saying a word. She smiled and nodded her head, acting as if what happened in his office didn't faze her.

When the door closed, her heart fell to the floor. She knew she had totally blown it with him. She made a mental note to never joke around with him again. She had to remember he was a client, and she needed to treat him like one.

She realized he was still mourning the death of John and trying to put his life back together, so he was probably a little on edge and not in a playful mood. While waiting for Antonio, she started making plans on how to get Jarvis back on her team again.

CHAPTER 14

After a few months of non-stop work remodeling the restaurant and office, Lisa was exhausted and unable to take on other projects because Jarvis and Antonio were demanding so much of her time. She didn't realize they would be so difficult to work with. Jarvis made all the decisions, and she basically was their personal shopper.

Although she wanted to complain, she didn't because he was paying her top dollars. Also, her company could benefit from having her name attached to his businesses. Every interior designer wanted this job, and she wasn't going to make him regret his decision to hire her.

She wanted to do a good job, so she worked day and night. The office was finished except for one final delivery the next day, and the restaurant would be done in about a month. She couldn't wait until it was over.

Out to dinner for a much needed girls night out, Lisa was looking forward to a break.

"Hey, Stacy, I'm glad you could make it," Lisa said handing her a drink.

"Thanks for ordering me some wine, because you know I needed it," Stacy said, taking a sip before she even sat down.

"Where's Candace?" Lisa asked.

"She couldn't make it tonight. She said she had something to do," Stacy said.

"She is always busy," Lisa added.

"How is the project coming along?"

"I'm done with the office and have a few weeks left to complete the restaurant. I'll be glad when it's over," Lisa said as she let out a long, tiresome breath.

"Is Jarvis talking to you yet?" Stacy asked.

"He only talks to me when it's about business. He's not into small talk with me. I guess I messed up," Lisa said, still a little frustrated.

Stacy snickered. "I told you about your big mouth."

"He's really successful, so I can understand the no-nonsense attitude. He's all about business," Lisa said before placing her order with the waitress.

"You're making a lot of excuses for him. He's probably just a rich, arrogant jerk," Stacy said.

"You're probably right. I'm going to finish this project and forget all about Jarvis Denttin," Lisa replied, trying to convince herself that she would.

"I know you're still attracted to him, and now that you are working closely with him, you're going to get in trouble," Stacy said, smiling as she took another sip of wine.

"I'm going to keep it professional. I don't like to mix business with pleasure."

"I need to tell you something before it kills me," Stacy told her.

"What?" Lisa asked curiously.

"Don't judge me. Just listen."

Stacy began telling Lisa about her relationship with Antonio. Lisa never said a word and let her finish talking. She could tell Stacy didn't feel good about dating someone else's man, but she didn't waste time telling her how she didn't approve of their relationship. After five minutes of Lisa telling her how wrong she was, Stacy stopped her.

"This is why I didn't want to tell you. I didn't want to hear your mouth. I know what I'm doing is wrong, and I'm planning on breaking it off with Antonio."

"I'm glad you're going to leave him alone. You will be the only one who gets hurt in this situation. He's not worth it," Lisa said, trying to comfort her.

"He really cares about me," Stacy stated.

"He has a girlfriend. He doesn't give a damn about you, because if he did, he would only be with you and you wouldn't be sneaking around."

"But the sex is great," Stacy said pouting her lips.

"You can find another man that will rock your world in the bedroom."

While Lisa continued to talk, Stacy started thinking about her sex escapades with Antonio. She thought about how every time they had sex he was rough and not romantic at all.

Was it because he didn't care about her? Was he making sweet, tender love to his girlfriend? She started getting upset. Every time they had sex he tried to bang her head through the headboard, and that was not love.

Antonio was very mechanical with her when it came to sex. There was never any foreplay. He wanted her to get naked, get in the bed, and spread her legs, but once they got started, the sex was great.

He did nice things for her, like send flowers and give her expensive gifts, but she felt like he was trying to be more like Jarvis than himself. She really didn't know him and was tired of keeping their relationship a secret. She was ready to date someone who she could love openly in public.

"I promise I'm going to leave him alone. I know I deserve better. It was killing me not to be able to talk to you about this. I was embarrassed," Stacy said.

"I'm your girl. You never have to be embarrassed in front of me. I won't judge you, but you need to leave Antonio alone for good."

"It's over," Stacy said, knowing this was something she had to do. She just wasn't sure how or when she was going to end her relationship with Antonio.

"Make sure you're available for the grand opening of Antonio's restaurant," Lisa reminded Stacy.

"I'll be there. What's the name of the restaurant?" Stacy asked.

"Antonio's! What else," Lisa said, laughing and shaking her head.

"Everyone is anticipating the opening, so you better make sure it looks elegant inside," Stacy said, poking fun.

Several hours later, they were leaving the restaurant after having planned their next dinner date. Lisa headed home to relax for the evening. She made it there in less than thirty minutes, and before she could open the door, her cell phone was ringing. She quickly opened the door and rambled through her purse to find her phone.

By the time she reached her phone, it had stopped ringing. She looked at the missed calls and noticed Antonio had called her three times. She then looked at the clock. Seeing that it was eleven o'clock in the evening, she contemplated returning his call. After learning about his secret relationship with Stacy, she didn't have the same respect for him.

"Why is Antonio calling me at this time of night?" she said out loud, but before she could decide if she was going to return his call, her telephone ranged again.

"Hello," Lisa answered, trying to sound peppy.

"Hey, Lisa, sorry to call you so late, but Jarvis wanted to know if you could meet him at the office," Antonio said.

"It's late!" Lisa responded, surprised by the request.

"You know we never sleep," Antonio said.

"Well, I do. What is this about?" Lisa asked, becoming disturbed. They had gotten on her last nerve, and she was now showing it.

"I don't know what it's about. Are you coming or not?" Antonio asked, sounding irritated by her hesitation.

"I'll be there in an hour. Goodbye," she said, then hung up her phone and closed her eyes frustrated.

Lisa flopped down on the couch and stared at the walls. She had enough of their demanding schedules, controlling ways, and disrespect of her time. Her patience was being tested, and she wasn't sure if she would last four more weeks. It seemed like things were getting out of hand, especially now that they were calling her after work hours.

Since she wasn't on the clock and just didn't care anymore, she decided to take her time going to the office. She jumped in the shower and then changed into a short, loose-fitting casual dress with flat sandals, which was unlike her usual business suit, heels and briefcase. She pulled her hair back into a ponytail, applied some make-up, and headed out the door.

An hour later, she pulled up in front of Jarvis' office. She sat in the car a few minutes, trying to get a positive attitude before she went in. They were on her schedule, and it was time for her to take control. She dragged herself out of the car, and to her surprise, Antonio was waiting at the door.

"There's been a change in plans. Jarvis would like for you to meet him at his house," Antonio told her as they walked in the office.

"You've got to be kidding me!" Lisa said, slightly raising her voice.

"He got tired of waiting for you, so he went home," Antonio replied while packing up his belongings.

"Can this wait until tomorrow?" Lisa asked.

"If you want to get paid, I think you need to go now. Jarvis is going out of town in the morning, and he wants to take care of this before he leaves. Go get your money," Antonio said, noticing she was agitated.

"Seriously, you guys are," Realizing that she still needed to handle this situation professionally and not show her personal feelings, Lisa stopped in the middle of her sentence.

"I'm sorry, Lisa. Here is Jarvis' address."

"Thanks, Antonio. Can you let him know I'm on my way," Lisa said, mustering up a smile.

She put Jarvis' home address in her GPS and headed to his house.

Lisa arrived in front of Jarvis' home thirty minutes later feeling uncomfortable to be visiting his house for the first time so late. Since he requested her presence, she let those thoughts fade away. She was impressed by the size of his home, and it made the statement that he was doing financially well.

"It's Lisa Cotus here to see Mr. Jarvis Denttin. He should be expecting me," Lisa said into the intercom at the gated entrance to his home.

"Hey, Lisa, follow the driveway to the front door," Jarvis said through the intercom speaker.

As instructed, she drove her car up the oval driveway, and Jarvis was waiting at the front door for her.

"Thanks for coming. Welcome to my home," Jarvis said, smiling as he escorted her into his house.

Lisa followed him down a long hallway and was impressed by the house layout and design. She touched almost every vase and piece of artwork out of amazement. They walked into a large office as she admired the beautiful, distinctively shaped mirror on the wall. Jarvis watched her as she looked around.

"I have something for you," Jarvis said as he handed her a glass of champagne and a white envelope.

"Thank you. What's in the envelope?" Lisa asked before taking a sip of her drink.

"It's your check. Open it and make sure the numbers are correct."

Trying not to act shocked while looking at the check, she said, "I guess you loved the office and restaurant." She was surprised he had actually doubled her salary like he promised.

"Yes, I loved it. I'm very satisfied with your work and professionalism. As you see, I'm a man of my word," Jarvis said, holding up his Champagne glass to toast.

"Thank you. I'm so happy you loved everything, but we still have a few things to do with the restaurant," Lisa replied, then took another sip of the sparkling bubbly.

"I trust it will be taken care of."

"Of course," she assured him, "thank you for the bonus." Lisa was still speechless that he actually doubled her salary.

"You're welcome. I wanted to discuss some more business with you." Jarvis pulled a folder from his desk and gave it to her.

"What's this?" Lisa asked as she looked over the documents.

"This is your next project," Jarvis said proudly.

"Whose house is this?" Lisa asked enthusiastically.

"This is my new home. I'm going to sell this house and build my dream home, and I want you to help me decorate it," Jarvis said, smiling.

Thrilled, Lisa replied, "I don't know what to say. I feel privileged."

"You will take the job, right?" Jarvis asked.

"Of course! Of course!" Lisa said, elated.

"We will go over all the details soon. Don't worry, you will be financially taken care of," he stated.

"Thanks, Jarvis," Lisa said, admiring the blueprint of the house.

"You're welcome. What do you think about this house?" Jarvis asked.

"From what I've seen so far, it's a beautiful house," Lisa responded. Before she could continue, Jarvis' cell phone started ringing.

"I'm sorry; I have to take this call. Take your time and look around the house, and I'll meet you back in this room so we can discuss all the details," Jarvis told her, than he answered his cell phone and walked out of the room.

Kora's mother suffered a stroke, and Jarvis allowed her to rush to her mother's side to be with her while she was in the hospital. Since Jarvis didn't trust her going alone, he sent Candace to accompany her to Atlanta. They were due back from their trip in a couple of days, so Jarvis wasn't worried about Lisa running into Kora while she roamed the house freely.

Anxious to look around his home, Lisa didn't waste any time. She entered almost every room and paid attention to every little detail. There was one bedroom that was locked, but she didn't force it because she thought maybe the dogs were in there. However, Jarvis had locked the door to the bedroom that he and Kora shared. Unbeknownst to Lisa, he was married, and there were no signs of a woman living in the house.

She noticed the floor-to-ceiling windows, the high ceilings and the extravagant kitchen. She spent a lot of time looking at photos, artwork and his custom-made furniture. Jarvis definitely had style, and it showed in his home.

She took the time to even sit in the dining room and appreciate the detailed crown molding. Twenty minutes had passed, and she was still looking around mesmerized at his enormous stylish home.

Lisa walked into what appeared to be the master bedroom. It was definitely a bachelor room. With a padded leather headboard, gigantic flat-screen television, seating area that had two chaises, a table with another flat screen television, and a bathroom that was every woman's dream, it was totally captivating. The thick aroma smelled of men's cologne, as if some was just sprayed in the air.

She rubbed her hand along the beautiful duvet and played with all the electronics in the room. With a push of a button, the television appeared out of the ceiling, and the curtains opened and closed on command. You could control the radio, central air system, and television, too.

Lisa walked inside the huge, half-empty closet that was just as big as the bedroom. It was obvious the closet wasn't regularly used since it only held a few suits, jackets, and shoes in it. This was actually Jarvis' private bachelor's bedroom that he didn't share with Kora. He slept in this room when he needed time away from her, and he also used it as a guestroom.

She opened a frosted glass door in the closet, curious to see what was inside. She realized it was another bathroom, just as impressive as the other ones, but only smaller. As she walked in and looked around, she noticed the huge shower that could fit at least ten people.

She also couldn't ignore Jarvis' naked body in the shower. He was standing with his back to her, leaning one arm on the stone wall as the cascade of water fell on his head. He had jumped in the shower to freshen up before he finished discussing business with her. His well-sculptured body mesmerized her, and she was eager for him to turn around so she could get a full frontal view.

She stood in the doorway without saying a word, looking at him from head to toe. She studied him as if she had never seen such a beautiful man before. It was something about Jarvis that made her lust after him, and watching him nude put her in a trance. Before she could stop herself from gawking, Jarvis turned around and quickly wiped the water out of his eyes.

Lisa jumped when he turned around and thought about running, but he had already seen her. He wasn't even startled by her existence. In fact, he acted as if he was used to people watching him. It didn't faze him that she was standing there uninvited and observing him take a shower. Their eyes locked, and he started slowly lathering his body with soap, never saying a word to her as he stared directly into her eyes.

Lisa stood frozen as she watched him put soap on every part of his body as he started to stroke his dick that was now standing at attention. He didn't show any emotions and never took his eyes off of her, and she never looked away. He was seducing her, and she was welcoming it.

Lisa couldn't believe she was still looking at him. It was something about Jarvis that commanded her attention, and she couldn't shake the feelings. Although it felt weird to her, she was fascinated by his sex appeal and was enjoying the perfect picture.

She was staring at the strong, confident, powerful, rich, handsome and calm-mannered man who she always yearned for. Even when she tried, she couldn't make herself walk away from the shower.

Jarvis signaled for her to join him, and as if hypnotized, she slowly walked towards him. As soon as she got close enough, he quickly pulled her under the water and gently pushed her up against the wall. He kissed her deeply and immediately put his hand under her dress, tugging hard at her panties trying to rip them off.

Not putting up a fight, Lisa enjoyed kissing his soft lips. When he slid a finger inside her, she took a deep breath. She couldn't help but to be hot and horny, with his hard dick poking her in the thigh. While he fingered her and held the back of her neck, she continued to passionately kiss him harder as the water poured down on both of them.

"I want you," Jarvis calmly said as he tilted his head to the side and looked at her.

Flabbergasted, Lisa couldn't say a word.

"I need you right now," Jarvis added, this time snatching her thong underwear and ripping them off her.

The way he handled her in a dominant way, she felt like he was teaching her. He demonstrated how he liked to be kissed with his lips, tongue, and eyes, without ever saying a word. Lisa felt like the student, and she was excited to have the teacher instruct her.

"Can I taste you?" Jarvis asked.

Lisa wanted to shout "Yes," because she wanted to feel him, but it was just too soon. However, she was already wrapped up in the moment and couldn't stop. At the end of the day, she was still a woman with sexual needs.

"I can't," Lisa said while continuing to kiss Jarvis' soft lips.

"Why?" Jarvis asked as he sucked on her breast.

"It's too soon," Lisa panted, trying to resist his touch.

"What are you waiting for?" He asked while attempting to insert his dick inside her.

Lisa moaned and forgot about the question.

"If you're trying to do that 'wait for a few months' thing before you have sex, what's the point? We will date for a few months, and then I will tap that ass. I mean, make love to you," Jarvis said as he stopped and stared at her.

Lisa was turned off by his choice of slang words, but was instantly turned on by it, as well. He knew exactly what she was thinking, and now that she heard him say it, it actually didn't make sense to wait. Not waiting for an answer, Jarvis lifted one of her legs up, but Lisa suddenly stopped him.

"Jarvis, I can't do this," Lisa said as she pulled her soaked dress down.

"Why not?" He questioned, while groping her body.

"This is happening too fast," Lisa said, becoming ashamed of her behavior.

"Are you sure?" Jarvis asked, looking sexier than before.

"Yes, I think we need to wait," Lisa responded, compelled by his eyes.

"Wait for what?" Jarvis asked, trying to kiss her again.

"I think I need to go," Lisa nervously said as she tried to leave the shower.

"Go get in my bed. I'll be in there in a moment," Jarvis demanded casually.

As if hypnotized by his voice, dripping wet, she walked out of the shower, back through the closet, and into the bedroom to get on the bed.

"What am I doing?" Lisa said out loud.

She realized she was about to do something she didn't want to. She was under his spell and doing what he told her to do, which was something she didn't like. For some strange reason, she was on the bed and waiting to make love to him.

After continuously talking herself out of it, she got off the bed and was ready to leave. Before she made it out the door, Jarvis was standing in the bedroom butt naked and dripping wet.

"Where are you going? I have condoms," he asked, confused.

"I'm sorry, Jarvis. I just can't make love to you," Lisa said, standing in the doorway.

"We're not going to make love. We're going to fuck. We have to be in love to make love."

His comment made her feel like a piece of meat, and she felt disrespected. She looked at him, then at his large erect dick, exhaled, and walked out of the room. She really wanted this man, even if he was being a jerk.

She knew she had to get out of there to protect her dignity. She walked out of the room and almost thought about going back in, but she pushed through the tingling sensation between her legs and headed for the stairs.

She walked down the stairs with her head hanging down, trying to resist the urge to go back. She was attracted to Jarvis, and was now horny and going home without fulfilling her needs. She knew sleeping with clients and friends could lead to a disaster. Her business was more important, so she got the motivation to keep walking.

When she almost reached the bottom of the long staircase, a woman was walking up the stairs with a bag on her shoulder. She never noticed Lisa because she was too wrapped up in her own thoughts. Once they saw each other, they were both shocked by each other's presence.

"Hello, I'm Lisa Cotus, Mr. Denttin's interior designer," Lisa politely said, extending her hand out to the woman.

Lisa wasn't sure who the woman was, but she wanted to be professional and not look like a booty call leaving in the middle of the night, although she was already embarrassed and the timing was horrible.

She instantly realized that her clothes and hair were dripping wet from almost having sex with Jarvis in the shower, which put her in an even stranger position.

"Hi, I'm Kora Denttin. Jarvis is my husband," Kora said shaking Lisa's hand with a smirk.

Kora looked her up and down, disapproving of her being there and letting her know from the frown on her face. Kora wasn't as naïve as people thought. She knew Lisa was not at her house in the middle of the night talking about decorating. She wasn't certain why she was at her home, but her intuition told her that she was sleeping with her husband.

Kora was trying to surprise Jarvis by taking a redeye flight home early, and Candace never called Jarvis to let him in on the surprise like he would have wanted her to.

"It's nice to meet you, Mrs. Denttin," Lisa said, trying to sound as cordial as possible, but it was noticeably showing all over her face that she was dumbfounded because she had no idea Jarvis was married.

"It's kind of late to be decorating, don't you think?" Kora asked in a condescending tone.

"I was just picking up some paperwork before Mr. Denttin left for his business trip in the morning," Lisa said. Looking at Kora, she knew she didn't believe her.

"Wouldn't the paperwork be downstairs in our office? Where is my husband?"

"Mr. Denttin is upstairs. This isn't what it looks like."

Kora looked suspiciously at Lisa, noticing she didn't have any papers in her hand, and it wouldn't possibly fit in the small purse she was carrying. Lisa was so uncomfortable that she could hardly keep her poise.

"Why are you all wet? Did you take a swim in our pool?" Kora asked, giving her a mean look.

"Oh! My clothes," Lisa said, straightening her dress. There was nothing she could say about her wet clothing. She couldn't find a lie quick enough.

"Ms. Cotus, I'm sure your husband is worried about you being out so late," Kora said, searching her hand for a wedding ring.

The look Kora gave Lisa told her, woman-to-woman, that she didn't believe a word she said and knew she was with her husband. But, she was going to act like a lady and walk away from Lisa.

"I'm not married, but I do need to get home to my boyfriend," Lisa replied, feeling the pressure to lie.

"I think you should go home now. Goodbye, Ms. Cotus," Kora said, then rolled her eyes and walked up the stairs.

"Goodnight, Mrs. Denttin."

Lisa rushed out the door mortified and pissed off at the same time. After Lisa got in her car and drove to the end of the driveway, she realized the gate was closed and wasn't going to open until someone let her out.

She slammed her hands on the steering wheel and then covered her face. She wanted to scream. She was still devastated that Jarvis had a wife and had the nerve to try to have sex with her in their home.

She couldn't dare go back into the house and face his wife again. She sat in her car for about five minutes contemplating about calling Jarvis, when suddenly the gates opened up. She glanced at the house and saw Kora standing in the window looking at her.

She wasn't sure who opened the gate, but she was thankful as she drove away without looking back. Not caring about how late the time was, Lisa grabbed her cell phone out of her purse and anxiously dialed Stacy's number. She had to tell someone what just happened.

CHAPTER 15

Sweating profusely and with her heart racing, Lisa felt like she had just relived a scene out of a movie. She couldn't believe Jarvis would be so disrespectful to try to have sex with her in his house knowing he was a married man.

Now that she had met his wife, she didn't know what to think about him. She wasn't even sure if she would have a job after seeing the look on Kora's face.

Lisa dialed Stacy's number a few times before she picked up the telephone.

"Stacy, you won't believe what just happened!" Lisa hysterically shouted into the phone.

"What's going on?" Stacy asked, trying to wake up from a deep sleep.

"Jarvis is married!" Lisa said, still in disbelief.

"What!" Stacy's said shocked, causing her eyes to pop out of her head. She sat up in her bed, ready to hear all the details.

Lisa shared with Stacy about the entire night. Her adrenaline was flowing, and she talked so fast that Stacy had to ask her to slow down a few times so she could get the whole story. Hearing all the juicy details, Stacy became just as stunned as Lisa.

"Jarvis is lowdown. I can't believe him," Lisa said.

"That is some stupid stuff. Who would have ever known he was married? Why didn't Candace tell you?" Stacy asked.

"I'm wondering that myself, but I will be calling her tomorrow to find out. I guess that's why she was so adamant about us not dating."

"Candace knows he's married. She works too close with him not to know. Candace is lowdown and dirty."

"Maybe she was doing her job and keeping it a secret since no one else knows."

Stacy wasn't trying to hear any excuses for Candace withholding that important information about Jarvis. "You're her friend who was trying to get with him. She could have told you. I don't like her anymore."

"Candace isn't on the firing line right now. It's Jarvis."

"I'm sorry. I know you really liked him."

"I thought things were really about to come together for us. I never saw this coming," Lisa expressed, disappointed.

"Are you going to continue working for him?" Stacy asked.

"I'm going to keep my job because he's paying me well. However, if he's not able to handle having a platonic relationship with me, then I will have to quit."

"You might not be able to have a platonic relationship with him," Stacy said, giggling.

"He has a wife! I'm not going to sleep with a married man. I don't know how to even face him."

"Let him take the lead and see how he handles it. If he acts like nothing happened, move on with your job. If he's mean because you ran out on him, then you need to quit."

"He doesn't even know I met his wife. He never came out of the room while I was talking to her," Lisa informed her.

"Now you know his wife told him all about meeting a strange woman in her house late at night. They're probably still arguing about you right now."

"His wife is probably telling Jarvis to fire me."

"Don't worry about her. Jarvis is the one who hired you," Stacy responded, trying to ease her fears.

"Maybe I should try to talk to her and clean things up."

"Lisa, what are you going to say? You're going to tell her that her husband tried to sleep with you, but you didn't have sex with him? Do you think that's going to make her feel better about you? The damage is done. You're not going to be able to explain why you were in her house late at night, so leave it alone."

"Maybe I should call Candace. She can let me know if Jarvis is upset or what's going to happen with my job."

"I wouldn't call Candace. Remember, she didn't even tell you about his wife."

Lisa kept coming up with ideas on how to clear the air with Kora. She really didn't want her thinking she wanted her husband. Well, she did want him at one time, but now that she knew he was married, she was not going to go down that road. She kept trying to include Candace in on her plan, and it started to drive Stacy mad.

She had never told Lisa about catching Candace and Jarvis having sex in the coatroom at the charity event, but she knew this was the perfect time to do it. Candace was starting to look really shady to her.

"I'm not trying to beat the nail in the wall further, but I need to tell you something." Unsure if she should discuss this with her, Stacy hesitated.

"What do you need to tell me?" Lisa asked.

"Okay, I'm just going to come out and say it," Stacy said, as she nervously took in a deep breath.

She knew Lisa would be upset with Candace, but she didn't know how she was going to feel about her not disclosing this information to her a long time ago.

"Now you're scaring me. Just say what you have to say," Lisa said eager to hear.

"Candace is sleeping with Jarvis," Stacy blurted out. "The night of the charity event I walked in on them having sex in the coatroom."

"Candace works for Jarvis. She's not sleeping with him. I don't believe that," Lisa replied, unconcerned.

"I know what I saw. You better wake up and look past his good looks and naked body. You know I wouldn't tell you this if it wasn't true."

Lisa didn't want to believe her, but she knew Stacy wouldn't lie. She also knew Stacy always had her back and would never make up such an elaborate story, and after hearing this information made Lisa forget all about meeting Jarvis' wife.

"I know Jarvis is probably still sleeping with Candace," Stacy added.

"I'm calling Candace right now!"

"Don't waste your time. She's only going to deny it."

"You're probably right. I'm going to act like I don't know anything about their relationship."

Lisa shook her head and started laughing. She couldn't believe he would have the audacity to try to sleep with her when he was also sleeping with Candace. She didn't take him to be that type of man.

"He doesn't even look like he's running game on women like this. Why the hell is Candace sleeping with him?" Lisa wondered.

"The same reason you almost slept with him."

"I can't believe her. I can't believe him. They deserve each other. I'm done!"

"I'm sorry I didn't tell you when it happened. I just didn't want to hurt your feelings."

"You should have told me. You're just like Candace," Lisa voiced, hurt behind everything that had just been disclosed.

"I'm not the one sleeping with Jarvis."

"But, you could have spared my feelings and told me that he was sleeping with her. I would have never let him kiss me if I had known. I can't trust anyone," Lisa said, frustrated.

"You can trust me. Please don't be mad. I was protecting your feelings."

"Well, my feelings were not protected tonight. So, thank you very much."

"Another reason I didn't tell you is because Candace knows about my relationship with Antonio, and she threatened to blackmail me with it. She knew I didn't want anyone to know."

"So, in other words, you were protecting your dirt."

"I'm sorry," Stacy said, knowing it was going to take Lisa some time to get over this and trust her again.

"People are never who they claim to be," Lisa said wondering how she was going to get over such betrayal from her friends.

CHAPTER 16

Stacy invited Antonio over for a nightcap. She wasn't able to visit his place because his girlfriend was always there, so they got together at her condo as much as possible. Their relationship only consisted of sex since they couldn't be seen together in public.

In the beginning, this arrangement was not a problem for her because she only wanted sex and lavish gifts from him. She wasn't looking for a serious relationship, but since they were spending much more time together, she became more attracted to him and now was yearning for a committed relationship.

Stacy opened the door and Antonio's cologne filled her nostrils, and she inhaled it like a drug. Before he walked into her condo, he kissed her. That's what she loved about him; he was always spontaneous. Even though he was sneaking around on his girlfriend, when he came to visit her, he made her feel like she was the only one he was interested in.

His muscular body made her dream of cuddling with him all night long. He was always well dressed, just how Jarvis trained him, and he took pride in his appearance. You couldn't help but notice his expensive watch and t-shirt that fit tight enough to reveal his muscles.

As they moved through her condo, he started peeling off her clothes. He never wasted any time getting right to the purpose of his visit. Stacy wanted him just as much as he wanted her, so she ripped his clothes off, too.

"Je vous veux," Antonio whispered in her ear while laying her down on the bed. He spoke French and Spanish fluently, which turned her on even more. His uniqueness was fascinating.

"What does that mean?" Stacy asked.

She loved when he spoke sweet French nothings in her ear, but not understanding the language, she always asked him to interpret what he had said.

"It means I want you."

"I want you, too, baby."

"Faites-moi l'amour," Antonio groaned. Before she could ask what he said, he beat her to the punch. "That means make love to me."

"Mon plaisir," Stacy replied.

Antonio looked impressed that she remembered those two words. 'My pleasure' was something she told him a lot.

"I see you've been working on your French."

"Let me show you what else I've been working on." She got on top of him and put his hard dick inside her.

After they finished their two-hour lovemaking session, Stacy rested her head on his chest as they watched television and had pillow talk like they always did. The closeness they shared is why Stacy felt herself falling in love with him and wanting a serious relationship.

"How do you feel about me?" Stacy asked.

"You know how I feel about you. Didn't I just show you?"

"I'm tired of sneaking around."

"Stacy, you knew the arrangements when we started seeing each other. I thought you were able to handle this," Antonio said, exhausted from having the same conversation with her again.

"I just didn't think I would fall in love with you."

"You love me?" Antonio asked, raising his eyebrows.

"I think I do. Now what are you going to do about it?" Stacy asked, looking for an answer.

"You know I have a girlfriend. I don't need this right now. I came over here to relax. I could have been stressed out at home." Antonio got up, interrupting their peaceful moment.

"You can't blame me for wanting to be with you. I can handle this," Stacy said, even though she knew she couldn't.

"So you want to be my girlfriend?"

"Stop teasing me."

"What would you do to be my girlfriend?"

"I think I've been showing you," she responded.

"We'll see how bad you want to be my girlfriend. Maybe one day you will become Mrs. Flink."

Stacy knew he wasn't serious about marrying her. This was just something he did when he wanted her to stop talking about a commitment. Wanting to enjoy the time she had with him, she dropped the subject so they could lie back down and continue talking.

They talked about their childhood and laughed at old memories. Antonio never talked much, but with three glasses of wine and two hours of incredible sex, he was more relaxed than usual.

Stacy had a huge family and always felt sad for Antonio because he didn't have any brothers or sisters. Antonio assured her that he had a great childhood without siblings. After hours of talking, laughing and drinking, Antonio said something that immediately caught her attention.

"I remember when I was young, my sister use to play practical jokes on me all the time. She drove me crazy," Antonio said, laughing as he remembered the happy times. "I miss my sister so much. I can't believe she's dead." Antonio's smile turned to a depressed frown.

Stacy's eyes bucked because he had always told her that he didn't have any brothers or sisters. She knew not to stop a man when he's talking and sharing personal information, because once you interrupt them, they wouldn't share any more. So, she let Antonio go on and on about how he missed his sister. He drunk two bottles of wine and continued being depressed about the sister Stacy never knew he had.

Once it seemed like he wasn't going to share anything else, Stacy asked,

"How did your sister die?"

"She committed suicide."

"What!" Stacy said, not expecting that answer.

"She killed herself," Antonio said as if he was reliving it over in his head.

"Oh my God, I'm so sorry to hear that.

"If I was around I would have been able to help her, but I was in the Army and we didn't talk much."

"Why haven't you mentioned her before? You said you didn't have any siblings."

Knowing he had said too much, he wanted to clean up the secret he had just exposed, but it was too late. "I'm sorry I told you that. It's just hard for me to deal with her death, and since she is dead, technically, I don't have a sister. So, I am an only child."

"But you once had a sister," Stacy pressed.

"Forgive me for not telling you. It hurts me to talk about her," Antonio expressed in a sorrow-filled tone.

Completely caught off guard, Stacy told him, "I understand."

"Please don't mention my sister to anyone. I like to keep my personal life private," Antonio told her, knowing he had really messed up.

"I won't say anything."

"Do you still want to marry me one day?" Antonio asked changing the subject that was making him show a side of himself that Stacy never knew existed. He was vulnerable and didn't want her to see him like that.

Feisty, she replied, "You have to get rid of your girlfriend before we can get married."

"Give me some more time, and I'll take care of it."

Stacy was ready to respond, knowing he was dangling the wife title over her head to see how high she would jump, but before she could comment, he got up and went to the bathroom. She wanted to know more about him than just how good he was in bed.

Even though their conversations were great, it wasn't enough for her. She at least wanted to see how his girlfriend looked or sounded to see what type of women he dated, but he kept that part of his life completely confidential.

As soon as the bathroom door closed and the shower started running, his cell phone started ringing. Trying to ignore it, she continued watching television. When it kept ringing, she couldn't help but want to peek at the caller ID to see who was calling. Since he had just shared some information he never mentioned before and basically was lying about, she was curious to know if he had told her any other lies.

She never felt a need to check his phone until now. Maybe it's his girl-friend, she thought to herself. She pulled his cell phone out of his pants pocket and looked at the name on the screen. The caller's name was private, which really made her want to know who was calling. Maybe it's some other woman he's dating, she thought. If he was cheating on his girlfriend, she knew she wasn't the only one he was seeing.

"Damn, I hate myself for getting attached to him. I know better," she murmured to herself. Growing bold, she did something she had never done before; she answered his cell phone.

"Hello," she answered in a deep, low tone, trying to disguise her voice.

"Bonjour peux je parler à Moe," the female caller said.

"What?" Stacy asked, not understanding a word.

Realizing she didn't understand French, the woman started talking in English. "May I speak to Moe?"

"I think you have the wrong number," Stacy said before the woman quickly hung up.

Stacy knew she wasn't the only woman, so she couldn't get upset, but it made her angry and it hurt her feelings.

When Antonio came out of the bathroom, he started putting his clothes on.

"Don't leave, baby." Stacy begged, ready for round two of their lovemaking.

"I got to get up early, so I'm going to call it a night," Antonio replied.

"I don't want you to leave," she said, knowing he was irritated. He hated when she brought up the subject of their relationship.

His cell phone started ringing again, and he answered on the first ring.

"Hello," Antonio said, then paused as the caller spoke. "Oh really," he said, turning and looking at Stacy suspiciously. "This is not a good time. I'll call you back later."

Cringing because she feared the caller had informed him that some woman had answered his phone, Stacy looked at him and asked, "Is everything okay?"

"Did you answer my phone?" Antonio inquired.

"It kept ringing, so I just answered it. I hope that wasn't a problem."

"I don't need to answer that because you know you shouldn't answer my phone under any circumstances."

"They had the wrong number. They asked for someone named Moe."

"Don't answer my damn phone again!"

"I hope I didn't get you in trouble with your girlfriend."

"I don't need this right now. I'm out of here."

"Fine! Leave! Get the hell out!" Stacy shouted, surprising herself by her response.

"What did you say to me?" Antonio said, walking close to her and forcing her backwards across the bedroom. He looked like he wanted to hit her.

"I'm just upset," Stacy replied, trying to clear the air after looking in his eyes and seeing that he was beyond angry.

"What did you just say to me?"

"I'm sorry, Antonio," Stacy said, as her back hit the wall, and she found that she had nowhere else to go. She tried to hug him, but he moved her hands out of the way.

"I want to be with you, but things are complicated right now. Just give me some more time. Things will work out. I promise."

"Okay, I'll give you some time," Stacy told him, knowing she was selling her soul and putting her life on hold for him. When there is something you can't have, it only makes you want it even more, and Stacy was dying to be with him.

"Let's get together in a few days."

"I can't wait," she said, trying to sound excited, even though she was unhappy.

"Can I trust you?"

"Yes, you know you can trust me."

"I need your help with something."

"What?" she asked.

"I'll talk to you about it later. I've got to get out of here," Antonio said, then finished getting dressed, kissed her goodbye, and left.

Stacy couldn't help but wonder if that was his girlfriend calling and maybe she didn't know he was cheating. She realized that he was not the man she needed to be in love with, and she had to back away from him to keep her mind from drifting his way.

CHAPTER 17

A week had passed since the incident with Lisa and Jarvis, and she was trying to throw herself into her work to stop thinking about it. Since she left Jarvis' house, she hadn't been able to stop thinking about him and his wife. She knew it was wrong to still be dreaming about him in a sexual way, but she couldn't forget his naked body. She hadn't called Jarvis, and he had not attempted to call her either.

When she talked to Candace briefly about Jarvis' wife, she tried to deny it, but Lisa kept pushing and eventually broke Candace down to the point where she gave up the information. Candace didn't give every detail about Jarvis and Kora's relationship but she did tell her that Jarvis didn't want anyone to know he was married. Although Lisa was furious with Candace, she never told her that she knew she was sleeping with him.

Candace actually thought it was funny. She told Lisa that she was supposed to call Jarvis to tell him that Kora was coming back from Atlanta early, but Kora begged her not to tell him so she could surprise him. Lisa never told her that she almost had sex with Jarvis that night. Instead, she decided to keep that piece of information to herself.

Lisa knew Jarvis was out of town on business and assumed he was either busy or just irritated with her for leaving him in the bedroom with a hard-on. She was a little embarrassed, but felt empowered knowing he didn't get his way. With Jarvis, she felt like she lost all control whenever she was around him, and that scared her.

She couldn't wait to talk to him about his wife and putting her in that situation at his home. Things could have turned out for the worst, and she couldn't understand why Kora was so calm about meeting her that night.

With only one week before the grand opening of the restaurant, Lisa was working overtime to prepare for it. She was satisfied with the results, and Antonio was more than ready to open his own business.

While the contractors were finishing the final touches of paint to the restrooms, Lisa took that opportunity to sit down at the bar and take a break. Antonio walked in, stopped, looked around the room, and almost had a tear in his eye.

"This place looks great. I couldn't have dreamed of a better restaurant," Antonio said, gazing around the room.

"I'm happy you like it. It's going to be a success. The grand opening will be amazing, so get ready," Lisa replied, excited yet exhausted.

"You did an excellent job. Thank you so much."

"You're welcome. I'm going to miss working with you guys, but I will be happy to get some rest," Lisa said, smiling.

"I know we've been working you hard, but look around. It has paid off. Jarvis told me that you will be working on his new house. See, it's already paying off," Antonio told her.

"I can't wait to get started," Lisa said, quivering at the sound of Jarvis' name.

After hearing him say that, she knew Jarvis had spoken to him and didn't have any negative feelings about her. Although she wanted to hit Antonio upside his head for not telling her that Jarvis was married. She was still a businesswoman and wasn't going to let this job get away from her.

"Let's celebrate. Have some champagne with me," Antonio said as he went behind the bar and grabbed the most expensive bottle, popped it, and poured two glasses.

Needing to relieve some stress, Lisa quickly grabbed the glass of champagne. They toasted, took a sip, and continued talking for the next fifteen minutes, almost finishing the entire bottle.

Lisa didn't realize how nice Antonio was and how much fun he could be. Even though they had been working together for the past few months, they kept a business relationship and never let loose until now.

Although she wanted to hate him for being a cheater and involving her friend in his doggish ways, he actually was a cool person and she enjoyed his company. She decided she would stay out of his personal life.

Jarvis was like a brother to Antonio, and Antonio respected him. Jarvis had always treated him well, and in return, Antonio repaid him with his loyalty. He knew Jarvis like the back of his hand and was forever indebted to him for helping him open up his own restaurant.

Lisa and Antonio felt good knowing they had succeeded in designing an elegant restaurant. They talked, laughed and started on another bottle of champagne, when the sound of footsteps could be heard entering the room.

"I see we're celebrating," Jarvis said cheerfully.

"What's up, man? You're home early," Antonio responded, standing up to give him a strong handshake.

"Hello, Lisa," Jarvis said.

Jarvis acted like nothing had happened between them, and Lisa went with his lead, pretending it didn't happen either. Even though she wanted to slap him right across the face, she wanted this to be over, so she didn't comment about the incident.

Jarvis grabbed the bottle of champagne to pour himself a drink, when he realized it was emptied. He grabbed the second bottle of champagne, but it was almost empty. So, he decided to have a different choice of drink. Going behind the bar, he grabbed a bottle of Cognac and poured himself a shot.

"How do you like the place?" Antonio asked, thrilled.

"It looks wonderful. Lisa, you really outdid yourself and my pockets," Jarvis commented, holding a glass up in the air to toast.

Lisa could barely look at Jarvis because of the spontaneous meeting with his wife.

"I'll be right back. I got to take a leak," Antonio said as he went to the restroom.

"I see you and Antonio are best friends now," Jarvis told Lisa with a smirk.

Lisa was taken aback by his comment. "What?"

"You guys finished two bottles of champagne while talking. I'm happy I got here when I did."

"What are you trying to say?" Lisa asked, trying to fight her anger. Just finish the job, is what she kept saying in her head.

Jarvis stared at her while he guzzled his Cognac down and poured another shot. Lisa was so uneasy she couldn't even speak. His presence made her tense. Jarvis didn't like seeing Lisa laughing, drinking and talking with Antonio.

"We were just celebrating completing the restaurant," Lisa said, wondering why she was explaining this to him. He has a lot of nerve, she thought to herself.

"I thought you were scared of men," Jarvis said.

"What are you talking about?"

"You ran out of my house so fast, I thought I scared you."

"I'm not going to discuss that with you, but I will discuss your wife."

"My wife?" Jarvis said.

He didn't know she had met his wife that night. Kora never mentioned it to him, and when he came into the bedroom two hours later, Kora pretended she had just arrived.

"The night you were trying to have sex with me, I met your wife on the way out the door. I'm surprised she didn't tell you that she met a strange woman in her house. I think that would have been worth her discussing with you."

"What are you talking about?" Jarvis asked, trying to think of something to say next. He didn't have a clue what happened that night between Lisa and Kora, and he was burning up inside that Kora didn't mention it to him.

"I'm talking about your wife who wore the large diamond ring on her wedding finger and who was in your house. Jarvis, you're busted. You have a wife, and you had the nerve to try to sleep with me. Are you that disrespectful?" Lisa wanted to tell him that she knew about him and Candace, also, but she knew he would deny it, and that would make her angrier.

"I don't think my personal business is any of your concern."

"It's my concern when you're trying to put me in a situation that could have gotten me killed. You disrespected me and your wife."

"You really need to stay out of my personal life because I never invited you in. Just because I tried to sleep with you doesn't give you the right to question me. You stop questioning me, and I will stop questioning you about getting with Antonio."

"There is nothing to question about Antonio. We worked together and were celebrating completing a project. You don't have to worry."

"Worry about what? We're not together," Jarvis said, smirking.

"You're right; we're not together." Irritated, Lisa stared at him for a moment before standing up to leave. "Good night, Jarvis," Lisa said as she started walking away.

"Don't walk away from me."

Just as she was told, she stopped, frozen stiff.

"What can I help you with?" Lisa asked, still trying to maintain control. She was annoyed with herself that she continued to do what he said, but it was something about him that made her succumb to his instructions.

"Come here. Please," Jarvis said seductively while turning around in his chair to face her.

She was frustrated with herself for not being able to walk away from him. He was reeling her in, and she couldn't stop it.

Walking over to him, she asked, "How can I help you?"

He stared at her, licked his lips, and made the moment more intense. With the silence, it became more awkward, but she did not show her feelings. She could never read him, so it was difficult to know what he was thinking. She stared back and tried to resist his sexy, hypnotizing eyes.

He pulled her close to him and kissed her, allowing her to feel every inch of his tongue. She didn't resist. Instead, she introduced him again to her tongue. His hands roamed over her body like he owned it. She instantly pulled away from him, remembering he had a wife and was sleeping with her friend.

"You disrespected me," Lisa said.

"Do you really think I would invite you to my house and try to have sex with you if I was married? You don't understand what's going on. It's not what you think. I'm not that type of guy."

Lisa wanted to believe him, but she knew he was lying. She had hoped he was the man of her dreams, but he was turning into her nightmare. She rubbed her head and wanted things to be perfect, but it wasn't. Still, she found him attractive and couldn't stop the urge of wanting him.

"Don't ever leave my house without kissing me goodbye," he whispered in her ear while pulling her body close to him again.

Lisa couldn't respond because she didn't know what to say. Her silence gave him the floor to keep talking.

"You left me hanging at my house, and that wasn't cool. You should have stayed," he continued whispering in her ear.

"I left because."

He interrupted her by gently putting his finger over her mouth. "Just don't let it happen again. Please," Jarvis said.

"I'm sorry," Lisa uttered, amused by his comment.

"When can I have you?" he asked.

"I'm not ready for that," she replied.

Jarvis laughed. "Oh, you're ready."

"Jarvis, I can't get involved in that type of relationship with you. We both know you have a wife, and I don't sleep with married men."

"We need to discuss this," Jarvis said.

"There's nothing to discuss," Lisa countered.

"So you're telling me that you don't want to know how I feel inside you."

"Honestly, I wish I could find out, but I can't do that because you're married," she told him, holding her ground.

Lisa was hoping Antonio would come back into the room to stop their conversation, but he never returned. It was as if he was purposely giving them time alone.

"Come to dinner with me tomorrow night," he said out of nowhere.

"Jarvis, I'm serious. I want to keep this professional."

"Antonio and I are having dinner here at the restaurant to taste all the food, and I thought you would want to join us. I respect your decision. I won't force you. That's not my style. We can work together, and that will be it," Jarvis said.

"Are you sure we can still have a working relationship?"

"You're a great interior designer, so I'm not firing you. It won't be a problem because business always comes first."

"Okay, I'll see you guys tomorrow then," Lisa told him as he got up.

Before leaving Jarvis spoke, "You don't need to continue celebrating with Antonio. That's not very professional."

"I think we're done here." Lisa smiled, but it wasn't amusing to him.

"Yes, you're done."

As Jarvis walked away, Lisa frowned, knowing that his comment sounded like he didn't want her to talk to Antonio anymore.

Before he reached the door, and without looking back at her, he said, "You're leaving now, right? Drinking with my partner doesn't look professional."

"I'll be leaving shortly," Lisa responded as she started gathering her belongings.

CHAPTER 18

Two weeks passed, and Lisa was trying to avoid Jarvis as much as she could. Because of his busy schedule, it wasn't hard for her not to see him. The grand opening of the restaurant was postponed for another month because Antonio couldn't get the event planning company he wanted.

Jarvis didn't question him about the delay because he knew Antonio was extremely nervous and wanted everything on point. He trusted him. He understood the feeling of opening up his first business, and he wanted Antonio to feel every aspect of the excitement. Antonio wanted the restaurant to be successful, and it showed. Antonio's hard work and dedication made Jarvis very happy to be his partner.

Jarvis requested a meeting with Lisa to discuss the details of the décor for his new home. She felt like he had gotten the message that she wasn't interested in a sexual relationship with him since he hadn't pushed the issue and had become very standoffish.

Lisa prepared for the business meeting she had with Jarvis in less than thirty minutes. When she arrived at the office, Antonio was standing in the doorway talking on his cell phone. Together, they immediately walked in and went into Jarvis' office as Antonio concluded his phone call.

Antonio took a bottle of wine from the mini bar inside the office and poured them both a drink. He also poured Jarvis a glass of wine and sat it next to his computer.

"Where is Jarvis?" Lisa asked before taking a sip of wine and sitting down.

"He had to run out for a moment, but he will be back shortly," Antonio replied, then swallowed his wine straight down and refilled his cup.

"No problem. We'll wait," Lisa said.

Antonio sat down and started discussing the opening of the restaurant. Thirty minutes later, she sat there still impatiently waiting for Jarvis, while Antonio went on and on about the restaurant.

"I see you and Jarvis are working well together," Antonio commented, raising one eyebrow.

"Yes, things are going really good."

"You guys make a cute couple."

"What are you talking about?" Lisa asked, trying to figure out where he was going with his comment.

"Aren't you guys dating?" Antonio inquired with a curious look on his face.

"No, we're just working together." Lisa started feeling embarrassed and wondered what he knew.

"That's all?" Antonio looked at her suspiciously while pouring himself another glass of wine, and then realized he was probably crossing the line.

"Why do you think we're dating?"

"I'm sorry. I must have gotten you mixed up with someone else," Antonio said.

Lisa looked at him strangely. She didn't want him to think she slept with her clients.

"I'm sure Jarvis has his hands full with other women," Lisa said, wondering if he was going to give up some gossip, but Antonio didn't give up anything.

"I'm not interested in his personal life."

"What's your story, Antonio? Why are you so loyal to Jarvis?" Lisa asked, putting the attention on him.

"Jarvis is a smart man, and I wanted to learn from him. He took me under his wing and showed me the ropes. I'm loyal to him for that. He also trusts me to run his business."

"What were you doing before you started working with Jarvis?"

"I was in the Army for a while, but I knew that wasn't the life for me. I became a sales manager for a local cable station in Atlanta and decided that wasn't what I wanted to do either. So, I got involved in the club scene as a promoter, which led me to being interested in owning my own business. When I heard Jarvis was hiring, I jumped at the opportunity. He had a reputation as being very successful in the club industry, so everyone wanted that position. I didn't mind starting at the bottom and working my way up."

"Wow, that's some story."

"I'm just a focused person, and when I set my mind to do something, I don't stop until I accomplish it, no matter how long it takes."

"Well, you've done a great job, because your restaurant will be opening soon. You're now an entrepreneur," Lisa said, impressed.

Antonio tried to hide his enthusiasm. "This has been a dream of mine."

"How do you deal with being away from your family?" Lisa pried.

"I miss my mother and father. I'm an only child, so my family is really small."

"Are you going to bring your girlfriend to the grand opening?"

"Unfortunately, she won't be able to make it because she will be out of town."

"Why is she out of town on such a special day like your grand opening?"

"She has to work," Antonio responded, giving her a peculiar look.

"So who will you be celebrating with while your girlfriend is away?" Lisa asked.

"It sounds like you're trying to get all up in my business," Antonio said, laughing as he looked directly into her eyes.

"I was just asking. You look like a ladies' man."

"I don't discuss my personal business, so I would appreciate it if you respect that. Unless, you're interested in me for yourself," Antonio looked her up and down with a smirk on his face.

"I'm sorry. I didn't mean to pry into your personal life. I was just trying to make small talk. And for the record, I'm not interested in you," Lisa told him.

"It's cool. I thought you wanted to go to the grand opening as my date."

"No, thank you," Lisa blurted out. "I was just curious who you were bringing. Sorry for snooping."

"Don't be concerned about who I'm bringing to the event. My love life is not up for discussion."

She knew he was not going to talk about sleeping with Stacy with her, so she decided to let it go. The more she looked at Antonio, the more she could see how well Jarvis had trained him to be identical to him. She also could see why Stacy was sneaking around with him. He was good-looking.

"I really didn't mean anything by it. I'm so sorry," Lisa said.

She really liked Antonio. They had spent a lot of time working together, and she didn't want ill feelings between the two of them.

"No worries. I said I'm cool," Antonio said, sounding and looking unflustered.

Before Lisa could ask another question, Jarvis walked in and was ready for business. "Have you guys started discussing the plans yet? We need to approve these last few details so we can officially open this restaurant."

"We were waiting on you," Antonio said as he gave him a handshake.

"Hey Jarvis," Lisa greeted as he gave her a hug.

Jarvis drank his wine and sat down to start discussing the plans regarding his new home and finalizing the restaurant. Three hours had passed, and they had everything ready to go. Antonio was excited about his new venture as a business owner and partnering with Jarvis. Lisa was going to get started right away on his new home, although she felt a little nervous about taking on such a huge and expensive project.

"I think we're done for tonight. We got a lot accomplished, so let's start implementing these plans," Antonio said eagerly.

"Everything's going to work out," Jarvis assured him.

"Lisa, I'll see you in a few days for our meeting. Goodnight, guys. I'm out of here," Antonio told them as he left the office.

Antonio called it a night and went home, while Lisa finished up her paperwork and planned to be heading home in less than ten minutes. It was silent in the office while Jarvis and Lisa completed the rest of the paperwork.

"I still want you," Jarvis voiced.

Feeling a bit caught off guard, Lisa didn't respond. She was upset for not leaving when Antonio did. She wanted him, also, and being alone in a room with him made it difficult for her to resist him. Still, she knew she was never going to cross that line.

Lisa shook her head. "You just don't give up do you?"

"I'm just going after what I want."

"I'm not going down this road with you. I think it's time for me to leave," Lisa said as she gathered her belongings.

"Lisa, you know you want me. So what's up?" Jarvis asked.

"Please respect me. Don't do this now. I thought we had an agreement. I'm not going to sleep with you. Ever!"

"If that's what you want to do."

"I've got to go." Lisa started moving faster, trying to leave.

"Let me walk you to the door," Jarvis said, disinterested.

He was not going to beg a woman for sex. Although definitely attracted to Lisa and wanting her badly, it wasn't his style to plead. So, he let her walk out the room. His ego was bruised and he was going to do what he did best; which was ignoring her.

"I just think it's best for us to have a platonic relationship while we are working together," Lisa expressed.

"No problem. You can't hate me for trying," Jarvis said as he unlocked the front door to the office.

"Great. I'll talk to you later." Lisa walked out the door comfortable that their business relationship had not been damaged.

"Contact Antonio if you need anything," Jarvis told her before closing the door.

Lisa knew they were back to where they had started in the beginning. Whenever he didn't get his way with her, he distanced himself from her, and she would have to talk to Antonio to get in contact with him. She still had her job and didn't have to be uncomfortable around him, even though she was still fascinated by him.

Not wanting to walk out on an incomplete job, she was going to try to deal with his sexual harassment as long as she could. Because of his behavior, she knew she probably wouldn't be able to take on the project of decorating his new home.

CHAPTER 19

It was rare for Jarvis to be home spending quality time with Kora, but it was Sunday, the day he gave her all of his attention. These were the days she always cherished and yearned for. Jarvis just wanted to relax at home, watch a movie, and cuddle with his wife. This was the man Kora had fallen in love with, and this was the person Jarvis loved being.

They didn't spend much time together, but when they did, they acted like two high school teenagers in love. Jarvis was most relaxed when he stayed home and hung out with his wife. No clubs, no women, no macho attitude and no employees. It was just Jarvis and his wife.

Lounging around in their pajamas, they were in heaven as they talked, laughed, and even had a pillow fight before collapsing on the bed to make love and fall asleep in each other's arms. When Jarvis woke up an hour later, he made sure not to wake her so he could start cooking dinner.

The aroma of spices woke Kora up, and she ran to the kitchen because she knew Jarvis was cooking her favorite dish of salmon, asparagus and garlic mashed potatoes. Jarvis was a great chef, and she loved when he cooked because that's when he seemed the happiest.

After eating the mouth-watering dinner, Jarvis topped it off by making a homemade strawberry pound cake. They both sat at the kitchen table feeling like stuffed pigs, happy, full, and in love. He was actually a nice, caring person, although he seldom showed that side to her, but when he did, she treasured it.

Jarvis really was in love with her. He adored the special moments they spent together when he could just be himself. He was actually a sensitive person and had revealed that side to Kora several times.

However, having lived with his father while growing up and wanting to be exactly like him, Jarvis had a tendency to duplicate every characteristic his father had. It seemed like he couldn't control having his father's personality buried inside him. It kept showing its ugly face. He wanted to be himself, which was a kind-hearted person, but his father taught him to be tough and not care about anyone but himself.

He learned from his father that being nice would get him nowhere. He wanted to please his father, and after showing him that he was willing to do exactly what he told him to do, his father was pleased. He had the approval from his father that he always wanted. His father was proud to have a mini version of himself.

During his younger years, Jarvis once dreamed of being an attorney, and his father encouraged him to pursue it. He said Jarvis had a way with words and knew how to manipulate people easily. Since he was a great liar and thought quickly on his feet, his father felt a career as an attorney would be profitable for him. However, the dream of becoming an attorney vanished quickly when he decided to own his own company.

His father taught him everything he needed to know about the nightclub industry. In addition to making Jarvis go to college to get a degree in Business Management, Jarvis' father filled his head with everything he knew about owning his own business.

His father was handsome, smart and a Casanova. Being impressed by his father, Jarvis wanted to be just like him, and that's exactly how he turned out. Womanizing came easy to Jarvis, especially when he saw that women would do anything for him because he had money. It became a game to see just what he could get women to do. His dad was right; money makes people do strange things.

When Jarvis told his father he was going to marry Kora, he wasn't happy. He felt Jarvis was too young to settle down, and he wanted him to stay focused on his career. Although Jarvis slept around, he truly fell in love in Kora.

Jarvis knew she was the person he wanted to spend the rest of his life with, and not wanting anyone to try to talk him out of marrying her, they eloped. He knew his father and friends didn't want him to hang up his player card, but he had no intentions of doing that. To him, marrying Kora just meant he would always have a woman at home. His player's card was still active.

Jarvis adored Kora and knew she was wife material the moment he met her. She was different from the other women he dated. Although he knew she was high maintenance, he also knew she was worth it. She just wanted the finer things in life, which wasn't a crime because he wanted that, as well.

He wanted to love her and make sure she never had to work a day in her life as long as she was married to him. Her breathtaking beauty attracted him to her the moment their eyes met.

Kora allowed him to be himself around her. She made him feel comfortable with revealing the true person that had been hiding inside him for so long. The careless, tough, money-hungry man he portrayed was only the person his father made him become. It wasn't who he truly wanted to be. He enjoyed spending time with Kora and acting like a loving married couple.

Jarvis threw a bag of popcorn in the microwave and grabbed a couple of beers from the refrigerator. This was another thing he really loved about Kora; she drank beer and was into sports. She was just like one of the boys.

"Let's go watch a movie."

"I'm stuffed and tired," Kora told him.

"Come on, baby. I just want to relax with you tonight. We can watch whatever you want," Jarvis said, trying to convince her.

Kora quickly jumped up, grabbed the beers, and ran to their home theater room to start searching through the movies. She knew he was just saying that to get her to watch a movie with him. So, she wanted to make sure they watched what she wanted to watch.

Jarvis picked up the popcorn and ran behind her, sliding on the floor and almost spilling the popcorn. Kora laughed at him when she saw him running in the room.

"Don't drop the popcorn," she said, laughing.

"I don't want to watch one of those depressing women flicks," Jarvis expressed as he flopped down on the large recliner.

"Let's watch a horror movie."

"Let's watch a stand-up comedy show, something with Mike Epps, Kevin Hart, or even Bernie Mac."

"Let's watch Bernie Mac. He's funny," Kora said as she put the DVD in the player.

She sat in the recliner next to him, opened her beer, and got comfortable. Their theater room had twelve large recliners situated in theater-style seating. Jarvis had splurged on this room since he loved watching movies on the big screen.

The wall-to-wall carpet and old-fashioned popcorn machine, gave the room the feel of a real movie theater. The sound system was remarkable, and it felt like they were sitting front row at the theater.

"I love you, baby," Jarvis said.

"I love you, too," Kora replied, blushing.

"Come sit on my lap." Jarvis smiled, ready for another round of lovemaking.

"Let's watch the video first. I'll put it on you later," Kora said as she threw popcorn at him.

After destroying the room from throwing popcorn at each other, they laughed and began to playfully wrestle on the floor. Jarvis kissed her as he lifted her shirt up, exposing her pink lace bra. She pretended not to be interested in his touches, but she loved spending those special moments together when he showed how much he cared.

"You think you're slick," Kora said, giving in.

Jarvis admired her. "I love touching you. You're so beautiful."

"You're not too bad looking yourself, although your pajamas are wrinkled." Kora laughed while tugging at his pants.

"These are Versace pajamas, and you don't iron them."

"If they're wrinkled, you need to iron them."

Biting his top lip while feeling the growth in his pants, he wanted her. "I can always take them off."

"Take it off, baby!" Kora shouted, waving her hands in the air like she was at a strip club.

Preparing to give her a show, Jarvis stood up and started giving her a striptease, while Kora sat in the chair enjoying the view. It wasn't hard for her to get turned on by him because he was gorgeous with a nice body. Those two things alone did it for her every time.

Jarvis removed his shirt, letting his muscular arms and ripped abs show. Then he teased her by delaying taking off his pants. Right when he was about to show her the goods, the doorbell rang.

"Use your keys," Jarvis yelled as if they could hear him at the front door. If they had the access code to get through the front gate, they had keys to his house. So, he knew it had to be Candace, Kevin, or Antonio.

Jarvis put his shirt back on because he wouldn't dare want someone to walk in on him half naked giving his wife a lap dance. He grabbed the remote, put in a code and turned to the security channel that displayed his entire house.

He clicked on the screenshot for the front door and tilted his head trying to see who was there. It was obvious it was a woman, but he didn't recognize her.

"Who is that, baby?" Kora asked.

"I don't know," Jarvis said as the woman continued ringing the doorbell. "Let me go see who this is. I'll be right back to continue my show." Jarvis smiled, turned the television back to the comedy show, and then rushed out the door.

As soon as the door closed, Kora tried to turn the television back to the security channel, but she didn't know the code. She was anxious to know why this strange woman was at her front door, but would have to wait until Jarvis returned to find out.

Jarvis opened the door with caution, wondering how she got through the secured gates and to his front door. "Can I help you?" he asked, looking at the woman who looked somewhat familiar to him.

"Hello Jarvis," the woman said.

"Do I know you?"

"I'm Jennifer Moeky's friend. I met you at her funeral. I've been calling your office. I'm Karen Law."

"Oh yeah, I remember you. You're the one that had a major attitude with me at the funeral," Jarvis said as if he was talking to an old friend. Then it suddenly hit him that this couldn't be a friendly visit. "What the hell are you doing at my house? How did you get past the gate?"

"I have no problems going where I want to go. Since I was in town, I just stopped by to say hello."

"We're not friends, so why are you here?"

"Nice house. I see you're living well."

Jarvis' eyes turned bloodshot red. He didn't like uninvited guests at his house, and he particularly didn't expect to see her at his front door. "I'm going to ask you one last time. Why are you here?"

"I just wanted to see where the person that drove my friend to kill herself lived. Are you going to invite me in?"

"Karen, let's not play these games. I want you to get off of my property."

"Where is your hospitality? I thought you would have better manners than that."

"Goodbye, Karen."

"I can see why women want to be with you. You're good looking and living large. It must be nice."

"I don't have any available time on my schedule to fuck you, so if that's what you want, I'm not interested."

"Jennifer did say you were arrogant. Please! Every woman doesn't want you. For the record, I'm one of those women who would never sleep with you, even if I was extremely horny and you had the last dick on earth."

"If you had a man, you wouldn't be at my door. So, I know you're lonely and horny. You look like a woman who hasn't had sex in a long time, and I'm sure you're wishing I would have sex with you. Now, go back to where you came from."

Jarvis was back to his regular self again. He no longer felt kind and sweet like he was feeling moments ago. His father had crept back up through his veins and out his mouth. The lion was back in rare form.

"I'll be back to visit you soon."

"Don't come back to my house. Don't underestimate me and get yourself hurt."

"See you later, Jarvis." Karen smiled and walked away.

Pushing the button to open the gate, Jarvis watched as she walked out the gate and got into her car that was parked across the street from his house. She had alarmed Jarvis, but he didn't show her. Although his legs felt a little weak from her visit, he still didn't know why she had showed up at his house.

Before returning to the theater room, he placed a call to Antonio and Kevin to let them know about his surprise guest so they could find out why she was in town.

He walked back into the room to find Kora laughing hysterically at Bernie Mac talking about beating kids. Jarvis was nonchalant and sat down on the recliner without explaining the strange woman at the door.

"Who was that?" Kora casually asked.

Thinking quickly on his feet, Jarvis replied, "That was someone looking for Antonio. She's helping with the restaurant and was supposed to meet him here. Antonio forgot about their meeting, so she's going to reschedule."

"Oh," Kora said.

Kora didn't question him because she knew she wouldn't get a truthful answer. She had never physically caught Jarvis cheating on her, but her intuition told her that he was. It was possible the woman could have been one of his girlfriends, but it was also possible she was there for Antonio.

The only question that still bothered the both of them was how she had gained access through their front gate. Kora wasn't going to let that ruin their night. So, she dismissed it in order to spend some much-needed time with her husband.

"Now, where were we?" Kora said, waving her hands for him to finish his striptease.

Jarvis didn't waste any time taking his shirt off and slowly moving his hips.

CHAPTER 20

Candace had tons of errands to run before she made it back to the office. For the past couple of days, Jarvis had been tied up in meetings and was waiting on some important paperwork that he sent Candace to his house to get. She pulled up in front of his home, pulled out her spare key, and headed to the door.

Once inside, she ran to the office to get the documents Jarvis needed and she decided to speak to Kora before she left. She ran up the stairs and opened the bedroom door without knocking. She saw Kora standing in front of the bed, and to her surprise, Antonio was standing right next to her.

It appeared she had walked in on them having a heated discussion. When they saw Candace, they both jumped and moved away from each other. Their body language told Candace that something peculiar was going on between them. Antonio would not have been in Kora's bedroom if there wasn't something seriously wrong.

"I'm sorry. I didn't mean to interrupt you. I should have knocked," Candace said, looking at them surprised.

"Come in," Kora told her.

Candace walked in slowly and closed the door behind her. She didn't know why Kora was inviting her in, but she wanted to know what was going on.

"Antonio, you know Jarvis would kill you if he knew you were in his bedroom with his wife," Candace said, looking back and forth at them like she was watching a tennis match.

Still looking at Candace, Antonio sat down on the edge of the bed.

"What's going on in here?" Candace asked since no one had said anything yet.

"Antonio was just leaving," Kora said, giving him a conspicuous look.

"I'm not leaving," Antonio voiced while getting more comfortable on the bed.

"Someone tell me something!" Candace said.

Still, only silence filled the room. Candace thought about the situation like she was trying to solve a murder mystery.

"Are you guys sleeping together? Why else would Antonio be in the bedroom? You guys are sleeping together!" Candace shouted like she had cracked the combination to a safe.

"Candace, it's not like that," Kora said, panicking.

"Relax, Kora. It's time people find out." Antonio remained calm, while Candace, on the other hand, started jumping up and down like she had won the lottery.

"Having Antonio in your house and in your bedroom, damn girl, I didn't know you were so scandalous," Candace said, smiling.

"Yes, Kora and I are sleeping together, but I better not hear anything about this," Antonio confessed.

"I've already figured that out," Candace told him.

"You haven't figured anything out, Kojak," Antonio responded sarcastically.

"Antonio, that's enough," Kora said, trying to stop him from telling Candace the truth.

"People are going to find out sooner or later," he said.

"I knew when Jarvis gave you a spare key to his home, it would lead to trouble. Jarvis is going to die if he finds out." Candace grinned from ear to ear, ready to run and tell the juicy gossip.

"He's never going to find out. Right, Candace?" Antonio asked, now standing up.

"Don't worry, I won't tell him. I'm not a snitch. I'm actually happy Kora is getting her groove on. So, while Jarvis is out doing who knows who, his wife is fucking his friend and business partner. Now, that's something," Candace said with a burst of laughter.

"This is not a joke. We're in love," Kora expressed. "You're in love!" Candace said, not expecting to hear that response. "What are you going to do about this?" she asked, amused.

"She's going to leave Jarvis," Antonio said, as Kora stood there looking stupefied. "You know the deal, Kora. It's time to divorce him," he continued.

"Can we talk about this in private?" Kora asked.

"No. Candace already knows about our affair, so it's out in the open now," Antonio said.

"Trust me; I'm not going to tell Jarvis. I don't care who you're sleeping with." Candace looked at Kora with a smirk on her face.

"Don't look at me like that," Kora said.

"I'm just shocked that you're cheating on your husband and bold enough to do it right under his nose. Jarvis thought you were perfect," Candace said, letting her bitterness show.

She hated when Jarvis threw in her face how great Kora was. She was happy that his perfect diamond was flawed.

"My husband is cheating on me with you, so why are you so surprised that I'm cheating on him?" Kora said with attitude she had never shown before. She was tired of Candace making her feel guilty.

"What are you talking about?" Candace asked, embarrassed.

"Don't act dumb. We both know you've been having sex with Jarvis. Bingo! Jackpot! Ah-ha!" Antonio said, elated and smiling from ear to ear.

"I'm not sleeping with him," Candace retorted.

"It's time to be honest. You've been screwing my husband for a long time, and you have the nerve to be in my face trying to be my friend," Kora said.

"That's not true," Candace said, still trying to deny it.

"I saw you sleeping with my husband in our family room. Don't you remember? You looked right at me, or did you think you saw a ghost?" Kora asked.

Candace tried to keep her legs from shaking, but she was busted and didn't know what to say or do. She did see Kora that night. She prayed it wasn't her and hoped she was just being paranoid. She was exposed and the truth was on the table. This was not the position she wanted to be in.

"Who do you think let you out of the dog cage?" Kora asked.

"It was you," Candace said, shocked.

"I should have let you stay in the cage, but even you didn't deserve that type of torture. I let you out of the cage," Antonio told her.

Ashamed, Candace said, "I don't know what to say."

"Thank you is appropriate," Antonio said.

"Why have you been so nice to me if you knew I was sleeping with Jarvis?" Candace asked Kora, needing answers.

"I've spent many nights in that dog cage, so I know how mortifying that feels. You're not the only woman my husband is sleeping with. I'm not in love with Jarvis any longer, and just like you, I want to live an extravagant lifestyle, too. We deal with what we have to so we can get what we want," Kora explained.

"You are really deceitful," Candace said.

"And you're a home wrecker," Kora blurted out.

"I'm sorry. I never meant to hurt you. Jarvis and I had a sexual relationship before he even met you."

"Correction, Jarvis and I had a relationship before he hired you. You were the side chick. He married me, remember?" Kora said.

"I had no idea," Candace uttered, listening to more than she wanted to hear.

"Game recognizes game. I know the type of woman you are because we are very similar. I can't get mad at you for trying to come up in the world," Kora said as Antonio listened.

"Damn, I thought I could read people." Still in complete shock, Candace sat down on the bed.

"Since you popped your nosey butt in the bedroom," Antonio started saying before Candace interrupted him.

"Nosey! I was just coming to say hello to Kora. I didn't know I would walk in on this," Candace said, pointing at Antonio and then at Kora.

"Look, Candace, I need you to keep your mouth shut about this," Antonio said.

"No problem."

"Thank you," Kora said.

"I know this might sound weird, but I really look at you as a friend, even under these bizarre circumstances," Candace told her.

"You took care of me, and I will never forget that," Kora said.

"I need to get out of here. Jarvis is waiting on me to bring these documents to him. If I don't leave now, I will be late, and you know how big Jarvis is on punctuality."

"Keep your mouth shut," Antonio said, warning her again.

He wasn't sure if he could trust that Candace wouldn't tell, but he would have to trust her for now.

"I hope you're not going to sleep with my husband tonight," Kora said sarcastically before Candace left.

"Kora, don't say that. I feel horrible about this already. I'm so sorry and embarrassed," Candace said, then closed the door and ran down the stairs and out the house.

CHAPTER 21

A few days passed, and Lisa was still working diligently on the final details for the grand opening of the restaurant. She knew she had taken on too much with trying to plan the party and finish decorating, but she was committed.

She had a couple other projects she was working on and wasn't giving them one hundred percent of her time. She needed to complete these projects with Jarvis and get back to her normal life and business.

Lisa was on her way to meet Antonio. Overly excited about opening his first restaurant, Antonio scheduled countless meetings. He wanted to make sure everything was covered and that meant meeting every time he had an idea or when he wanted to confirm that everything was going as planned.

Candace was joining them to assist Lisa with the planning. Jarvis had backed off again, so Lisa was dealing directly with Antonio, which was fine with her. Lisa and Candace were looking forward to meeting with Stacy after the meeting so they could have their girls' night out dinner.

Once inside the restaurant, Lisa found herself pleased by her own designs. The restaurant looked impeccable. She couldn't help but admire the beautiful hardwood floors, the expensive artwork on the walls, the elegant table settings, and the striking light fixtures that hung from the ceiling strategically over each table. She knocked on Antonio's office, and he quickly invited her inside.

"Look at you Antonio, with your own private office. Congratulations!"

Lisa said with enthusiasm.

"I love my office. You gave me everything I wanted." Antonio's wide smile displayed his satisfaction as he leaned back in his large, high back leather chair and looked around. "We only have a few things to finalize, so this should be a short meeting. I can't believe we will be opening up in two weeks. I didn't think I would be this nervous," he said while typing on his laptop.

"It's scary starting your own business, but it's so rewarding. Those are good nerves you're feeling. The restaurant is going to be a huge success."

"I feel really good about it. Plus, having Jarvis as a partner, it will be prosperous."

"He's a smart businessman."

They continued talking, and Lisa was happy their last conversation hadn't affected their business relationship. They had a great working connection, and she couldn't be happier that it wasn't damaged.

Ten minutes past their meeting time, Candace opened the office door without knocking.

"Do you ever knock? Damn!" Antonio said aggravated.

"I'm so sorry I'm late," Candace said as she rushed in and sat down.

"Time is money. Where were you?" Antonio asked.

He didn't like people being late, and he wasn't going to allow her to get off easy without giving an explanation.

"I had to stop by the bank. You know Lake Shore Drive is bumper-to-bumper traffic at this time of the day," Candace said while pulling her notepad out of her purse. She knew Antonio wasn't going to let it go, but she hoped her answer would be sufficient.

"Were you making a personal deposit or a deposit for Jarvis?" Antonio asked, still inquiring about her tardiness.

"I was making a personal deposit. So what did I miss?" Candace quickly asked, trying not to sound bothered by his questioning.

"You didn't miss anything because we were waiting on you to start the meeting. If you were making a deposit for Jarvis, then I could understand why you were late because that would come first. You could have taken care of your personal business after the meeting," Antonio said, sounding peeved.

"I'm sorry, Antonio. I just needed to make my deposit today because I didn't know how long the meeting was going to be, and I didn't want the bank to close," she explained.

"If you're going to work with me, you need to be on time. I don't accept tardiness for bullshit excuses. I run the same tight ship as Jarvis, and I will not accept anything less," Antonio said looking at Candace like he really didn't care for her.

"I apologize. It won't happen again," Candace responded, swallowing her pride.

Embarrassed that he was chewing her out in front of Lisa, she wanted their conversation to end quickly. She knew not to get smart with him because he would tell Jarvis, and he would do something to make her pay. Not commenting, Lisa continued listening to them.

She had never heard Antonio talk in such a superior tone, and it was strange to hear. She also didn't know he could be so mean with such a cruel attitude.

Knowing that she had a little dirt on him, Candace was surprised that Antonio was talking to her so rudely. She knew he hadn't forgotten that she knew all about him and Kora's love affair. She couldn't believe he was pushing the envelope and trying to aggravate her in front of Lisa.

Maybe he's trying to impress Lisa, she thought to herself, but she didn't know why he would be that comfortable with testing her. She wanted to chew him out, but stayed in her lane.

Antonio eventually let it go and they started their meeting, with Candace being extremely quiet while taking notes the entire time. Lisa kept looking at her because this was not the strong, outspoken person that she knew.

She saw a submissive, insecure, desperate woman, and she didn't know how to take Candace. She couldn't wait until the meeting was over and they were at dinner so she could drill her on her new manner.

Ever since Lisa spoke to Candace about knowing that Jarvis was married, she had been acting very strangely. She didn't come around as much as she used to and seemed to be extremely busy all the time. Candace begged Lisa not to tell anyone that Jarvis was married because that would affect her job, and Lisa agreed.

Candace had been acting bizarre, and since she agreed to go to dinner after the meeting, Lisa had a list of questions ready in hopes of getting some answers. She would demand to know what was going on with her friend because she was concerned.

Antonio asked Candace to go and get them something to drink from the bar. When she got up to leave, her purse fell dumping everything on the floor. To Lisa's surprise, Antonio turned into the perfect gentleman and jumped up to help her pick up the items that had fallen out of her purse.

He immediately picked up a piece of paper that had flown over by his feet. He glanced at the paper and noticed it was a bank deposit receipt. Not trying to be discreet, he read the receipt, frowned, and wrinkled his forehead.

Lisa looked at Candace, who was so busy trying to pick up her tampons that she didn't notice the look on Antonio's face. Lisa looked at him and frowned back, wondering what he was looking at that had changed his whole attitude. Antonio never picked up anything else. Instead, he waited for Candace to finish. Once Candace gathered all of her belongings off the floor, Antonio handed her the piece of paper.

"You dropped this."

"Thanks," Candace said as she took the piece of paper out of his hand without looking at it.

"Since when do you make a personal deposit for fifty thousand dollar," Antonio asked, raising both of his eyebrows.

"What?" Candace asked, taken aback by his question.

"You told me that you made a personal deposit today, and the bank receipt I just handed you said you made a deposit today for fifty thousand dollars. Where did you get that type of money from?" Antonio asked.

"That's none of your business," Candace shot back.

Lisa smiled inside because this was the aggressive woman that she knew.

"I know how much you get paid, and you don't have that type of money to be making such a large deposit."

"My personal finances shouldn't be any of your concern," Candace replied, slightly raising her voice.

"I think I have a right to inquire about this deposit, especially if someone is stealing from Jarvis' business," Antonio voiced, now standing up and sounding angry.

Lisa continuously looked back and forth at Antonio and Candace while they started to have an intense argument. Lisa was astounded at what was going on and also wanted to know about the large deposit Candace had made.

By Candace becoming very defensive, Lisa knew something was wrong. She wanted to ask what was going on, but knew she needed to stay out of it, so she continued to be an innocent bystander.

Antonio's cell phone kept ringing, which forced him to be distracted from his argument with Candace.

"What's up, Jarvis?" Antonio answered, making sure he let Candace know who was on the other end of his phone.

He looked at Candace like he was going to tell Jarvis everything that was going on, but Candace had her game face on and didn't seem alarmed.

"I'll be right back," Antonio told them as he stood to leave out of the office, obviously needing some privacy. "Don't you leave this room!" he said, pointing at Candace. He then walked out and slammed the door behind him.

As soon as the door closed, Lisa didn't waste any time getting to the bottom of things. She let the questions flow from her lips rapidly.

"What the hell is going on? Where did that money come from?"

"It's my money," Candace said.

"Now we both know you don't have that type of money lying around. Where did you get that money from?" Lisa whispered.

"It was a gift from someone, so that makes it my money, and I deposited it into my account," Candace said in a snippy tone.

"Did Jarvis give you the money?"

"Why would Jarvis give me the money?"

"I'm not going to pretend that I don't know you're having sex with Jarvis," Lisa said as Candace's mouth fell open and almost hit the floor. She didn't plan on discussing this at that particular time, but for some reason, it just came out. "What I do care about is where you got that money from, because Antonio is really upset."

"I'm sorry, Lisa. I didn't mean to hurt you. It just happened. I know you really like Jarvis," Candace said, revealing the truth. Her dirt was revealed, and she was tired of hiding.

"I don't give a damn who you are opening your legs to," Lisa said. Even though she was crushed, she wouldn't let Candace know it. "What's important now is where you got that money from. I've built my company and earned my money the legal way, and I'm not going to be a part of some shady shit. You're going to be on your own if you don't tell me something."

"You don't have anything to do with this."

"Candace!" Lisa shouted, demanding to know the truth.

"Okay, okay. I stole the money from Jarvis," Candace whispered.

"What?"

"He doesn't even miss the money."

"Just because he's rich doesn't mean he doesn't know when his money is disappearing. How long have you been stealing from him?"

"Enough to retire at an early age."

"Oh my goodness, you have lost your mind. I can't believe what I'm hearing."

"You don't know what Jarvis has put me through. If you only knew, you wouldn't care if I were stealing his money. I have to take care of myself, and if that means increasing my bank account with someone else's money, then that's what I'm going to do. Jarvis is an asshole, and I hate his guts. I'm just dealing with his abuse until I have enough money to open my own business and live securely. I'm almost at my goal."

Lisa was speechless. She looked at Candace trying to understand her actions. Candace continued telling her side of the story and explaining why she had become a thief.

"If you knew what I've been through, you would think differently," Candace told her.

"You know how men are when you mess with their money. There's no telling what they are going to do to you," Lisa said fearfully.

"I don't care anymore," Candace replied, fed up.

"We need to think of something fast to get you out of this."

"It's nice to know that you're down with me," Candace said, making light of everything.

"I'm not down with you. I'm trying to help you from getting killed. I'm not going to jail for you, but I'll help you try to get out of this situation." Lisa didn't know why she was helping her, but for the first time, she felt sorry for Candace.

Before they could discuss anything, Antonio came back into the office. "Candace, we need to talk. Can you excuse us, Lisa?" Antonio said sternly, getting right back to where he left off.

"She can stay," Candace said, while Lisa looked at her.

Lisa really didn't want to be a part of her scheme.

"Is Lisa your partner in crime?" Antonio asked, looking at Lisa with an uncanny look on his face.

"I don't have anything to do with this. This is my first time hearing about this," Lisa stated convincingly.

Antonio sat down, inhaled and exhaled slowly, then leaned back in his chair. "What were you thinking, stealing from the hand that feeds you?" Antonio asked Candace.

Candace didn't respond, but she never took her eyes off of him.

"If you have nothing to do with this, I really think you should leave. If you stay, then you are involved, too," Antonio told Lisa.

"Okay, that's my cue to leave," Lisa said slowly as she looked at Candace to try to read her face. Candace's poker face was on, and she never looked at Lisa. "Is everything going to be okay?" Lisa asked, concerned.

"Things are going to be fine. You just go home and finish finalizing the details for the opening," Antonio instructed her.

Lisa stood up and looked at the both of them. She was afraid to leave Candace alone in the room with him, but she didn't know what to do to help her at that moment.

"Are you leaving?" Antonio asked impatiently.

"Yes. Sorry, I'm just a bit alarmed by all of this. I'm actually worried about my friend's well-being," Lisa said while standing still.

"This is none of your business. Leave now so I can take care of this," Antonio said.

"What's going to happen?" Lisa continued to inquire.

"Either you leave now or stay and become her partner in crime. I know you want to help your friend, but if you have nothing to do with this, you need to leave. Get out of my office, Lisa!" Antonio shouted.

Lisa looked helpless and didn't know what to do.

"It's okay. I'll be fine," Candace said, finally breaking her silence.

Lisa left the office feeling apprehensive.

"Candace, I thought you were loyal, but you're nothing but a stealing bitch!" Antonio said as soon as Lisa closed the door behind her.

Candace was mute.

"Are you going to explain yourself?" he asked.

"It was a gift from someone I'm dating," Candace lied, knowing once it got back to Jarvis that she was dating someone else, he would be mad. At this point, she didn't care.

"So you're going to hang on to that lie?"

"It's not a lie!" Candace said.

They had a staring contest for a moment as Antonio tried to figure her out.

"You can go."

"That's it? That's what you had me stick around for?" Candace asked.

"You didn't steal the money, right?"

"No, I didn't steal anything."

"Then leave. If you didn't steal the money, then we don't have a problem," Antonio said, knowing she was lying through her teeth. He had every intention of investigating and watching her like a hawk.

"I'm glad you believe me," Candace said.

"I didn't say I believe you," Antonio replied while still casually leaning back in his chair.

He stared at her while taking in her entire body with his eyes. Candace knew he would be a problem for her. She also knew he was Jarvis' right-hand man. Without a plan, she didn't know how to handle the situation she was in, so she decided to do what she did best. Go with the flow.

"I'll just leave," Candace said as she headed for the door.

Antonio had no intentions of letting her leave. She was the thief in the company, and he had to do something about it.

"You didn't think I was just going to let you leave my office, did you?" Antonio asked, quickly rushing up behind her.

"Damn," Candace mumbled to herself, as she stopped and dropped her head.

If she was able to leave, she was going to keep moving and never look back. Today would have been her last day of work. Unfortunately, Antonio wasn't going to let her leave that easily.

He put both of his hands on her shoulders and whispered in her ear, "I know you're the one stealing Jarvis' money. I've been watching you for some time now. You know how he feels about people stealing from him, so what are you going to do for me to forgive and forget about this situation?" Antonio pressed his body against hers.

Candace twisted her lips and closed her eyes. She knew exactly what he wanted, and by the hard bulge in his pants that was pressing against her butt, she knew she wasn't going to leave without giving him what he wanted.

Antonio had always been a man of little words, and although she knew he was a mini version of Jarvis, she would have never predicted this side of him.

"What do you want?" Candace asked.

"You know what I want, but first, I want to know why you've been stealing."

"I'm not stealing," Candace said as he pulled her closer to him and fondled her breasts. She smacked his hands away, but he went right back to touching her more aggressively.

"Jarvis would kill you if he knew what you were doing."

"What am I doing? I'm just rubbing on your breasts. What does Jarvis have to do with what's going on with us?" Antonio asked.

Candace knew Jarvis would be angry if he knew Antonio was trying to have sex with her. She didn't understand why he was crossing the line; she didn't understand his motive.

"Don't act like you don't know about my relationship with Jarvis."

"Don't act like you don't know what Jarvis does to people who steal. So, I wish you would stop acting like you're not a thief. The truth is out, and right now, you're going to give me what I want or I'm calling Jarvis," Antonio threatened.

Candace gritted her teeth as he pushed her up against the wall. She wasn't going to confess to stealing, but knew she had to do something. She had never seen this side of Antonio after working with him for a couple of years, and truthfully, she was a little frightened.

If she slept with him that would be admitting her guilt, and if she tried to leave, he would definitely tell Jarvis. She was torn.

"I thought you were in love with Kora. Now you're trying to have sex with me."

"I do love her, but this situation has nothing to do with love."

"What is this about?"

"It's about getting what I want."

"Why now?"

"This is the perfect time."

She wasn't finished with her plan and getting caught was not on the list. She needed the protection from her ex-boyfriend that Jarvis provided, and she needed more money to put her where she wanted to be financially. She had come this far, so she wasn't backing down now.

Jarvis had taught her how to have a hardened heart and a cold soul. She only cared about one thing and that was making money. Occasionally, she dreamed of being married with children.

"Take your shirt off," Antonio ordered while kissing her.

She looked into Antonio's eyes, and it was almost like seeing him for the first time. She couldn't resist the fact that he was gorgeous, but his eyes told a story of pain.

"I said take it off, now!"

When she didn't do what she was told, he grabbed the back of her neck hard.

A large lump grew in her throat, and tears formed in her eyes from the pain in her neck. She became angry that she was not in control of the situation. There was no way he was going to take 'no' for an answer.

She wanted to fight back, but she had sense enough to know she wouldn't win. So, instead of fighting back, she decided not to feel the torture and just give in.

"You're not going to do what I tell you to?" Antonio asked as his cell phone started ringing. He reached in his pocket and grabbed it, never letting go of her neck. "What's up, man?" He answered then showed the telephone to Candace to let her see Jarvis' name and number across the screen.

Candace heard Jarvis' voice, which verified he was talking to him. Antonio continued rubbing on her breast with one hand while putting his other hand underneath her skirt. When she pushed his hands away, they got into a little struggle.

She tried to leave, but he snatched her back, locked the office door, and pulled her to his desk. He sat down in his chair and held her hand tightly as she stood between his legs. He continued talking to Jarvis while he squeezed her hand, causing her to moan.

"I want to talk to you about the person that's stealing from you. We will definitely make them pay," Antonio said as he looked at Candace and unbuckled his pants.

This time, Candace didn't try to leave; she stayed put. She started helping him unzip his pants. She didn't want him to think he had scared her, even though she was terrified.

He forcefully pulled her close as she straddled him on the chair. He continued talking to Jarvis, holding the phone between his shoulder and head, while he moved her panties to the side and inserted himself inside her.

He eased in slowly and then pumped hard, which made her let out a loud shriek. She never thought he would be so large, and she definitely wasn't prepared for him to be inside her so fast.

It was obvious Jarvis heard her moaning, because he asked, "What's that noise?"

"One of my female friends stopped by for a little fun. You know what I'm saying," he replied, laughing as he cupped her butt with his hand and banged her harder.

Enjoying the feeling, Candace started to ride him wildly. If she was going to have sex with him, she was determined to enjoy it. She started breathing heavily as she leaned in and kissed him. It got so good to him that he almost dropped the phone.

"I'll call you when I'm on my way," Antonio told Jarvis before ending the call.

He slapped Candace's butt hard enough to send a rippling sound through the room.

"Stop," Candace said, panting for air.

"Chill out."

"I thought you were in love with Kora," Candace said again, while continuing to move her hips slowly as he squeezed his eyes tight from the pleasure.

"This is not the time to be worrying about Kora," Antonio said.

"I see you're a cheating dog just like Jarvis."

"Don't try to act like you're a good girl. I know you think you're tough, but I know your type," Antonio said.

His grip got tighter, and Candace tried to relax and enjoy the ride. She rode him like her life depended on it, and unable to control himself, he wailed out. She knew how to work her magic on a man, and she was giving it to him well. By the sound of his moaning and groaning, she knew he was enjoying it.

Neither of them ever thought they would be having sex with each other, but the way they were going at it, their true feelings were showing. There was definitely an attraction between the two of them, and it was beyond blackmail sex.

She was a woman on a mission, and that mission was to save her job for now and get what she wanted. She knew Antonio and Jarvis didn't care about her, just like she didn't care about them. But, right now, she needed Antonio on her team to buy her some time.

Antonio slowed down and looked at Candace, then sucked on her bottom lip. He kissed her wildly and rotated his hips, while she duplicated his every move even better.

"All is forgotten," Antonio said.

"Is that right?" Candace asked.

"I think I might be addicted to you," Antonio said as he showed her how much by moving faster.

Candace knew what that meant, but she didn't want to start a sexual relationship with him, especially if she wasn't getting any funds out of it.

When she was about to explode, he lifted her up off the chair and put her on the edge of the desk to get full access. By now, Candace was so turned on that she forgot who she was having sex with and pretended he wasn't blackmailing her.

She was determined to get something out of this ordeal and that was an orgasm, which she received hard and strong. Afterwards, they collapsed on each other and tried to catch their breath.

"So I guess we're even," Candace said.

"You stole thousands of dollars from Jarvis and you think since we just fucked we're even?" Antonio asked as he caught his breath.

Candace quickly got up. "You're an asshole!"

"Let's make sure we have an understanding that you're not going to steal another dime. Don't get yourself killed making the wrong mistake."

"Jarvis is not a hoodlum. He isn't going to kill anyone," Candace said, snickering.

"He won't, but I will." Antonio's comment sent chills down her spine.

"I didn't steal from Jarvis. He's my boss, and I respect him."

"I see you're sticking to your story. Now that's how you play the game. Watch yourself, because I definitely will be watching you. I won't tell Jarvis about your sticky fingers or how good it felt to be inside you, but you better not steal anything else," Antonio warned her.

Candace refused to admit anything. She knew Antonio meant what he said, and because they both were stubborn, this was going to be challenging.

Candace leaned closer to him and calmly said, "Don't think I'm afraid of you," even though, at that moment, she was scared.

"You should be."

"You just remember I know you're sleeping with Jarvis' wife. Don't forget that little secret while you're trying to threaten me."

"You're trying to blackmail me? You think you got something over my head?" Antonio started laughing. "Go ahead and see who Jarvis will believe. His friend and partner who he trusts or a sneaky, lying, stealing bitch," Antonio said.

"Whatever!" Candace said, knowing she was defeated.

"We were trained from the same person, so I know how you think. Hell, I even know what you're thinking right now. I know you will never admit to stealing, but you know I know the truth. If you want to live, let me know you understand and agree with what I'm saying. I will forget what happened, and I won't mention this little episode to Jarvis, but you need to do whatever I tell you to. Now, if we have an agreement, kiss me," Antonio said, then waited.

Candace resisted, but she knew she had to make a move. So, she leaned over and kissed him softly on the lips, sealing the deal.

As soon as she pulled away from him, he quickly grabbed her neck and choked her hard.

"Don't fuck with me, Candace. I'm not Jarvis. You don't know me."

"Okay," Candace softly said, struggling to talk. She was wondering where the old Antonio disappeared to, because this wasn't the same kind man who was hired with her.

"Good. I'll call you when I need you," Antonio said, pushing her away.

"What are you going to need me for?" Candace asked, still trying to sound tough as she rubbed her neck.

She was a strong woman and able to handle herself, but Antonio rubbed her the wrong way. Something about him told her that he was serious and would kill her if she didn't play by his rules.

"For work," Antonio said, ignoring her as he played on his laptop.

Candace adjusted her clothing and walked out of the office not knowing what to expect next. She knew she needed to find out who Antonio was; she needed to research him.

Candace missed dinner with Stacy and Lisa that night and went home shaken. She would have to walk around on eggshells until she figured out what to do next. She knew Antonio's blackmailing would eventually run out, and hopefully by then, she would be long gone with enough money in her bank account to last her a lifetime.

CHAPTER 22

A week passed, an as usual, Candace was at the office working. She kept her word by not mentioning Kora and Antonio's affair to Jarvis. She wasn't worried about their situation because she had her own issues to deal with. Jarvis never mentioned anything and acted like everything was normal.

She was so nervous that she kept dropping things and looking over her shoulders. She didn't know if Antonio had kept his word or if he had told Jarvis everything. She could only imagine what Jarvis would do to her if he found out she was stealing from him and that she had slept with Antonio. She tried to keep her distance from both of them.

"Candace, can I see you in my office?" Jarvis' voice came through the intercom on the phone that was sitting on her desk.

"Sure, I'll be right there." After grabbing a pen and notepad, she headed to his office.

With only a week left until the grand opening of the restaurant and the planning of parties at the club, Jarvis was working her overtime.

"Close the door behind you," Jarvis said. "I want you to take Kora shopping to get an outfit for the grand opening," he told her, then slid his black credit card across the desk to her.

"No problem." Candace smiled, but inside, she was dying.

"How many people are confirmed from the guest list?"

"All two hundred and fifty people are confirmed."

"Great. I think everything is taken care of," Jarvis said, reading over some paperwork.

"I've got everything under control."

Jarvis finished reading his paperwork, pushed his chair back, leaned backwards to rest his head on the chair, and folded his hands on his lap.

"What's this I hear about you flirting with my employee?"

"What?" Candace asked as a huge lump grew in her throat.

"Antonio told me you were flirting with him."

That son of a bitch, she thought to herself. "I wasn't flirting with Antonio. He's mistaken," Candace said, enraged.

"I don't know what happened, but I know you have more sense than to try to date my boy."

"I would never disrespect you. I'm not sure why he thought I was flirting with him, but I can assure you that I wasn't."

Jarvis chuckled. "A little flirting never hurt anyone."

"I wasn't flirting with him," Candace said, sounding like she was pleading her case.

She didn't know what type of game Antonio was playing and couldn't wait to find out. She figured Antonio needed something on her to discredit her. That way, Jarvis really wouldn't believe her and think she was just trying to get back at Antonio if she ever told his secret.

"My boy wouldn't lie to me, but don't worry about it. Just don't let it happen again."

"I'm sorry he thought I was trying to get with him."

"I've let you get away with a lot of things. I didn't even say anything to you about Kora coming home early from her trip and you not calling to inform me."

"I didn't know."

"Don't give me any excuses. I don't know what you were on, but that wasn't cool. I've let that go, but I won't let you disrespect me."

"Jarvis," Candace said before he interjected.

"I'm done with this conversation."

"Are you going to fire me?"

"I'm not going to fire you. Now go take Kora to buy something sexy and expensive," Jarvis said, knowing that would piss her off.

"No problem," Candace responded sadly as she walked out of his office.

Degraded and livid, she knew one day she wouldn't have to deal with him any longer.

Forty-five minutes later, Candace pulled up in front of Jarvis' house to pick up Kora for her mini shopping spree courtesy of Jarvis. She didn't want to go inside the house, but she knew she had to. As always, she hid her pride, took a deep breath, and walked inside. She knew Kora wouldn't answer the door, so she used her spare key.

She walked up the stairs and knocked on the bedroom door. She didn't want to walk into her bedroom unannounced, especially since the last time she found Antonio there. She didn't want to know any more of her secrets.

There was no answer, so she knocked again. This was odd, because usually Kora was in the bedroom. She knew not to leave the room unless instructed by Jarvis.

It was unusual for Kora to obey him the way she did. Candace had never seen anything like it before. Kora didn't move unless Jarvis told her to, and she submitted to him one hundred percent. However, lately, it seemed like she was a different person and moving to her own beat.

Candace thought maybe she was in the shower, so she waited by the door. Ten minutes later, she knocked on the door again, but still no answer. She prayed that Kora wasn't in the room with Antonio again. She really couldn't face her, knowing she was sleeping with Jarvis and now Antonio. She was starting not to even recognize herself.

Candace walked around the house looking for Kora. She was excited that Kora had taken a stand and stopped being confined in her bedroom. Candace headed to the kitchen looking for Kora, and before she made it there, she saw her walking out of the family room.

"Kora," Candace called out to her.

"What are you doing here?" Kora asked.

"Jarvis sent me here to take you shopping."

"Great! Let me get dressed and we can go," Kora said, knowing she needed to change from the jogging suit she was wearing. Jarvis wanted her to look nice whenever she left the house, and that included wearing high heel shoes.

"What were you doing out of the bedroom?" Candace asked, almost sounding like Jarvis.

"I came down here to get something to drink and noticed the television was on in the family room, so I turned it off," Kora said as she walked to the bedroom, while Candace followed behind her.

"Now you know if Jarvis was here, he would be pissed at you being out of the bedroom. You better be careful."

"You're not going to say anything, are you?" Kora asked.

"You know I'm not going to say anything. I don't care if you leave the room. I actually think it's crazy that he makes you stay in the bedroom until he gets home. I also think it's even more ludicrous that you allow him to control you."

"I get so tired of staying in the room and in this house. I'm so miserable," Kora expressed as she started to cry.

"Don't cry, Kora. Things will get better," Candace said, even though she knew it wouldn't as long as she was still married to Jarvis. "Why don't you just leave and be with Antonio?" She asked, lowering her voice.

"I can't. It's not that easy," Kora said.

"You deserve to be happy."

"I'm going crazy! That's why I'm so happy when he sends you to take me shopping, because it gets me out of the house. I feel like I'm in jail."

"Let's do something you want to do today," Candace said, ready to break all the rules and also feeling extremely guilty about sleeping with Antonio.

"You're crazy. You know if Jarvis finds out, he will kill both of us."

Candace smiled. "If he finds out, then blame it all on me. I don't care anymore, and technically, you don't either."

"Sounds like you're just as frustrated with these arrangements as I am," Kora said.

"I've got my own problems with your husband."

Concerned, Kora asked, "Do you want to talk about it?"

"I'm good. Let's get you dressed so we can get out of the house and have some fun," Candace said.

"You know I'm here if you need to talk."

"You're so sweet, Kora. You shouldn't live this way. I'm sorry."

"What are you sorry for?"

"I'm just sorry for the life that you have," Candace responded.

Candace was wrong for being Kora's friend, and she knew Kora would never forgive her if she knew all the dirt she had done. Although she liked Kora, she couldn't be concerned about her feelings because she had a life to build. They jumped in Candace's car and drove off, ready to go shopping and enjoy Kora's free pass out for the day.

Five long hours later, Candace was just making it home from a long day of shopping with Kora. She finally found something for Kora to wear to the grand opening of the restaurant that would get Jarvis' approval. Kora even suggested that Candace purchase something for herself, but she declined because she wanted the day to be all about Kora. She was starting to feel drained by the lifestyle she had chosen.

She kicked her shoes off and plopped down on the couch to relax. Before she could reach for the remote for the television, there was a knock at her door.

"Who could that be?" Candace said as she reluctantly got off the couch.

Exhausted, she opened the door without looking out the peephole.

"What's up, Candace?" Antonio said as he pushed his way in.

"What are you doing at my house?"

"We need to talk."

"I don't talk to liars."

"Now I'm a liar?"

"Let's talk about why you told Jarvis I was flirting with you!" Candace said with much attitude.

"I could have told him we had sex."

"I also could have told him you're having sex with his wife, but I didn't!"

"Shut up!"

"Get out of my house!"

"Sit down!"

"Don't tell me what to do in my house!"

"Sit the fuck down!" Antonio said, pointing a gun to her head.

"What are you doing?" Candace nervously asked as she sat down slowly while trying to keep her teeth from chattering.

"You're a thief, and that's one thing Jarvis won't tolerate." Antonio put the gun back in his pocket, but never took his hands off of it. He sat down on the couch next to her.

"I told you I didn't steal anything," Candace pleaded, persistently hanging on to her lie.

"We both know the truth, so please stop lying. You're really pissing me off with that shit." Antonio's corporate business persona was nothing but a cover-up for his true thug mentality.

She wasn't going to go out that easy. She had plans for her future to live well and be happy. She almost had her finances set to purchase a home in Paris, open up a high-end clothing boutique, and live comfortably. She wanted to move far away from Jarvis and her ex-boyfriend, who was out of jail and possibly looking for her. She wasn't going out without a fight.

She tried to remain calm as she nervously scanned the room for a weapon. It's like Antonio knew what she was thinking, and he followed her eyes. When she locked her sights on the letter opener that was underneath a small pile of mail on the table in front of them, Antonio grabbed it before she did.

"Don't try anything stupid," he said. Then he bent the letter opener and threw it to the other side of the room where it landed behind the curtains.

"Why are you here?" Candace asked trying to control the nervous twitch she had just developed.

"Jarvis sent me here to kill you."

"Kill me!" Candace yelled.

"Chill out. He sent me here to fire you and make sure you leave town."

"Fire me! Leave town! Why?" Candace asked, overreacting.

"You were flirting with me, and he feels you disrespected him."

"Stop it! I wasn't! What type of game are you playing?" Candace yelled.

"Would you rather be fired because you flirted with his friend or because you stole money from him? Being a thief will make it very hard in this industry to get another job."

"Jarvis said it wasn't a problem. He told me that he wouldn't fire me."

"I guess he lied. It's a lot of that going on around our camp."

"Why did you have to say anything? I thought we had a deal?"

"My loyalty is with Jarvis. I think I did you a favor."

"You don't know what you've done. I'm not going to be protected."

"Protected? What are you talking about?"

Candace told Antonio the story about her ex-boyfriend and the promise Jarvis made to protect her as long as she was still working for him. Now that her ex-boyfriend was out of jail, she was not going to be protected, and now she was paranoid. She broke down crying uncontrollably.

Her life was crumbling right before her eyes. She felt like she was having a bad nightmare, but this was reality. She started pacing back and forth, panicking and remembering the type of person her ex-boyfriend was, knowing he would definitely come after her.

"Calm down."

"I can't."

"I'll help you, if you help me."

"Help you with what?" Candace asked eager to hear what he had to say.

"Sit down. Let's talk."

He knew Candace didn't have to worry about her ex-boyfriend, because he was still in jail serving his time and was not getting out anytime soon. Jarvis told Candace that to keep her paranoid and keep her dedicated to him.

Antonio knew fear always made people do what they were told. He was going to allow her to continue thinking that Mark was out of jail and keep that fear in her to get what he wanted.

"You're not going to coerce me into some stupid stuff," Candace said, now feeling relieved that he wasn't there to harm her.

"You're going to do whatever I tell you to do," Antonio blurted out.

"No, I'm not."

"I can always call the police and have you arrested for stealing," Antonio said seriously. "How much do you have in the bank now, a little over five hundred thousand dollars?"

"You don't know what you're talking about," Candace said. However, he was exactly correct on the amount she had in the bank. He's really been watching me, she thought to herself.

"I know all about your sticky fingers," Antonio said.

"I'm sure Jarvis would love to know you're sleeping with his wife in his home. Maybe he will be more interested in knowing who you really are," Candace said, now feeling confident that she had some dirt on him.

"What are you talking about?" Antonio asked, remaining unruffled.

"What's up, Moe?"

"Who is Moe?" Antonio asked, knowing that was his nickname.

"Maybe I should say Jennifer Moeky," Candace said. She had definitely struck a nerve. "That was your sister who committed suicide because Jarvis broke her heart. Jarvis doesn't know that, does he?"

After Stacy revealed to Candace that Antonio had mentioned he had a sister that committed suicide, it gave Candace the fuel to look into his background further. She wasn't sure why Stacy told her, but after a few glasses of wine, and Candace probing about Antonio's past, Stacy gave her enough information to start looking into his past.

After doing some research, Candace remembered the name Jennifer Moeky from a lady named Karen Law who called Jarvis' office a while back. She contacted Karen, who told her all about Jennifer Moeky and her brother, Antonio. Being in the Army for eight years, Antonio was never around. That's why it was easy for him to slip under the radar.

Jennifer and Antonio had the same mother but different fathers. Antonio was the oldest. When his mother remarried, she gave birth to Jennifer, and Antonio was adopted by her husband. Antonio had a good relationship with his biological father and wanted to keep him a part of his life, so he kept his last name Flink.

Honoring his adopted father, he took his last name as his middle name, creating Antonio Moeky Flink. Most people thought the name Moeky was his middle name, so he went with that scenario. His family and friends called him Moe for short, and that nickname stuck with him throughout his life.

Jennifer wrote letters to Antonio all the time while he was enlisted in the Army. He loved his sister, and after she told him all about Jarvis, he wanted her to leave him alone because he knew Jarvis was no good for her. But, his sister was in love and didn't want to break it off.

Antonio was so devastated over his sister's death that he didn't even attend the funeral. Instead, he put all his thoughts into getting revenge on Jarvis. He was going to make Jarvis pay for her death, even if he had to wait.

With the training from the Army, he learned how to be patient, and he could wait for years to attack his enemy. Jarvis made it much easier for

Antonio to continue to conceal his identity, when he moved him to Chicago to help run his nightclub. He was able to live comfortably and make Jarvis trust him.

"I'm sure Jarvis would want to know why the brother of a woman who killed herself over him is working for him. Is Jennifer Moeky your sister?"

Not one to back down from the truth, he answered without hesitation. "Yes, that was my sister. And?"

"And you know Jarvis wouldn't have hired you if he was aware of that. Why didn't you tell him? Better yet, why are you really here?"

"I'm going to get revenge for my sister, and you're going to help me," Antonio said, putting everything on the table.

Dumbfounded, Candace was surprised by his honesty. It seemed like everyone had their own motives and she never saw this one coming. This was not what she signed up for, especially since it had nothing to do with her. This was his personal vendetta, and she didn't want any parts of it.

Even though Jarvis had fired her and she was now jobless, she wasn't sure what Antonio had in mind and if she would benefit from it. She had a love-hate relationship with Jarvis, and right now, she definitely wasn't in love with him any longer.

With nothing else to lose, Candace asked curiously, "What do you want me to do?"

CHAPTER 23

Two days later, Lisa had been calling Candace all day, but she never answered. She hadn't spoken to her since the incident with Antonio. She knew Candace was avoiding her, but she was determined to get to the bottom of things and find out why she was stealing from Jarvis.

There was no way she would just let this go. After Lisa contacted Stacy and informed her about everything that was going on, they jumped in the car and went to Candace's home to see how she was holding up.

"I can't believe Candace stole from Jarvis. I'm not mad at her. He has enough money to share," Stacy said, laughing as they knocked on her door.

"It's not cool when you get caught. No one looks good in that situation," Lisa responded as she knocked on the door again.

"She needs to take that money and run. The gig is up. The cat is out of the bag. The fat lady has sung," Stacy said, cracking up laughing while she amused herself.

"I'm glad you think this is funny. She could get herself in some serious trouble."

"I guess she deserves it. She's hasn't been truthful, and now we're seeing who she really is. Let's not forget she slept with your baby daddy, Jarvis, and didn't tell you that he had a wife. She's a hot mess."

Lisa ignored Stacy and continued knocking on the door. She reached in her pocket and got the spare key that Candace had given to her in case of an emergency. This was definitely an emergency. She put the key in the lock, turned it, and opened the door. Not knowing what to expect, they walked into her house slowly while looking around.

Engulfing their nostrils was Candace's favorite scent of lavender, which lingered in every room. As always, her luxury condo was immaculate. Nothing was out of place or seemed abnormal. They were finally feeling peaceful, thinking she was just out for the night, until they walked into her bedroom.

The bedroom looked like a windstorm had passed through it. Her drawers were pulled out, clothes were everywhere, and no longer hanging in her closet were any of her expensive designer clothing. Her bed was untouched and looked picture-perfect with the five-hundred-dollar duvet that Lisa couldn't understand why she had to spend so much money on. But, because it had a designer label attached to it, she had to have it.

"What happened in here?" Lisa and Stacy said in unison as their eyes frantically searched the room.

"Either she's been robbed or she has left in a hurry," Stacy said, stepping over the clutter on the floor.

"I should call the police," Lisa said.

"Don't start freaking out. Let's see what's going on first. Call her," Stacy told Lisa.

"I'm dialing her number now." Lisa punched in the numbers quickly on her cell phone. When Candace's voicemail picked up, she left a message.

"Ooh, I love these jeans," Stacy said, picking up the pants.

"Stacy, put those down."

"If she got robbed, then she wouldn't miss these. The burglar could have stolen them," Stacy said jokingly.

"I'll call her again, and if she doesn't answer, I'm calling the police."

"It doesn't look like someone broke in, so let's wait until she calls us back before you call the police. Stop jumping the gun," Stacy said.

"I guess you're right. Let's just get out of here."

"She's a big girl and can take care of herself, so stop worrying. Try her one more time and see if she answers," Stacy said while closing the front door behind them. She was becoming a bit concerned, but she didn't want Lisa to know.

Before they went home, Stacy and Lisa decided to stop by an Italian restaurant to get something to eat and indulge in some Bruschetta, Lasagna, and for dessert, Cannoli's. Eating was something they enjoyed, and because of their large appetites, they had to work out daily. After sitting down at the table, they ordered their food and two glasses of red wine.

They talked about Candace, but decided she had probably gotten dressed in a hurry to go out of town or on a date. They wanted to give her a chance to contact them so they could figure out what was going on. Even without Candace, their third wheel, they laughed, talked, and enjoyed their spontaneous girls' night out.

Soon after their food arrived, a lady walked up to their table interrupting their conversation. "Are you Lisa Cotus?" the lady asked.

"Yes, I'm Lisa Cotus. How can I help you?"

"Sorry for intruding. My name is Karen Law," she said while extending her hand out to Lisa. "I was dining in the restaurant and saw you walk in, so I had to meet you. I've heard so much about you and your work, and I would love to hire you."

"Great. Here's my business card. Just give me a call and we can discuss the details."

"Thank you. I will call you in the morning. My husband and I are ready to get started right away on remodeling our new home," Karen told her, making up a story. "Candace told me so much about you, and I'm excited to meet you," she added.

"You know Candace?" Lisa asked.

"Candace and I are both from Atlanta. I've known her for many years."

"That's great!" Lisa said. She loved referrals, and it was great that she knew one of her friends. "When is the last time you've spoken to Candace?"

"I just spoke with her yesterday. She's in Atlanta visiting her family."

"Oh, that's good to hear, because we've been trying to get in contact with her." Lisa sounded relieved that Candace was fine.

"Candace said she needed a break from work and that her boss had been stressing her out. It sounded like she just needed some space from everyone."

"I guess she just needed to get away. I wish she would have told us, because she had us worried," Lisa said.

"When I talk to her, I will tell her to give you a call."

"Where is your new home located?" Lisa asked.

"We just move to Highland Park, Illinois."

"There are beautiful, expensive homes in Highland Park. Michael Jordan used to live there."

Karen's cell phone started ringing, and she glanced at the caller ID to see who was calling. It read 'Moe'.

"I'm so sorry, but I have to take this call," Karen said politely, but looking slightly edgy. "I look forward to working with you. I will call you in the morning. It was nice to meet you, and I'm sorry for interrupting your dinner."

"No problem. It was nice meeting you, and I will look for your call in the morning." Lisa said.

Karen walked away quickly, as she finished her phone call speaking French.

"Look at you getting recognized out in public," Stacy commented. "She seems nice, and if she lives in Highland Park, then she has money."

"If she calls, I will know that she's serious," Lisa said.

She was used to people asking for her business card and telling her that they wanted to hire her, but then she never heard from them. Only serious people with money contacted Lisa.

CHAPTER 24

Jarvis walked into his restaurant with a pleased look on his face while admiring the room. He felt like he had accomplished another dream. His father was so proud of him, and he couldn't wait until he flew in for the grand opening.

Jarvis had exceeded his dream of opening up one nightclub. Now with five clubs in different cities under his belt, he had plans of opening up more restaurants, as well. Life was good, and he had no complaints.

Being at the club every night, flying back and forth to Miami and Atlanta to check on his other clubs, he was extremely tired and ready for a vacation. Kora had been begging him to take her to the Bahamas, and he was ready to give in to her request. Business always came first in his life, but now he needed some personal time and space. His body had been telling him to relax for a while.

He was proud of his employees for keeping his businesses running smoothly. He knew without good, loyal employees, he couldn't run a thriving business, which was something his father always told him.

He ran a tight ship, but he also paid everyone well. Even though he was tough on them, they respected him. His philosophy was to treat his employee with respect and pay them well. In return, they would be loyal.

Right in the middle of his admiration of his own success, Jarvis and Kevin walked in.

"You're wasting my money sitting around doing nothing," Antonio said, teasing Jarvis.

That was something Jarvis would tell his employees if he caught them sitting around not working.

"I'm glad you made it in safely," Jarvis told Kevin.

"Thanks, man. I'm only here for a few days, then I have to go back to Miami for the big party we're having. I hope you're going to make it to the event."

"I should be able to make it. Just remind me," Jarvis said.

"We have some big celebrities coming through that night," Kevin informed him. "So, it would be nice if you were there to greet them."

"There are always superstars at our club. That's what we're known for. You know we got the hottest clubs in town," Antonio commented, bragging.

"Sit down and have a drink with me," Jarvis said with weak eyes. He was physically and emotionally fatigued.

"What are you drinking?" Kevin asked.

"I'm doing shots of Tequila," Jarvis replied.

"You're trying to get fucked up," Antonio said, laughing.

"You need that every once and a while. Have a shot with me," Jarvis said.

"What's wrong? You look worn out," Antonio told Jarvis, then swallowed the shot quickly.

"I've just been so exhausted lately. I need to take a vacation. I'm going to plan something soon."

"You have to take care of yourself, man," Kevin told him.

"We need you around here. We can't run this empire without you." Antonio poured himself another drink. "You work too hard. You need to start getting some rest."

Jarvis rubbed his head. "You're right. I really need some sleep. I'll be cool."

"I don't need you falling out somewhere. I'm not going to be babysitting a sick person," Antonio said teasingly.

"Did you take care of that situation with Candace for me?" Jarvis asked Antonio as soon as Kevin went to the restroom.

"Yeah, I got her packed up real fast that night and sent her back to Atlanta. She should be settling in now thinking about what she did to mess her life up. I think she just got too comfortable," Antonio told him.

"She knew better than to try to get with my boy. I don't know what she was thinking. These women think they can get away with anything. Just because the sex was good doesn't mean she was irreplaceable. Thanks for letting me know," Jarvis said.

"No problem. I'm just doing my job."

"Did she give you any problems?"

"You know how Candace is. She wasn't going to go without a fight, but usually, no one argues with a gun pointed in their face."

"Man, you didn't hurt her, did you?" Jarvis asked.

"No, but I did fuck the shit out of her before I sent her to Atlanta."

"Really!"

"Since you were sending her home and you didn't want her anymore, I thought I would see what she had going on between her legs. You cool with that, right?" Antonio asked, even though he knew he didn't have sex with her that night.

"Normally, I don't share my women, but since I don't want her and you're my boy, you can have her. I don't care about Candace. I got a beautiful wife who loves me, waiting for me at home," Jarvis said, knowing he was furious. "By the way, how was she in bed?" he asked curious.

Antonio smiled. "It was good. I might have to visit her when I go to Atlanta."

He knew Jarvis was livid, but he wasn't showing it.

"Candace had been trying to get with me since I started working for you. I was so focused on my job I didn't know she had such a sexy body. Damn, that girl really put it on me," Antonio said, then downed another shot of Tequila.

"I guess you really don't know people. I didn't know she was stepping to you like that," Jarvis said, shaking his head.

Jarvis tried to have sex with every woman in town and didn't want his friends to sleep with any of the women, even though he didn't care about them. His friends found it hard to find a woman to fool around with because Jarvis had put his mark on most of the women in the club scene.

"You sure you don't have a problem with that?" Antonio asked.

"I've already had her, so she's fair game to whoever wants her," Jarvis said as steam started rising from his head from anger. He grabbed the bottle of Tequila, poured two shots, and drank them both.

"Can I ask you a question?"

"What's up?" Jarvis asked as he leaned on the bar. He was feeling the intense buzz that had grabbed a hold of him.

"No disrespect, but why do you cheat on Kora? She seems like a good woman."

"I'm not cheating. I'm just being a man. I love Kora, and I know she will never leave me."

"You've got a lot of confidence in her. As much as you step out on her, how do you know she won't leave you?" Antonio asked.

"Kora loves the lifestyle I'm providing for her. She's an undercover gold digger wrapped in a beautiful, sweet package. You think I don't know that she probably loves my money more than she loves me? That's why I keep her ass on lockdown. No one plays me. I'm always one step ahead of her," Jarvis said while Antonio stared at him. "I can't blame her for wanting to be with someone wealthy. What woman doesn't?"

"You better be careful before someone steals her from you."

"I'm not worried about Kora leaving me. She knows what she's got, and she's not going anywhere."

"You got a good woman," Antonio said.

"She's off limits to you," Jarvis said, smiling. He would never think that Antonio would try to sleep with his wife. It was the least of his concerns.

"What was up with you and Candace? Did you have feelings for her?"

"Hell no! She was just a piece of ass. Being in this type of business, I run across a lot of women, and it's hard to say no. You must understand, because I see you getting your share of women also," Jarvis said.

"You ain't shit," Antonio said, laughing.

"I'm the best person you will ever meet. Just because I sleep around with other women, I still love my wife. I treat her like a queen and give her anything she wants. I guess my downfall is I just don't give a damn about the women I sleep with, and once I've slept with them, I don't want to be bothered. I've got a weakness for beautiful women, but I'm a good guy."

"You're a selfish bastard," Antonio said as they both cracked up laughing.

"You might be right," Jarvis agreed. "I just love women. I'm a man."

Antonio smiled. "I'm trying to be more like you. I'm trying to figure out how to juggle all of my women at one time. I'm just a student willing to learn."

"You're a quick learner, and I think you got it down," Jarvis said, laughing. "Just make sure you keep a good woman at home so you always have someone to come home to."

"I have to find a good woman. I keep running into these women looking to hit the lottery from my pockets."

"Never make your girlfriend someone you meet from the clubs. They are not marriage material," Jarvis schooled him.

"I've learned that the hard way."

"I tried to warn you."

"Thanks for taking me under your wings," Antonio said humbly.

"Antonio, you're like family to me. You've done an excellent job, and I trust you. I normally don't trust people, but I know I can trust you."

"Thanks. You're like family to me, also."

"Just make sure you don't run after these women, because you don't have to. They are already running after you. Make money your main focus, and everything else will fall in place."

"You have a different way of living your life."

"It's the right way. Stick with me, and you'll be living exactly how I am, rich and happy," Jarvis said as Kevin returned. "Where have you been?" Jarvis asked him.

"I had to make some calls," Kevin replied as he grabbed his glass and drunk the liquor straight down, trying to catch up with them.

"I'm not going anywhere. I've got your back," Antonio said, continuing the conversation they were having when Kevin rejoined them.

Antonio was managing his businesses and had keys to his house and cars. He knew Jarvis trusted him.

"You've proven that you have my back," Jarvis said, feeling the effects of the liquor even more.

"We have two more days before the opening," Antonio said.

"This is the first of many more restaurants to open," Jarvis told him.

"It's going to feel good to have my own business. Thank you for making this happen for me," Antonio said gratefully.

"Jarvis is hooking you up. You're about to have a whole new life. I remember when Jarvis and I opened my first clothing store. Man, I was scared to death, but ready to be the CEO of my company. Two years later, I opened another store that was bigger and better. I'm still going strong to this day. Jarvis looks out for his friends," Kevin voiced.

"I respect Jarvis, and I appreciate everything he's doing for me. He's got my loyalty and dedication."

"I didn't trust you when I first met you. I told Jarvis not to hire you, but he saw something different. Honestly, I didn't think you would last this long. You've proven me wrong and turned out to be cool," Kevin expressed.

"Trust is the major component in this equation. Having your own business is powerful. You are in control. Run your business like you run your life," Jarvis advised.

"Money first and women second," Kevin and Antonio said in harmony.

Jarvis' telephone started ringing, but he ignored it. When it continued ringing, he knew that was his signal to deal with some business.

"Let me take this call," Jarvis said.

A minute later, he quickly ended the phone call with his eyes bulging out of his head.

"Is something wrong?" Kevin asked after noticing the distressed look on his face.

"Come with me!" Jarvis franticly told Antonio and Kevin.

"What's going on?" Antonio asked.

"My club is on fire!" Jarvis said as they all ran out of the restaurant.

CHAPTER 25

The flashing lights from the police cars lit up the entire block. The sirens echoed through the busy streets as several fire trucks pulled up in front of Jarvis' nightclub. Blazing flames were shooting out of the windows of the stand-alone building while firemen tried to put out the fire. Things were hectic as a crowd started gathering across the street.

Fifteen minutes later, Jarvis, Kevin, and Antonio pulled up. Jarvis watched as his hard work and dreams went up in flames. Kevin immediately tried to get some answers from the firemen and spectators, but no one had seen anything and didn't know how the fire started. Antonio tried to get closer to the club, but the firemen stopped him and told him to wait by the curb.

"I can't believe this is happening," Jarvis said.

"The club was not open tonight, so how the hell did it catch on fire?" Kevin asked.

"Somebody has to know something." Antonio walked away to find answers.

"Maybe you should call the insurance company to let them know what's going on. They will probably send someone out here to help," Kevin suggested.

"You're right. I'm going to call them right now," Jarvis said.

Jarvis started arguing with the person on the telephone, as Kevin tried to interrupt to ask what was going on. Out of frustration, Jarvis ignored him and walked away while the insurance agent informed him that his insurance policy had expired a few weeks ago and was never renewed.

"This has to be some kind of mistake," Jarvis yelled at the agent.

When Antonio heard Jarvis shouting on the telephone, he went to see what was going on.

"What's the problem?" Antonio asked, trying to calm him down.

Jarvis never answered him. Instead, he kept yelling at the insurance agent. Antonio took the cell phone from him in an attempt to rectify the problem.

"You better fix this!" Jarvis shouted at Antonio.

Antonio spoke to the agent for at least five minutes before he hung up the telephone obviously upset.

"What happened? Did you clear it up?" Jarvis asked as Kevin listened.

"They said there's a problem with the insurance because it was never renewed," Antonio told him.

"But I signed those papers and renewed my insurance a while ago," Jarvis said.

"Jarvis has always taken care of things like that. There has to be some type of mistake," Kevin voiced in a troubled tone.

"The agent said she will look into it further and give us a call when she gets more information," Antonio said.

"I don't need this right now. This is the wrong time for me not to have insurance," Jarvis said furiously.

"Did Candace send them the paperwork?" Kevin asked.

"I signed the renewal papers and watched her fax it to the insurance company," Jarvis replied, frowning.

"Get her on the telephone so we can find out what's going on," Kevin said.

"She doesn't work for me anymore," Jarvis informed him.

"What!" Kevin said, shocked.

"Jarvis fired her," Antonio said.

"I'll kill her if she didn't renew my insurance." Jarvis balled his hands in a tight fist.

"Let's not panic. Maybe she did send the renewal form. The insurance company will call us back, and we can clear this up," Kevin said, trying to calm him down.

"I'm not going to worry about this. I'll pay for the damages with my own money if I have to," Jarvis said.

He knew he had no control over what was happening, so he decided to just let it go. His club would be up and running in no time. Since he had money to repair his club, he shook off the angry feeling that was burning in the pit of his stomach.

It took two hours for the firemen to put the fire out. They didn't have an explanation as to how the fire started, but they were going to investigate it. Once they got the clearance, Jarvis, Antonio, and Kevin went inside to survey the damages. When they walked through the doors, Jarvis instantly had to hold back tears as he looked around at his club that was smoldering and dripping wet.

The club was a total disaster. He would need to do a complete remodel of the establishment to get it back up and running, and that would cost him tons of money. Antonio looked at the once uniquely shaped bar that was now burned, and he put his hand over his mouth to keep it closed.

Kevin didn't know what to expect when he walked into the club, but he stumbled when he saw how much damage the fire caused. He wasn't sure if Jarvis would even want to try to repair it. Looking at the condition of the club, he didn't think it was even worth rebuilding.

"Don't worry, we'll be back on top in no time," Antonio said.

"We won't be back any time soon. This is too much damage to recover quickly. Maybe I need to rethink reopening," Jarvis said feeling depressed as his mind started to race. He felt like it was time to cut his loses.

"Don't make any irrational decisions right now. It's going to work out," Kevin tried to assure him.

"I found something," the fireman yelled out.

Splashing water from the wet floor, they all rushed to where the fireman was standing. Then they walked inside the kitchen along with the other firemen and quickly jumped back when they saw a body lying on the floor. They tried to get closer to see whose body it was, but the firemen stopped them and made them leave.

"Who could that be?" Kevin asked as they huddled together outside the kitchen door.

"The person has a skirt on, so I guess it's a woman," Jarvis whispered in shock to Antonio.

"Candace was the only woman who had keys to the club," Kevin said.

"Do you think that's Candace?" Antonio asked

Jarvis' heart raced. "I don't know. I couldn't see her face."

Thirty minutes later, the coroner carried the body out of the room in a body bag. Needing a moment, Jarvis walked out of the building. Antonio followed behind him to make sure he was going to be alright. Jarvis was broken down.

Not only was he upset about his business, he had to deal with a death on his property. The police quickly surrounded them and started asking questions about the body that was found.

Jarvis explained it could be one of his employees that he fired, but he wasn't sure. They wanted to know if anyone was supposed to be in the club, and Jarvis told them no one should have been there because the club was closed. If it was Candace, he was wondering what she was doing back in town and in his club.

The police told Jarvis to give them a minute because they wanted him to see if he could identify the body. So, Jarvis waited around patiently.

"Why the hell would Candace be here?" Jarvis asked Antonio.

"I don't know. It might not be her," Antonio said.

"I thought you sent her home?" Jarvis asked, furious.

"I did. I dropped her off at the airport. Either she didn't leave or she came back into town," Antonio told him.

Jarvis started putting the pieces together. "She probably started the fire."

Just then, the police signaled for Jarvis to come and identify the body. Kevin and Antonio followed behind him as they took the longest walk of their lives to the coroner's van. They tried to prepare themselves for what they were about to see. As the police officer unzipped the bag and opened it, Jarvis' heart stopped beating.

He quickly looked away because he didn't want to see Candace lying in the bag. However, when he slowly looked towards the body, he saw it wasn't Candace. The person had been burned so badly that they were almost unrecognizable, but he knew it was not Candace.

After being questioned for ten minutes, Jarvis was drained and ready to go home. The police officer informed him that he would contact him once they found out the identity of the woman. Antonio, Kevin, and Jarvis' cell phones started ringing all at the same time.

They ignored the calls and continued talking to the police. When they noticed their phones were not going to stop ringing, they excused themselves from the police officers and answered the calls.

It was as if they all got the same news at the same time because they looked at each other with their mouths open. Jarvis immediately sat on the curb and put his hand on his head while continuing to listen to the caller.

Antonio and Kevin hung up their call and waited for Jarvis to get off the phone. Looking at the expression on Jarvis' face, they knew they had gotten the same phone call he just received.

"Why is this happening to me?" Jarvis asked in a daze.

"You obviously got the same call we just did," Antonio said.

Jarvis couldn't hide the distressed look on his face. "This is fucked up!"

"I don't know what to say," Kevin said as he sat next to Jarvis on the curb.

"All five of my clubs are on fire! What the hell is going on?" Jarvis said hysterical. "Do you think Candace set me up?" he asked, looking for answers.

"Maybe. She was pissed off when you fired her," Antonio replied.

"She couldn't have pulled this off all by herself," Kevin said.

"If Candace had something to do with this, I'll kill her," Antonio promised.

"I've worked my entire life to build this empire, and now it's gone up in flames. How will I recover from this?" Jarvis said, distraught.

"Calm down," Kevin told him.

"I got a dead woman in my club, and you're telling me to calm down!" Jarvis yelled.

"Let's get out of here," Antonio said.

"My life is over!" Jarvis shouted out into the night air that smelled like charred wood.

CHAPTER 26

Jarvis' clubs burning down seemed to be a big catastrophe. The news broadcasted about it every hour on the hour, especially since there was an unidentified body found on the premises. Stacy couldn't help but hear about it the very next morning because the radio stations were talking about the hottest clubs going up in flames. They were already trying to find the next hot spot to tell their listeners to patronize.

"Hey, baby, I was calling to see how you were doing," Stacy said in a serene tone.

"I'm good, considering everything that's going on," Antonio told her, sounding disappointed.

"I can't believe all of his clubs burned down. That sounds like foul play to me."

"Don't remind me of the details."

"How is Jarvis holding up?"

"He's hanging in there as much as he can. This has been extremely hard on him, and I think he's planning on moving back to Atlanta."

"I just heard on the news that the body found in Jarvis' club was Karen Law. Lisa and I just met her. I can't believe she was found dead in his club. What was she doing there?" Stacy asked. She had tons of questions and wanted answers.

"This is so bizarre," Antonio said sounding exhausted.

"Did you know Karen Law?" Stacy asked him.

"No."

"Did she know Jarvis?"

"I think they used to date, but I'm not sure," Antonio replied.

"Jarvis better hope they don't try to link him to her death."

"Things are really messed up right now," Antonio commented.

"What's going to happen to the restaurant?"

"As of now, we're still planning on opening it."

"Are you guys still having the party with all of this going on?" Stacy asked.

"We have to because we've invested too much money and time not to have the grand opening."

"I thought Lisa was joking when she said she was still preparing for the event. I guess I will see you tomorrow then."

Antonio paused before speaking. "It might be good if you stay at home."

"Why?"

"Because my girlfriend will be there with me, and I don't need any problems."

"I don't care about your girlfriend. It's not like I don't know she exists."

"Stacy, please stay home."

"I've been planning for this event for weeks. I even bought a new dress to wear."

"This is not a good time," he told her. "Can you please just do this for me? I will come see you after the event."

"I'll think about it," Stacy said. She was hurt and never thought he wouldn't want her to attend the party.

"This is such a stressful time right now, and I need your support."

"You know I support you."

"I'm on my way to your house. I miss you."

"Okay," Stacy said, knowing this was going to be another all-night sex session.

"I'll see you in thirty minutes," Antonio said before he hung up.

Just as he promised, Antonio was ringing Stacy's doorbell thirty minutes later. Even though she knew she shouldn't be with him, her body craved him. Being single and lonely, she had nothing else to do but entertain herself with Antonio's presence. She was quick to open the door and glad to see him. She hugged and kissed him, then invited him in.

"Hey baby," Stacy said, excited as she sucked on his neck.

"No talking. Just take your clothes off," Antonio told her.

She didn't hesitate to rip her clothing off, revealing her beautiful black lace bra and panties that made Antonio take a deep breath. He stared at her body like he could eat her for dinner. He was always turned on by her beauty and body. She never disappointed him.

"I've missed you," Stacy said while kissing his lips.

Antonio picked her up and carried her to the bedroom.

After they made love, he kissed her passionately and stroked her hair.

"You're so beautiful," he said, admiring her good looks.

"Thanks, baby. You're not too bad looking yourself," Stacy replied, smiling as she lay back on his chest and watched television. She tried to fight the feeling of love from creeping up in her heart again. She wanted to be with him, but knew that would never happen.

"I've always cared about you. I never meant to hurt you," Antonio said as he wrapped his arms around her from behind.

"What are you talking about?" Stacy asked, puzzled.

"I didn't know I would meet you and fall in love with you so fast. I didn't want you to get involved in my crazy world, but here you are. I only wanted to make you happy."

"You have made me happy. I just wish I didn't have to share you. I want you all to myself. You hurt my feelings when you told me not to come to the grand opening of your restaurant. I want to be there to share your accomplishment with you."

"Then you should be there. Make sure you look pretty," Antonio said.

Looking at her face, he could see the desperation to be with him, and he didn't want to disappoint her.

"Thank you. I really want to be there."

"You deserve to be there. We will have a good time."

"What about your girlfriend?" Stacy asked.

"I will tell her to stay home. It will be all about you," Antonio said, knowing he didn't have a girlfriend at home. It was all a lie to keep her feelings from getting too involved with him.

"Really?" Stacy said, although she felt degraded. She needed to be number one in his life, but she knew she was second or even third on the list of his priorities.

"You didn't mention anything to Candace about my sister's death, did you?" Antonio asked, even though he knew she probably did.

"I...I...I might have mentioned something," Stacy stuttered, knowing she wasn't supposed to say anything to anyone. She also knew Candace must have told him if he was asking her about it.

"I asked you not to say anything, and you promised to keep your mouth shut."

"Antonio, I'm sorry. It just slipped out when we were talking one day. I didn't mean to tell her."

"You told me that I could trust you, but I can't depend on someone who can't keep my personal information private."

"It's not that serious. I made a mistake. She is the only person I told. You know you can trust me," Stacy said, trying to get back to the loving moment they were just having.

She looked at Antonio, who looked like he was in deep thought. He knew he could never trust her again.

"I love you, Stacy," Antonio said sincerely.

He knew Stacy loved him more than he loved her. He just wasn't that into her. He enjoyed her company and the sex was great, but he knew she wasn't wife material. He just didn't want to break her heart by telling her that he didn't want to be with her.

"I love you, too," Stacy responded as her heart melted.

She continued laying on him, nestling her back on his chest while watching television.

"I'm really sorry," Stacy said.

I'm sorry, too, Antonio thought to himself as he held her until she fell asleep. His plan was to make love to her one last time, then kill her for revealing his secret, but he couldn't do it and realized he did care about her. His feelings for her spared her life. He eased his body from under hers and covered her with a blanket. He put his clothes on, took one last look at her, and quietly walked out the door, knowing the only way for her to get over him was for him to never see her again.

CHAPTER 27

Two days after Jarvis' clubs burned down, he decided to finally go home. He was staying at a hotel to try to get his mind right. He still couldn't believe what had happened. Having always been strong and unbreakable, he was embarrassed to let Kora see him in such a depressed state.

While trying to cope with the loss of his businesses, he was contacted by the police, who let him know the badly burned body found in his club was Karen Law. Now he started feeling like she had something to do with the fires.

With her showing up at his house and now dead in his club, he couldn't digest it. The police questioned him like he was a suspect and told him not to leave town. He knew he had to try to explain to Kora why the same woman who was at his front door was now dead. This didn't look good for him.

He was also trying to figure out a way to get back on track, but he was miserable thinking about all of his hard work destroyed. The only business he had left was the restaurant, and it was scheduled to open the next day. Even though he was in no position to attend the grand opening, he knew he had to be there and keep moving forward with the one business he had left.

He spoke with his father, who told him to come home and cut his losses. Even though it would take time and a lot of money, his father knew he could bounce back, but he didn't want him to spend too much time dwelling on the clubs. He needed to focus on a plan to move forward. After taking his father's advice into consideration, he decided to get the restaurant up and running and then move back to Atlanta to get his life back on track.

Antonio and Kevin knew not to bother him and respected his space. They knew he needed time to let everything sink in. The next day, Kevin flew out to check on the condition of the other clubs and give Jarvis feedback. Jarvis was in no condition to go with Kevin, but he planned on checking on the clubs after the restaurant's grand opening. Antonio decided to stay in Chicago with Jarvis and handle things while he got back on track.

Antonio informed Jarvis that Candace didn't renew the insurance for none of his clubs. Therefore, they were not covered, and if he wanted to reopen, he would have to use his own money. He didn't think he would be able to restart all of his businesses again.

Kora had already heard about the fires on television and had been calling Jarvis, but he didn't want to talk to anyone. He told Antonio to let her know what was going on and tell her that he would see her soon so he could clear his head. Jarvis had always been on top and never knew what it felt like to hit rock bottom.

Now, he was experiencing it full strength. This was the breaking point of his career, and although he knew he had his father to help him get back at the top of his game, he still felt distraught.

He needed to be with his wife; he needed her support. Kora always had the right words when he wanted to hear them, and he knew she would make him feel more relaxed and help figure out a plan. He had to tell her that they were going to move back to Atlanta, and he wasn't sure if she would be happy about that decision. He loved Kora and wanted the best for her, so moving was ideal for them.

As he made the drive home, he started reminiscing about his life and how much he had accomplished. He was proud of himself, but he wanted to know where he went wrong and how could he have prevented the fires. He knew his controlling, selfish ways probably drove his staff over the edge, but he thought he took care of them financially and didn't have to worry about them.

Such a major tragedy in his life had made him ready to start his life over and do right by Kora. Why he was thinking this way he didn't know, but the loss of so much made him rethink his life.

He knew Kora was a good woman, and she didn't deserve the way he was treating her. It was time that he pleased his woman and loved her in ways she never knew he could. He thought about how she had always been by his side and never left him even though she knew he was cheating. He loved her and wanted her in his life forever.

Now that he felt like he had nothing, he needed her more than ever. She was the only woman he really trusted. Hitting rock bottom opened his eyes to what was important.

For Kora, he knew he had to pull it together and start over for the sake of his career and marriage. Always having money and being successful, it drained him to think about being without and having to go through the process of rebuilding his empire.

Jarvis thought about all the wrong he had done to people and how he always laughed because karma hadn't hit him in the butt yet. He thought he was dodging it, but now, he figured the fires were his karma finally catching up to him. He would accept it for now and then start over bigger and better.

By the time he made it home, he felt much better and had a reasonable plan on what he needed to do next. He sat in the car for a moment looking at his home and at the Bentley he was driving.

"Life is good," he said out loud.

He loved being rich; that's what made him who he was. He was determined to keep his wealthy status and rebuild his business.

"Money is power," Jarvis said as he got out of the car trying to motivate himself.

Before he could open the front door of his home, his cell phone started ringing. Ready to focus all of his attention on his wife for the night, he ignored it.

Once inside, he almost lost his balance when he saw that his house was empty. All the furniture, chandeliers, light fixtures, and artwork were gone. Baffled by the large empty room, he walked around the house thinking he had gotten robbed. Why is this happening to me? He checked the kitchen, and even the food in the cabinets was gone.

"Damn! I've been robbed," Jarvis said as he slammed his fist on the kitchen counter.

He couldn't handle anymore turmoil. He instantly became concerned about Kora and her safety.

"Kora! Kora!" He shouted while running up the stairs.

Jarvis opened the bedroom door and stopped so fast that he almost fell. He saw Antonio sitting in his empty bedroom in a chair facing the doorway.

"I've been robbed! Is Kora okay?" Jarvis asked after seeing Antonio.

"Kora is fine," Antonio replied calmly.

"What the hell are you doing in my bedroom?" Jarvis yelled.

"Don't you mean my bedroom?" Antonio said with a wicked expression on his face.

"Where is all my furniture?"

"In my new house," Antonio told him.

"You stole my furniture?"

"I just took what was mine."

"Antonio!" Jarvis screeched. "What are you doing here?"

"Why don't you come in and have a seat." Antonio pointed to the only other chair in the room.

"I don't want to sit down!" Jarvis said, continuing to holler.

"Sit!" Antonio roared.

"Where is Kora?" Jarvis asked then looked around the room frantically. "Kora!" he yelled out.

"Come here, baby, so he can shut the fuck up," Antonio said.

Kora came out of the bathroom and walked over to Antonio, kissing him softly on the lips. Jarvis shook his head and blinked as if he were seeing a ghost. Anger started boiling inside him, and he lunged at Kora.

"What are you doing?" Jarvis screamed.

Still seated, Antonio quickly pulled a gun out of his pocket and pointed it at Jarvis. "Sit down!"

Jarvis wanted to kill them both, but knew he had no defense against a gun. So, he stood still, breathing heavily before he unwillingly sat down in the chair and looked intently at Kora.

"Are you sleeping with Antonio?" Jarvis asked.

"I'm in love with him," Kora responded.

Antonio grinned. "That's what happens when you don't take care of home."

"You bitch!" Jarvis shouted.

"Watch how you talk to my woman," Antonio said as he continued to point the gun at him.

"Here I am coming home to be with you to get our life together, and you're sleeping with my boy. You're just like all the other gold-digging whores!"

"I'm sorry, Jarvis," Kora said sincerely.

"You know the rules, man. You know my wife is off limits," Jarvis said irately.

"You weren't thinking about your wife when you were screwing Candace in your home and at the office. You're a selfish punk!" Antonio said as he became upset.

Jarvis looked at Kora, and as he watched her expression, he knew she was already aware of his infidelity.

"Wait a minute. Did you have something to do with the fires at my club?" Jarvis asked, now connecting the dots.

"Bingo!" Antonio howled like he had won a prize. "That was my best work ever. I couldn't believe we pulled that off. You have to admit that was classic, with all your clubs burning down at the same time in different cities. Hot damn, I'm a bad man!" Antonio felt proud of his conniving plan.

"I treated you like family," Jarvis said sadly.

"I'm just treating you how you treated my family," Antonio told him, while Jarvis stood there looking perplexed.

Jarvis shook his head as he gritted his teeth and growled, "I can't believe this! You were my boy, my right-hand man."

"You can't abuse women and throw them to the curb. You don't care about anybody's feelings but your own. A woman killed herself because of you, and you don't give a damn," Antonio said.

"What are you talking about?" Jarvis asked, completely baffled.

"Remember Jennifer Moeky?"

"Yes, I remember her," Jarvis replied, still puzzled by the conversation.

"She was my sister. She killed herself because you broke her heart. What really drove her to the edge was when our mother confessed to her that she was sleeping with you, too. How could you do that, you heartless piece of shit! Do you really have to sleep with every woman?"

"Jennifer Moeky was your sister," Jarvis mumbled in awe.

Jarvis never would have guessed in a million years that Jennifer Moeky was his sister. How did he not know this? He was baffled and now thinking about if he had ever seen Antonio. Since he never met any of Jennifer's family except her mother, he never knew she had a brother, and she never mentioned him because Jarvis didn't want to hear about her personal life. He only wanted her to sex him down and do her job. Nothing else mattered to him.

Kora listened intently as Antonio spoke. Not knowing this information, she was just as shocked as Jarvis and didn't know what was going on. When she looked at Jarvis, she knew what Antonio was saying was true. She wanted to know more about Jennifer Moeky, but this wasn't the time to ask questions. Instead, she stood by her man waiting for the next step.

"Yes, Jennifer Moeky was my sister," Antonio said while his lips quivered from anger.

"I'm sorry about your sister, but I didn't have anything to do with that. Her death had nothing to do with me. You're accusing the wrong person."

"Don't play the role with me. You know what I'm saying is true. She wrote a suicide letter, and you were all up in it. I should kill you right now!"

Antonio pointed the gun closer to him.

"Wait!" Jarvis begged.

"My only reason for working with you was retribution for my sister. You will pay for breaking her heart, which drove her to end her life," Antonio said while Kora frowned, unaware of his strategies.

"Shit," Jarvis muttered. He was in an awkward situation.

"I've been sleeping with your wife not long after I moved to Chicago with you. You didn't follow your own rules. You left me in the house with your lonely wife and trusted me too soon. I guess you don't practice what you preach."

"You son of a bitch!" Jarvis barked.

"You can't blame me for sleeping with Kora. You didn't treat her the way she deserved to be treated, because you were too busy sexing every woman in town. Oh, and you were busy trying to make money that she couldn't enjoy unless you wanted her to."

"Whatever, man," Jarvis said. It was hard for him to think about Kora being with another man. Even though what Antonia was saying was true, he was hurt.

"Right now, I'm just doing what I have to do, for the sake of my sister's memories."

"Why did you wait so long to reveal all of this? You could have told me this a long time ago."

"And spoil all the fun? The Army trained me to be patient. The longer you wait, the better things get."

"What do you want from me?" Jarvis asked, now frustrated.

"It's not what I want from you. It's what I've already taken."

Jarvis knew he had trusted Antonio and allowed him into his life. He was usually a good judge of character, but he dropped the ball on this one. He was totally caught off guard and never saw this coming.

Antonio had been such a great employee and never gave him any reasons to distrust him or think negatively about him. After working with him for a few years, and being such a dedicated hard worker, Jarvis didn't hesitate to treat him like family. In his eyes, he was trustworthy. Jarvis couldn't believe that Antonio sat for this long contemplating revenge.

CHAPTER 28

This was a situation Jarvis didn't want to be in. Now he was dealing with his wife cheating on him and his best employee pulling a fast one. Distraught, he tried to keep his composure. He didn't know what to expect next, but his mind was trying to think of a way out of the bedroom. Although he was traumatized and felt drained, dying was not an option for him.

He couldn't stop thinking about Kora having sex with Antonio. The thought of any man touching, kissing, and caressing his wife almost made him want to pass out. Although he treated her horribly and cheated on her every chance he got, he never expected her to sleep with another man. He never thought she was deceitful. His feelings were wounded, even though he knew they shouldn't have been.

He kept looking at Kora, trying to figure out who she was. He no longer knew her. He thought he was keeping tabs on her by keeping her locked in the house, but he was only pushing her into someone else's arms.

"So now that I know you're dirty, what do you want? You want money?" Jarvis asked, trying to get out of the situation.

Antonio laughed loudly. "I've already taken your money. Candace has also taken your money. She's been stealing from you for a long time, and you didn't even know because you thought you controlled her."

"You've taken my money? The last time I looked I was still a millionaire," Jarvis said boastfully.

"Well, you need to check your bank account again, because the last time

I checked it had a zero balance."

"I'm not broke."

"When I found out Candace was stealing from you, I was pissed, but when I found out she had access to all your accounts, I was thrilled. You once said money is power and without money you're nothing. So, I guess it's over for you."

"Candace set me up!" Jarvis shouted.

"You set yourself up. Candace was just a big help," Antonio said.

"You and Candace," Jarvis said angrily under his breath.

"Candace was such a big help. That's why I kept her around. It's amazing how you can get people to do whatever you want them to if you offer them some money. Candace had already stolen money from you, and with the additional money I gave her, she was willing to do anything. She also purposely didn't renew your insurance on your businesses. I've been working with Candace for a while planning this," Antonio said.

Kora's eyes were glued on Antonio, unaware of his plot. "You were working with Candace?" Kora asked, amazed.

"Candace was a major part of this," Antonio told her.

"I didn't know she was in on this with you," Kora said, looking peculiar.

"Don't worry about it, baby. She just made things a little easier. Now you don't have to worry about Candace sleeping with your soon-to-be ex-husband."

"Ex-husband," Jarvis said, surprised.

"When I kill you, Kora will become a widow. She will collect big off of your life insurance. I believe its ten million dollars. Not to mention I'm the beneficiary of your accounts and businesses. Ha! I bet you're straining your brain trying to figure out how I did that," Antonio said arrogantly, while smiling the whole time.

"How?" Jarvis asked, perplexed.

"Let's not forget I served in the United States Army." Antonio gave a salute. "I was trained very well."

"The Army should be proud that you're using that training to do malicious things."

"I'm not crazy. I'm just like you," Antonio said, smiling and looking like a madman.

"I don't have time for this. What do you want? You're already sleeping with my wife and said you stole all of my money. So what else do you want from me?" Jarvis asked, sounding overwhelmed and exhausted.

"I want your life," Antonio replied as he pointed the gun at him.

"Antonio, this wasn't part of the plan," Kora said anxiously.

"Kora, you had a plan with this man? Who the hell are you? I've done nothing but treat you to the lifestyle you always wanted. I gave you everything you ever wanted, and this is what you do to me. You set me up?" Jarvis' emotions started getting the best of him.

"I was tired of being locked in this damn house. I wanted you to love me the way I needed to be loved. I tried to tell you that, but you wouldn't listen. You only cared about your businesses," Kora explained.

"I do love you, and I thought I was showing you that. You're nothing but a conniving bitch," Jarvis said.

"That's the last time you're going to call my woman out of her name. You had your chance to love her. Now that I've shown her what real love feels like, she's happy and doesn't need you."

"I helped you open your own restaurant, and this is how you repay me!" Jarvis yelled.

"I did all the legwork to open that restaurant. All you did was fund it with your money. I mean, my money," Antonio said.

"Kora, this is who you want to be with?" Jarvis asked.

"I love him," Kora responded as Antonio rubbed her butt.

Jarvis gritted his teeth while watching him touch his wife. He didn't even like men looking at her, and now he had to watch Antonio grope her. He wanted to rip his head off, but was reluctant because of the large gun he was holding in his hand.

"Is there anything you want to say before you die?" Antonio asked

Jarvis.

"You don't have to do this," Jarvis said.

Antonio stood to his feet and told him, "You will die tonight."

As Jarvis sweated, he pleaded for his life. "Don't do this, man!"

Scared to death, Kora's hands were shaking. With her nerves getting the best of her, Kora tried to save Jarvis' life. "You don't have to kill him."

"Do you want to be with him? Now you want me to save his life? You didn't care too much about him when you were helping me steal his money," Antonio said.

"What!" Jarvis said.

"That's right. Your innocent wife is the head person of this little scheme. She's the one who showed me where everything was in this house. Where you kept your checks, insurance papers, deed to your businesses, and oh yeah, your passwords to your computer," Antonio divulged, knowing he was pushing the nail further into his heart.

"Kora, I can't believe you," Jarvis said.

"It wasn't like that," Kora responded.

"Don't tell a lie, baby. Let the truth set you free. Tell this man exactly who you are," Antonio told Kora.

Jarvis looked at Kora as tears ran down his face.

Fearful of the person she was looking at, Kora didn't know who Antonio was and what he was talking about. She had found out about things she didn't have any knowledge of, and now she was starting to regret her thoughts of being with him. She looked at Jarvis, who was now weeping out of fear, anger, and pain.

Kora started to feel sorry for Jarvis. Even though he misused her and treated her poorly, she couldn't stand seeing him in pain. She didn't realize it would be this difficult for her. Trying not to be sucked into his agony, she looked away. Antonio didn't seem to have a care at all. In fact, he appeared to be enjoying every bit of it.

Kora knew Jarvis was humiliated and felt overpowered. She also knew he was burning up inside from rage because he didn't like to feel this way.

After what he'd put her through, she didn't know why she was feeling sorry for him, but the feeling took over her body. She watched Antonio as he held the gun to his head. Jarvis didn't want to die, but he found himself looking death in the face.

"I think this has gone too far," Kora said nervously.

"No, it hasn't. Things are going as planned," Antonio told her.

"This is not what we planned. We didn't plan on killing anyone," Kora said.

"We didn't, but this just feels right," Antonio said.

Kora grew flustered. "What is wrong with you? I'm not going to be a part of this."

"You're just as guilty as I am. Besides, this was your idea, remember?" Antonio said.

Jarvis swung his head around fast to look at Kora. He was still stunned to hear that she had something to do with this. He couldn't process her being involved with something so vindictive.

"Let's just stick to the plan and then we can be together," Kora said, wanting to get out of the house.

"Let me pop him real quick. I need to do this for my sister," Antonio said, cocking the gun.

"He's not worth it," Kora told him, trying to save Jarvis' life.

Antonio's jaws tightened and his lips started to tremble.

"He's worth every bit of pain I went through when they buried my sister. He's worth every bit of pain when she cried to me on the telephone. He's worth every bit of pain when she told him she was going to kill herself and he hung up the telephone, not giving a damn about her. He needs to feel some pain."

"Don't do this," Kora begged.

"I have to do this for my sister. Jennifer Moeky. That's the last words you're going to hear before you die."

"Antonio, stop! We can be together whether he lives or dies," Kora said, trying to prevent him from killing Jarvis.

Ready to pull the trigger, Antonio cocked the gun. "He deserves to die. I've waited too long for this day."

Kora had to think of something fast. "Don't you want him to suffer for the things he did to your sister, instead of putting him out of his misery without any anguish?"

Antonio thought about what she said as he continued pointing the gun at Jarvis. "You might have a point," Antonio said as he finally lowered the gun.

Stillness was in the room for what seemed like a lifetime before anyone made a move.

"You made the right decision," Kora told Antonio as she looked at Jarvis, who had the fear of death in his eyes.

His eyes told her that he was thankful for her saving his life.

Candace startled them when she suddenly opened the bedroom door. "Are you ready to go, Kora?" she asked while walking in.

Candace looked like a deer caught in headlights because she didn't expect to see Jarvis and Antonio in the bedroom with Kora.

"What the hell are you doing here?" Antonio blurted out as he swiftly put the gun back into his pocket, concealing it from Candace's view.

"I'm…I'm…" Candace said stuttering.

"Why are you here? Didn't I fire your ass?" Jarvis yelled, letting the rage control him and forgetting that he almost just died.

"Does it matter?" Candace replied in a feisty tone as she looked at Kora for answers.

"Why are you in my house? Did you steal my money? What the hell is going on? Somebody tell me something!" Jarvis shouted uncontrollably, alarming them. He had a million questions for Candace to answer. "Antonio told me all about you helping him to take me down. Is this true?"

"Shut up, Jarvis," Candace said.

"That's how you're going to play the man that helped your broke ass? I made you! I gave you the life that you're living. You're going to answer my damn questions!" Jarvis yelled loud enough to shake the walls.

In a sassy tone, Candace told him, "I came to pick Kora up. That's why I'm here."

"Pick up Kora! What the hell are you picking her up for? What's going on?" Antonio asked, confused by the diversion in their plan.

"You're early," Kora told Candace. She was annoyed that she was put in this situation where she would have to explain herself.

"I was trying to be on time. Let's just go," Candace said while looking at Antonio and Jarvis oddly.

"You're not going anywhere until you answer my questions," Jarvis said.

"Kora, you're going to tell me what the hell is going on," Antonio demanded, just as confused as Jarvis.

"Let's answer these questions for them because they need to know," Kora said, giving Candace the signal to tell the truth.

"You have been so dirty to people, but you can't handle it when it's done to you. You're so cocky, thinking no one will ever do any harm to you. You treated me like dirt, and all I ever wanted was for you to love me," Candace told Jarvis as he looked at Kora.

"Don't look shocked. I know all about you and Candace's sex life in our house. I should kill you myself!" Kora told Jarvis, feeling the pain he had caused her.

Candace continued. "I stole from you. Hell, everyone was stealing from you. You thought you could control everybody by giving us a few dollars, but that wasn't good enough when you were the one inflicting pain on everyone. I wasn't going to leave until I got all the money I wanted from you. That is until Antonio found out about my scheme. In order to keep stealing your money, I joined him in his plan to take you down. So guess what? I win and you lose."

Antonio looked at her, shaking his head, amazed that she was sneakier than he thought.

"I can't believe you," Jarvis said as he sat down in awe.

"I helped her steal your money. You had sex with her and then had her be my assistant. Jarvis, that is so low. You even had the nerve to have sex with her all over our house. Why would you treat me that way? I loved you and you misused me! I was loyal to you, but you took advantage of that!" Kora screamed.

"Relax, Kora. He isn't worth it," Candace said, trying to calm her down, but Kora needed to get it off her chest.

"I had your back, but since you didn't care about me, I don't care about you. I stole your money and helped Candace steal your money, also. So, thank you for introducing me to her. As for Antonio, he put it down in the bedroom because you were too busy having sex with other women to have sex with your own wife. Antonio was a big help in doing what I needed to be done. I didn't know about his sister, but now that I do, maybe you should die," Kora said.

"Baby, I'm sorry. I never meant to hurt you," Jarvis said.

Candace rolled her eyes at Jarvis. "Why do men say that when they get busted? Well, that's not going to work this time. It's over for you, and you have nothing. You really should have had Kora working for you, because she's a smart woman."

"You were working with Candace all this time? What about us, Kora?" Antonio asked.

Before Kora could answer, Candace responded, "Antonio didn't care about you, me, or Jarvis. He only cared about getting revenge for his sister."

"I do care about Kora," Antonio said, getting wrapped up in the mushy moment.

"We all got what we wanted," Kora said, feeling sad that she was hurting Antonio.

"I can't believe you guys. This is incredible. Kora, I didn't think you would do me this way," Jarvis said as his anger boiled inside him.

"You left me no choice," Kora stated.

"Your wife isn't so perfect after all," Antonio said, happy that he was getting under Jarvis' skin.

"It was her idea to have all your clubs burned to the ground," Candace told Jarvis.

"Kora!" Jarvis said, staggered.

"Kora knew how to hit you hard. She knew taking what you loved the most would completely bring you down. Take your clubs and money away, and you will crumble and fall. Of course, she couldn't plan this all by herself. That's why I enlisted Karen Law to help with this master plan," Antonio said, smiling.

Jarvis' face showed that he was putting the pieces together.

"You remember Karen Law?" Antonio asked.

"Yes, I remember her dumb ass. She showed up on my doorsteps a while ago and was found dead in my club. What does she have to do with this?" Jarvis asked. If he was going to die, he wanted to hear all the details.

"Since she was my sister's best friend and hated your guts, she was happy to get revenge. It's amazing how a hundred dollars can get a crack head to set your club on fire, but Karen wanted to personally come to Chicago and set your club on fire herself. Unfortunately, something had to go wrong, and that's why she was found dead in your club. I guess she died happy," Antonio explained.

With sweat beading on Jarvis' head and running down his face, it made his tears invisible. "Unbelievable!"

Trying to pound the nail in deeper, Candace was happy to see Jarvis miserable. "It was also Kora's plan for me not to renew your insurance for all your clubs," Candace added.

Candace was always jealous of the way Jarvis treated Kora. He never looked at her the way he looked at Kora, and she still couldn't handle it. Now that Jarvis saw that Kora was just as dirty as she was, she couldn't help but feel gratified.

"I signed the renewal papers and saw you fax it to the insurance company," Jarvis said.

"You were actually signing the deed to your house and businesses over to Kora. Although Antonio thought he was going to be on the deed, we didn't need a third person. I didn't want your properties. I just wanted the money," Candace said.

Listening to their conniving ways, Antonio chuckled. "So you guys cut me out of the deal."

"You got everything you wanted, so don't be greedy. You still have the restaurant and a nice bank account," Candace told him.

"I gave you everything you wanted and more," Jarvis said.

"But you didn't give me respect," Candace retorted.

"You didn't have to do this to me. I would have given you guys anything you wanted. All this isn't necessary," Jarvis expressed, disappointed.

"This is karma. It's payback!" Candace said.

"Let's go, Candace," Kora said.

"Where are you going?" Jarvis asked Kora.

"We are getting away from here," Kora told him.

"I can't believe you guys set me up. You are no better than me. Get the hell out of my house!" Jarvis shouted to the top of his lungs.

"This isn't going down like this. I helped both of you guys, and you're not going to leave me out to dry. Jarvis screwed all of us. This is what I get for trying to help you. I loved you, Kora," Antonio said.

"Love! You don't know what love is. Kora, I know you don't love him," Candace said, frowning.

"I don't want to discuss this," Kora responded, now feeling uncomfortable about the decision she had made.

"The closest people in my life are the ones screwing me," Jarvis said, still traumatized.

"So you were going to leave me after everything I did for you?" Antonio asked Kora.

"I didn't mean to hurt you. I needed help, and you were the one person I knew I could get to set it all up," Kora said.

Antonio chuckled. "So you used me. I should kill you, too."

"Let's not get drastic," Candace said.

"I didn't use you. I love you," Kora said while Candace glared at her, wondering if she was telling the truth.

Kora wasn't in love with Antonio, but she had grown to care about him. She had no intentions on spending the rest of her life with him. The sex was great, but that's all that connected them.

Jarvis was infuriated. "I'm not going to listen to this bullshit."

"What type of life would we have? We can't be together because people will put all the pieces together. You can't be with the wife of the man you brought down. We will still see each other, but this is best for all of us," Kora said, sounding heartfelt.

She knew she had to say the right things because Antonio still had the gun in his pocket and she didn't want to die. She wanted to walk out of the house as planned.

"I don't know what type of All My Children scene this is, but I'm ready to get out of here," Candace said, aggravated. She didn't care what was going on. She was ready to live her new life and put this situation behind her.

"Antonio, you got everything you wanted out of this deal and more. It's over, so let's get out of here," Kora said, anxious to taste her freedom.

CHAPTER 29

Antonio knew he had gotten more from Jarvis than he anticipated. Killing him was the icing on the cake. He developed feelings for Kora and wanted to be with her, but he never thought it would look strange for them to be together in public after everything they've done to Jarvis.

Even though he was a person who didn't trust people much, and he knew Kora was no different, he somehow allowed her to play on his feelings. He needed to shake it off.

"Let's stick to the plan. Come with me," Antonio said, looking at Jarvis. He pulled the gun out of his pocket and pointed it at him. Too emotionally drained, Jarvis started walking.

"Where are we going?" Jarvis asked.

He knew it was a bad idea to be moving to another location. He thought about fighting for his life, but after what he had witnessed so far, he was ready to be put out of his misery. He was ready to die.

"Shut up and keep moving!" Antonio shouted.

When he walked into one of his dog rooms, Jarvis started to figure out what was going to happen next. Kora frisked him and made sure he didn't have his cell phone on him. She also took his wallet.

"Get inside!" Candace shouted powerfully.

"Where are my dogs? Don't hurt my dogs!" Jarvis said.

"You shouldn't be worried about your dogs. They will be safe at my new home," Antonio told him.

"This is ridiculous," Jarvis said.

"As many days as Candace and I have spent inside this cage, you need to know what it feels like to be trapped like an animal. I hate you!" Kora said.

"So you guys are just going to leave me in here to die?" Jarvis asked, infuriated.

"You won't last that long without food or water. As much as I want to kill you right now, I want you to suffer. Let's see how long you can last in this cage before you die," Antonio said.

"I'm not getting in that cage," Jarvis said.

"You can either get in this cage, or I can put a bullet in head. Which one would you like?" Antonio said, tired of hearing his mouth. "Who knows, you might live a few days in the cage," he added, smiling.

"We're leaving you where you love putting the people you claim to care about," Candace said, remembering her time spent in the cage.

After Jarvis walked inside the cage, Kora secured it with a padlock.

"Enjoy your new home," Kora said, then smiled and waved goodbye with no remorse.

They turned the television on and made sure the windows and curtains were closed. They looked at each other, nodded their heads, and smiled because they had pulled off a brilliant plan. They couldn't believe they were getting away with it.

"Baby, can't you see Candace and Antonio are trying to play you? They want our lives. Wake up, Kora, please! Let me out so we can live our life together and get away from them. I love you," Jarvis desperately pleaded.

"You don't love me. I always knew you were cheating on me. Hell, I even saw you screwing Candace in our house. I just thought that maybe you would be faithful to me one day, but that never happened. I guess that's every woman's dream when she stays with an unfaithful man. She just hopes he will love her the way she needs him to. I did love you, and I also loved the lifestyle you provided. But, I couldn't enjoy the money the way I wanted to. I don't know how long you thought I would put up with the way you were treating me. You created this monster inside of me, and it's your fault that all of this is happening right now," Kora said, pouring out her heart for the last time.

"Let's go," Candace said.

Jarvis continued trying to convince her. "Kora, don't let her manipulate you. Please, baby."

"Meeting Candace was the best thing that ever happened to me. She helped me with this entire plot, and it worked. So, she is not influencing me. She has encouraged me to wake up and get the hell away from you. She just showed me a better way to do it."

Outdone, Jarvis' mouth fell open. "I'll be damned!"

"No one would have ever thought a wife and her husband's mistress would pull off such an elaborate scheme and get away with it. Not to mention, involving the husband's business partner and friend in on the action," Candace said, grinning.

Shockingly, they became good friends and leaned on each other for support. They refused to allow Jarvis to continue to destroy their lives any longer. Instead, they took things into their own hands and did something about it. Although Antonio was furious with Kora for crossing him, he had gotten what he wanted and was happy for his sister's retribution. So, he decided not to retaliate against Kora and just walked away.

They closed the door behind them, leaving Jarvis locked in the dog cage. Candace watched Antonio and Kora kiss and say their goodbyes before he left out of the house. Kora looked at him as if she was going to miss him. Deep down inside, she cared about him, but she refused to let her feelings blossom into anything.

Standing in the hallway in awe, Kora was enthusiastic. "I can't believe we did it!"

"Ahhhhhhh!" Candace screamed to the top of her lungs, just as excited as Kora.

"Thank you," Kora said, sounding extremely grateful.

"No, thank you," Candace said.

"I'll never forget what you've done for me," Kora told her as she exhaled and finally felt free.

Candace smiled. "Freedom feels good. Now let's get out of this house so we can enjoy it."

"I forgot my purse upstairs. I'll be right back, and then we can leave," Kora said, then rushed up the stairs.

While Candace waited for Kora, she went to the kitchen to get something to drink. The kitchen was completely empty, and there was nothing left but a few bottles of water in the refrigerator. She grabbed the water, twisted the top off, and guzzled it down.

Water went flying out of her mouth and onto the floor and granite countertops when she saw Antonio standing in the doorway with a gun pointed in her direction.

Candace almost choked on the water. "What are you doing?" she asked. "You scared me." When she realized Antonio was still pointing the gun at her, the beat of her heart increased. "You're pointing the gun at the wrong person," Candace said with a frown.

"You're the right person."

"Put the gun down."

"I can't do that," Antonio said, still pointing the gun as he walked slowly towards her.

Candace couldn't believe what was going on. She was so close to being out of the house and starting her new life. She knew he was not going to put the gun down.

"What are you doing?"

"I'm doing what I have to do."

"Where's Kora? Does she know about this?" Candace asked, flinging her hands and knocking a glass cookie jar to the floor.

Glass flew everywhere as she jumped out of the way. Antonio didn't move; he never flinched. As tears filled Candace's eyes, she felt death in the room.

"So you're going to kill me? Does Kora know what you're doing?"

Antonio never responded. Another thing he learned while training in the Army was that it's never good to communicate with the enemy, especially when you're about to kill them. He cocked the gun, squint his eye for a direct shot to her head.

"Did you really think Kora would team up with her husband's mistress? Do you think she's that stupid? You slept with her husband in her home and then stole his money. That was her money, too. By the way, your bank account also has a zero balance. Kora is no fool. You deserve to die, but I will spare you the torture and kill you quickly," Antonio finally said.

"How could she do this to me? You guys set me up!"

"No, Kora set you up."

"So this is how it's going down?"

"This is exactly how it's going down," Antonio replied before squeezing the trigger.

Pop! Pop! Pop! The sound of loud gunshots filled the room. Large holes formed in the front of Candace's head and chest. She fell to the floor, clenching her chest and moaning in pain as blood squirted everywhere.

Antonio couldn't take the sound of Candace struggling to breathe. So, he stood over her and shot her in the head again, stopping her movement instantly. Antonio watched as she took her last breath of life.

Kora heard the gunshots and rushed to the kitchen. Breathing hard and afraid of what she would see, she walked into the kitchen slowly. She quickly glanced around the room, locking eyes with Antonio before spotting Candace on the floor. She covered her mouth with her hand.

"Is she dead?" Kora asked.

"Yes," Antonio said.

"You're a stupid bitch. I'm glad you're dead," Kora said while standing over Candace's body.

"We need to get out of here," Antonio said, then kissed Kora on the lips.

They exited the house leaving Jarvis locked in the cage and Candace dead on the kitchen floor.

Epilogue

Time stood still when Kora and Antonio walked out of Jarvis' house two weeks ago. They went their separate ways and agreed not to contact each other until they felt it was safe to resurface. They had plotted a foolproof strategy that they carried out smoothly, and it was exhilarating and frightening for them.

Kora decided to continue her modeling career since she still had the looks and body. She moved to Milan, where she had been paying for an apartment for the last year. She had planned every little detail and needed people to think she was living in Milan all this time.

Since no one really knew she existed as Jarvis' wife, she was confident her alibi would be believable that she and Jarvis were separated and she was living in Milan pursuing her modeling career.

Once Kora officially moved to Milan, she signed with a modeling agency and started her career with a boom. She instantly started booking jobs and was already hired to shoot a major layout for an Italian magazine. Life was good, and she was living her dreams in such a short time.

She felt bad about how everything went down, but she felt she deserved more. It was unfortunate about Jarvis, but at this moment in her life, she didn't care about him anymore.

She had a love-hate feeling for Candace. On one hand, Kora has happy she helped her pull off such an elaborate scheme, but on the other hand, Candace was dirty. She just couldn't forgive her for sleeping with her husband, especially after they became friends. She knew she wasn't important to Candace and she was just using her, just like she had been used. It was unfortunate that she had to die, but that was best.

Kora kept her telephone close to her at all times waiting on the call from Antonio. She hadn't seen him since the incident, and she missed him. She was lonely in her new life. Once Jarvis was dead, they wouldn't have to walk around on eggshells.

Kora also knew she would be extremely wealthy once he was dead and she cashed in on the life insurance policy. Although she had stolen enough money from him to live off of, her big pay would come after his death. So, it was just a matter of time.

She always thought about Candace, Jarvis, and Antonio, but she had to put that life behind her, and it wasn't easy. She walked around looking over her shoulders and jumping every time her doorbell rang, thinking the police was coming to arrest her. The more time that passed, the more comfortable she became with her new surroundings.

Being paranoid all the time was starting to wear on her. She didn't think she had made the right decision, and her newfound freedom was sucking the life out of her.

Antonio was living his life as normal and kept a smile on his face because he felt he'd given his sister's death justice. Although he felt a little guilty because Jarvis had been actually good to him, he knew Jarvis had no respect for woman, including his sister and mother, and that just didn't sit well with him.

He had no thoughts about Candace. He continued to live in Chicago to keep his plan going. During his successful grand opening for his new restaurant, he explained to everyone that Jarvis had gone out of town to handle business.

Antonio kept Jarvis' cell phone with him. He never answered his telephone, but he checked all voicemail and text messages. He also made calls from the phone and hung up before there was any answer to make it look like Jarvis was calling people and living his life as normal.

He returned all calls by text message only, making people think Jarvis was busy dealing with trying to reopen up his businesses.

Antonio knew Jarvis' friends and family wouldn't bother him if he told them to leave him alone. He controlled everyone around him, so it made it easy for Antonio to manipulate them. He never got any frantic messages from anyone because they were too busy respecting his space. He only received heartfelt messages saying they were there for him if he needed to talk.

Antonio continued to return texts from Jarvis' cell phone, telling everyone he needed time alone and to respect that. He strung them along and actually enjoyed every minute of it. Gratification filled his body every time he sent a message to Jarvis' friends and family.

Three and a half weeks later, an important newsflash interrupted Antonio's television program. A flashing headline ran across his screen. Successful nightclub owner, Jarvis Denttin, found in his house locked inside a dog cage. Stay tuned for more details.

Antonio sat up in his bed. The television had his full attention. He stood up and started pacing the floor while eagerly waiting for the commercials to end. His heart started racing and his palms were sweating as the excitement made his heart rate speed up.

When the news reporter appeared back on the television screen with Jarvis' picture displayed over her right shoulder, Antonio almost had a heart attack waiting to hear the details. He had been waiting for this for a while, and it was finally here. The news he had been waiting for, the death of Jarvis.

The newscaster continued reporting the story about Jarvis, stating, "Police officers arrived at Jarvis Denttin's house, the owner of the worldwide Denttin Nightclubs, a little after one o'clock this afternoon. Calls flooded 911 early this morning with concerns from his family and friends who demanded a well care visit. Mr. Denttin hadn't been seen since his nightclubs burned down a month ago. Once inside the home, shockingly, police found Jarvis Denttin locked inside a dog cage, where it appeared he had been restrained in for a long period of time. They also found the body of Candace Mourton, Mr. Denttin's assistant, dead in the kitchen of the home, with three gunshot wounds to the head and chest."

During the news reporter's announcement, pictures of Jarvis' home, businesses, and cars were flashed across the screen. They also talked about his nightclubs burning down and the turmoil he had been in ever since the tragedy of his businesses.

As he listened intently to the reporter, Antonio couldn't breathe. He started nervously shaking his legs and rubbing his hands together while anticipating the news he had been desperately waiting to hear.

"Hurry up!" Antonio yelled at the television.

The news reporter continued her story. "Jarvis Denttin's parents flew in town, and wanted to make sure the police were with them when they entered their son's home because they felt something was wrong. The police found Jarvis Denttin's body…"

Antonio screamed out of excitement when he heard the word 'body'. He couldn't control his enthusiasm. He wanted him dead, and he wanted him to suffer. He was happy he was getting everything he planned. He worked long and hard getting Jarvis to trust him, just so he could plan such an intricate scheme against him. He patted himself on the back as he jumped up and down.

"I did this for you, little sis," Antonio said, looking up and blowing a kiss in the air. He loved his sister and felt what he was doing was justification for her death.

He continued listening to the news reporter, who stated, "Miraculously, Jarvis Denttin is alive! He was extremely malnourished and unconscious when found, but he is alive and in intensive care. More on this story as we receive more details.

Antonio couldn't believe what he had just heard. Distressed, he fell back on the bed. His plan was destroyed. How did he survive? Antonio thought to himself.

"You're fucking up my life!" Antonio shouted out loud. "Damn, I knew I should have killed you, and this would have been over."

Quickly, he changed the channel on the television to see if the other news stations were covering the story. He stopped flying through the channels when two familiar faces appeared. It was Lisa and Stacy being interviewed by a reporter outside of the hospital where Jarvis was in the intensive care unit.

He listened as Lisa spoke about working as Jarvis' interior designer and calling the police department because she hadn't spoken to Candace or Jarvis in weeks. Stacy added to it by saying it was unlike Candace to disappear and not return calls. That's why they got involved.

They both stated they were going to miss their friend and wouldn't sleep until they found out who was responsible. They were both distraught by Candace's death and unable to comment long.

For the first time, Antonio felt sorry for killing Candace. He knew the feeling of missing someone you loved, and he never wanted to feel that again. Watching Stacy break down on television filled his heart with pain.

As the reporter continued talking about the death of Candace and Jarvis' condition, Antonio grew scared. He knew Stacy and Lisa would help in the investigation and tell everything they knew.

He hadn't spoken to Lisa or Stacy since the grand opening of the restaurant and had been avoiding their calls. If it were up to him, he would have killed them both, but Kora didn't want anyone to die. That is until he convinced her that Candace had to go and he would be the one to kill her.

His mind was racing and his heart was pounding. He was angry with himself for not shooting and killing Jarvis. He had let his anger and revengeful mind get the best of him, and now Jarvis was alive. Instantly, Kora's face appeared in his mind.

He didn't know what he was going to tell her. How would she handle this? They never had a plan B, because they were so sure he wouldn't survive. He felt like he was letting Kora down.

He needed to think of an idea on how to get out of the situation. He knew the police would be contacting him soon. It was only a matter of time before Jarvis started talking, and he didn't want him and Kora to live the rest of their lives in jail. He needed time to think.

Just as he felt like he was about to go crazy, his phone started ringing, bringing him more unbearable stress. He looked at the caller ID, and it read Kora. How was he going to tell her that she would no longer have her freedom? She would once again be on lockdown, but this time, it wouldn't be so comfortable.

Be careful what you put out,
because it always comes back to you.
-Karma-

More Novels by
W I N K Katme

TOUR SECRETS

TOUR SECRETS 2

W W W . W I N K K A T M E . C O M